Advance Praise for MISSISSIPPI COTTON

"In *Mississippi Cotton* a 20th century Huck Finn has a real adventure. No matter that his raft is a Trailways bus along the river, the trip is no less toward maturity. If you like a good story, this is your book—a book told by someone who knows the terrain—its history, people, landscape and culture. Only a proper native could have his narrator say that his daddy taught him never to hold onto anything with Lincoln's face longer than you had to. If you want to meet a close cousin of Faulkner's well-mannered little gentleman Lucius Priest in *The Reivers*, then read *Mississippi Cotton*."

~Dr. James Everett Kibler, retired professor of English at the U. of Georgia; author, *Walking Toward Home, Memory's Keep* and *Our Father's Fields*.

"First time novelist, Paul H. Yarbrough, masterfully transports readers deep into the world of *Mississippi Cotton*, where life is not as simple as it seems."

~Julie Cantrell, editor, *Southern Literary Review*; author, *Into the Free*.

"A wonderful Southern story that flooded me with memories. Yarbrough has captured time, place and meaning in *Mississippi Cotton*."

~Coach Billy Brewer, former player and head football coach at Ole Miss.

"Paul H. Yarbrough has painted wonderful images with his words. His writing brings back so many memories. Even if you didn't grow up in Mississippi, you will enjoy *Mississippi Cotton*."

~Mary Ann Mobley Collins, former Miss America, Miss Mississippi.

"Mississippi is a state with a rich, deep history and once you've had an emotional connection with it, the state never leaves you. Paul H. Yarbrough knows and feels that complex history—he knows the pain of those who lived in and loved the state and he has brought these things to light in *Mississippi Cotton*, his first novel.

"Yarbrough's writing style is solid, with terse, tight dialogue and prose. The numerous allusions are rich, sparking one's memory of all things Mississippi. Set in the Mississippi Delta, the novel takes us through layers of lives and conflicts that one can only experience in the South. Yarbrough has a good eye and ear and he has missed few details. If you love the South, this is a read you will enjoy."

~Rickey E. Pittman, Grand Prize Winner of the 1998 Ernest Hemingway Short Story Competition; author, *Red River Fever*, *Jim Limber Davis: An Orphan in the Confederate White House*, and *Stories from the Confederate South*.

"Having been born and raised on a farm in rural Mississippi during the time setting of this book, I am blown away with the fantastic authenticity regarding the descriptions of the bus stations, cotton fields, hoeing/picking cotton, the sights and sounds depicting the Mississippi Delta; and the common everyday Southern dialogue from that era.

"I was transported back in time as I read how the author described farm life, characters who were mutual to small towns, and the reflections of family authority relevant to raising children.

"I believe Mississippians, as well as Southerners in general, may appreciate the underlying themes of family unity, value of honesty and hard work, and the pride in one's loyalty to community, state and way-of-life."

~Don "Scooter" Purvis, halfback on L.S.U. 1958 National Football Champion team and coach in 13 Bowl Games

Mississippi Cotton

by
Paul H. Yarbrough

WiDō Publishing • Salt Lake City

WiDō Publishing
Salt Lake City, Utah
Copyright © 2011 by Paul H. Yarbrough

ISBN 978-0-9830238-0-7

Manufactured in the United States of America

www.widopublishing.com

To my wife, Marion, and my son, Douglas.
The most loyal people I have ever known.

And
Mississippi. The finest land; the finest people

I am a face in the Southern collage of
Gentlemen and scholars, belles and writers,
Soldiers and sharecroppers, Cajuns and Creoles,
Tejanos and Islenos, Celts and Germans,
Gullah and Geechi, freedman and slaves,
We are all, the South.
Deo Vindici

PROLOGUE

The river gave up manifold jetsam—roots, silt, limbs and a number of dead fish; and human flotsam—beer bottles, food wrappers and an occasional automobile license plate. Yesterday under the Greenville Bridge, it gave up a body.

The Mississippi river basin is the second largest in the world, covering almost two million square miles. Its watershed encompasses almost forty percent of the lower forty-eight states.

Along its length of over 2300 miles is a marked path: areas, regions, neighborhoods and homes, all with indigenous qualities born of some function of the river with its strength and power and sometimes gentleness, like a midwife allowing new birth. But as it gives life, it takes life. It could also be a monster, as in the 1927 flood. Death is the beginning of life as life is the beginning of death, and all floods start a movement that cycle from scouring to sediment building. The same sediments that build also bury.

One such area, the Delta, spread across three states—Mississippi, Arkansas and Louisiana. Though the river had created an alluvial plane it adopted the area as a delta child, and the richness of life it brings. The Mississippi region of this area is the Mississippi Delta. Someone described the Mississippi Delta as, "Beginning in the lobby of the Peabody Hotel in Memphis and ending on catfish row in Vicksburg."

Bounded geographically on the east by the Yazoo River and the west by the Mississippi, the region has been cleared, farmed, invaded, fought over in THE WAR, and farmed again. Originally occupied by Indian tribes living in swamps and marshes the Delta was cleared by pioneers and made due for farming from its fertile sediments grading into rich soil; a soil, whether fallow or plowed, that hid ghosts.

Central African Negroes, enslaved by West Africans, sold to and transported by English and New England slave traders to the New World, and their agrarian masters moved in and developed their world. Before The War white and black worked side by side: free and slave, master and servant. After The War white and black worked side by side: free and free, together and apart, shaped by Yankee Black codes; codes that would uncover that which had been planted.

An old Negro man and his son had been fishing when they discovered the body. They thought they had hooked a big channel cat; a downward pull on the line, like a catfish, not moving side-to-side. It was when the cane pole broke he saw the back of the neck, a man, a white man just below the water. His shirt collar was hooked.

The Negroes were not brought to the station, as they weren't suspected as having done anything. They had simply discovered the body, and because the sheriff knew them, they were allowed to leave. They lived in the Delta not far from the river and often fished, like many, under the bridge. The old man was upset. He had not seen anything like this.

"I usually just catch fish." He watched as the body was placed in the hearse.

The sheriff told him he could go on home now if he wanted to. The department would get in touch if it needed him. The hearse pulled away from the edge of the river, climbed the hill and drove to the county morgue in Greenville, the body of John Doe wrapped in a plain white sheet. The Negro man and his son loaded their old '37 Ford pickup with cane poles, bait buckets and tackle.

"Come on, Daddy, we seen 'nuff for one day. Let's git home."

"Okay, Julius. I guess I'm ready."

They had found a ghost.

The coroner had tagged the toe of the body with John Doe. The man appeared to be in his late sixties or maybe early seventies. The cause of death was gunshot wounds. Two shots-- one to the chest, one to the head-- .22 caliber. The heart was punctured, as well as other organs, but either shot would have killed him. It was hard telling how long the man had been in the river, though the coroner had guessed maybe a couple of days at most.

The sheriff had no missing person reports on anyone matching the description of the body, his original appearance having somewhat changed after spending time in the Mississippi. Catfish, gars, minnows, snakes, whatever carnivores could get a taste had been at him. Maybe surrounding counties had a missing person. The deceased could have been from anywhere.

CHAPTER 1

My mother gave me last minute reminders while my daddy checked my suitcase and rechecked the schedule. It was Friday morning, early in August, 1951. The bus station was full of people. Some coming, and some, like me, going.

I always liked to watch the guys in military uniforms, especially the sailors. There was a war going on in some place called Korea. I had no idea where Korea was, but the men looked real sharp in their white uniforms and sailor hats.

I'd wanted to be a sailor since my brother and I had seen The Fighting Sullivans at the picture show a couple of years earlier. It was the story of five brothers in World War II who were all killed at once. I almost cried when their parents got told they'd been killed. I didn't cry, though. All the guys at school would have found out, and that would have been the end for me. Anyway, I always kind of thought I'd be in the Navy one day.

"When you get to Cotton City, be sure to tell the driver that you need to get off at Cousin Trek's. It's just outside of town, you tell him," my mother said. "He'll let you off right in front of the mailbox. But you have to ask him. You're sure you understand?"

"Yes, ma'am."

I was about to get on the Trailways bus for a three week visit with cousins in Cotton City, Mississippi. My parents had taken me to the station. If I was old enough to drive, I guess I might have been driving myself to Cotton City.

Although my older brother Farley said when guys got old enough to drive, they drove to New Orleans, not Cotton City. He had been driving over a year, but he still hadn't been to New Orleans by himself, so it made me think he was talking about something over my head. That's what he said about things I didn't understand—that they were "over my head."

I didn't see what was so great about New Orleans. My mother and daddy had taken us there for a weekend once when I was seven. Mostly I remember Canal Street and the giant billboard sign of OLD CROW WHISKEY with a monster cutout of a crow that looked like something Walt Disney might have had in one of his cartoon picture shows. And there was a sign, even bigger, that advertised Jax Beer. My daddy didn't drink beer but was always singing the Jax commercial:

"Hello, Mellow Jax Little Darlin',

You're the Beer for Me...,"

There was this place called the French Quarter that all four of us went to during the daytime. We stayed at the Roosevelt hotel at night. Our parents said Farley and I were too young for the French Quarter at night, but during the day we walked through it and I remember some pretty odd people walking around. Some of the men had beards, scraggly beards that looked like they just didn't shave very much. And they carried brown paper bags under their arms like a woman's purse. We had no idea what was in the bags. And some of the women had earrings that were as big as the ones on our shower curtain, and there was one very fat guy who looked like Oliver Hardy without a derby. Farley and I kept looking for his skinny friend, Stanley.

I asked my daddy where these strange people worked. He said most probably didn't, which made me wonder how the fat guy got so fat. Farley and I saw one guy with an eye patch who Farley said may have been an heir of Jean Lafitte. It made me wonder that if someone wore an eye patch, would all their children wear eye patches. Actually, it didn't make sense. But, Farley was older than me.

The one thing that looked good to Farley and me was the Voodoo House of Marie Laveau. My daddy let us go in, although my mother had not been a hundred percent in favor of it.

Marie Laveau was some old voodoo queen or priestess who was part of New Orleans history. She died a long time ago, but she had been, supposedly, able to call up demons and make voodoo magic and a lot of other weird stuff. I guess her shop was run by her grandchildren or something. They had all these different charms and stuff you could buy, like Gris-Gris bags and charms and even custom made dolls. I guessed the dolls were for voodoo-ing people you didn't like. And all the rooms were lighted with nothing but a bunch of candles, so the rooms were dark and strange. Daddy said Marie Laveau was a legend of the city, but voodoo and black magic weren't something we needed to get into, he said.

New Orleans was the biggest town I'd ever been to. One day we tried to catch the Canal St. trolley. There must have been a special signal because Daddy never could get one to stop. Finally, he shouted at one that passed and sort of pointed at it with his hand turned toward his face and one of his fingers sticking up. Farley was twelve and pretty much a man-of-the-world by then, so when I asked, he told me Daddy was doing something called 'giving the finger.' I wasn't sure what that meant, but my mother seemed to know. She bellowed the word mor-ti-fied; then bellowed it again. That's all I remember about New Orleans.

Ten was old enough for a boy to take a bus to Cotton City, alone, my daddy had said, although my mother wasn't wild about the idea and had belabored the notion to the point where she had done everything but pin a note to my shirt regarding her earlier reminders. These instructions also included telling me to be sure and eat the sandwiches she had wrapped in wax paper and put in a small brown sack, folded two folds over from the top. She didn't want me wasting money on bus station hamburgers when we stopped. Although my daddy had given me three dollars, which had to last me the three weeks of my visit, I had always been instructed not to spend money. Save it. And there would be several stops on the way to the Delta.

"What if he doesn't wanna stop?" I asked.

"He'll stop. It's his job. But you be polite when you ask him or you'll wish you had. Cause your daddy and I will find out. We will." Her light smile had gone straight-faced at the thought that I might be impolite. And somehow she always held that strange power over us, my brother and me, "…we'll find out."

When Farley was just a kid like me, and I was just starting kindergarten, he said our parents must have friends with the FBI or something. That was all he could figure. Now that he's grown with his driver's license and everything, he says it was just something they said to make sure we didn't 'screw the pooch.' That was over my head, too.

"And don't you put any money in those dad-blamed pinball machines," my daddy said. He let my mother give most of my instructions—eat your food, be polite and all that stuff. But when it came to the important things, like pinball machines, he stepped forward as chief disciplinarian. He just let my mother go on about the sissy stuff, so she wouldn't worry that I might misbehave out of her sight.

"Those dad-blamed things are there to take your money," he said. He could never speak enough of the evils of pinball machines. "Electrical parasites," he called them. And "dad-blamed" was the only profanity he allowed himself in front of Farley and me—most of the time.

Instructions were interrupted by the blaring intercom: "Trailways scenic cruiser for Flora, Yazoo City, Belzoni, Indianola, Greenville, Cotton City and Cleveland, with final destination for Clarksdale now boarding from dock number two. Leaving in ten minutes. All aboard, please."

"Okay, son, I checked your grip." My daddy always called a suitcase a grip. "Better hurry if you wanna get a window seat. But don't run, you're liable to knock somebody down."

"Yes, sir." I hated to look at my mother because she was about to get all weepy and stuff. This was my first trip alone out of the county, but she acted like I was off on a mission to find King Solomon's mine.

She pulled me toward her and gave me one of those colossal mother hugs while she was crying. Of course, she got snot on my shirt. "Oh dear! Give me your handkerchief, Zack."

"Well, if you don't quit slobberin' on him he's gonna miss the dab-blamed bus, Leslie."

"Just you never-mind, this is my baby and he's leaving home

by himself. He's not going to miss the bus."

We walked outside to the buses, and went straight to the slot where the one had 'Clarksdale' printed above the front windshield. Its engine was idling with the diesel smells in your nose.

Last minute instructions came from my mother. "Now be nice. Don't roughhouse in your good clothes, and don't scratch yourself on the bus."

"Yeah, only off the bus," my daddy said.

This got him a stern look from my mother. "I'm trying to teach him manners. And you should be helping and not making your cute little stale remarks. If you want him to grow up to be an animal, well you can just jump off a barn."

I climbed the steep steps. The aisle was narrow and lined on both sides by huge cushion seats sewn with white cloth patches where your head could rest. The bus hadn't filled and there were still plenty of window seats, as everybody who had gotten on so far was pretty old and probably didn't care whether they got a window or not.

I got the first window seat I saw, on the station side of the bus. I knew my parents would want to wave goodbye when the bus pulled out. My daddy would want to as much as my mother, but he wouldn't do all that slobbering snot stuff like her. Course it's not so bad if snot just gets on your shirt, but sometimes some gets on your face or neck and that's pretty horrible.

I had no sooner sat down than I saw my parents. They appeared distorted through the window, like what funny mirrors do to your image in the house of mirrors at the State Fair. I thought at first there was something wrong with the window so I pushed it with my finger, revealing the problem. The last guy who had been sitting here must've been leaning his head on the glass with a dose of Wildroot Cream Oil in his hair. I wiped my finger on the back of the seat, then jumped up and moved down the aisle to select another seat.

Through the window I could see my mother mouthing something, probably trying to ask if something was wrong. I just waved and shook my head. If she knew why I had moved she probably wouldn't let the bus driver leave until the whole bus had been steam-cleaned.

The bus pulled out onto Pascagoula Street and moved eastward. Then along the main artery, State Street, which was lined with crepe myrtles and old white-column houses. It turned north onto Woodrow Wilson Avenue, where its final turn would take it through town and onto Highway 49, straight to the Mississippi Delta. I could feel the big engine switching gears, building and losing power as it moved through several stoplights, often stopping, then re-gunning its engine.

Most of the passengers seemed settled for their trip, wherever it was they were going. I pulled on the window latch and slid the window backward in its frame. I wanted to reach out and grab some berries off the crepe myrtle bushes, like Farley and I did on the city buses, but the Trailways' windows were too high for me to reach the bushes. The air streamed into the bus and though it was almost a hundred outside, the flow of air felt good.

The seat next to me was empty, which suited me just fine. I was afraid somebody about a thousand years old would sit next to me and try to talk to me, asking me questions like: "What's a little fellow like you doing going off on a trip by himself?"—or "How far are you going?"

I would rather sit by myself until I got to Cousin Trek's house, unless it was someone my age who had something to say I wanted to talk about. And even at that, I liked having the extra room. I put my sandwich sack on the seat hoping to discourage anyone who might stroll down the aisle looking for a seat.

I was riding all the way to Cotton City without changing buses. There were a handful of stops but no changes. All I had to do was wait until I was outside Cotton City and walk to the front and tell the driver I wanted to get off at the Mayfield mailbox. Daddy had said that Cousin Trek knew when the bus came by and he would be waiting.

These last three weeks of summer would be spent with my country cousins, Casey and Taylor, in the Delta. We could stay out past dark and come and go as we wanted, as long as we were home for dinner and supper and didn't destroy anything.

We had almost done that a couple of Christmases ago, when we were out in somebody's field. The grass was dead and dry, and we were throwing firecrackers around.

Casey, who was in the first grade at the time, started striking matches and setting small clumps of grass on fire. Then before it spread he would stomp it out. For some reason, Taylor thought it would be a brilliant idea to throw firecrackers in the fire while he was stomping. But a gust of wind came up, and the fire began to spread. At first we began stomping as fast as we could, but the fire was gaining faster than the stomping. Finally it occurred to us that if we could get some of the pond water we had a chance. The fire had spread and it wouldn't be long before the wind really took over and half the county would be on fire.

We pulled our t-shirts over our heads and soaked them in the pond. We then began to beat the edges of the fire with the water-soaked shirts. Driven by survival, as we could only imagine the whipping each would have gotten for his part in a county-wide disaster, we slapped the fire like professional smoke jumpers, finally putting it out. Each of us said a prayer that night that our t-shirts would somehow not be missed. I guess God gave us an extra present that year because my mother never asked; and that in a day when every dime was accounted for

There were open fields with ponds, and creeks and branches to fish in. Everything seemed fun in the Delta. And there was the windmill to climb. It stood next to the chicken house by the garage and was the first thing you'd see as you drove down the gravel road from Cousin Trek's mailbox to the farm. For those who had the courage to climb it, you could see all the way to the highway and beyond.

There was a porch swing where we sat sometimes after supper and listen to my cousin play, slightly off key, on his harmonica, Dixie and Loch Lohman and Swanee River. In the back of the house on one of the big oaks there was an old Firestone without any tread tied to a rope and hanging from a limb. We would swing and spin until we got so dizzy we could hardly walk. One of the games was to see who could walk the farthest without falling down, after the others had spun him into dizziness. If he didn't fall, someone would trip him or give a gentle nudge, because no one was supposed to be standing following a spin.

My grandmother had written about the family farm and our family in little notebooks and things. She had been a teacher, too, and had taught lots of things as best as I could tell. Music and painting and things like that. She had even taught at the Mississippi School for the Blind. I don't think she sold her stories to anybody or anything like that. My mother gave me one of the notebooks to take with me for the family in Cotton City. My mother said they should have it for the home place. She also had given me instructions to not leave it on the bus or lose it.

Cousin Trek was going to let me work this summer in the cotton fields, hoeing or chopping, or whatever else you did before it was picked. I was going to get twenty cents an hour, enough to go to the picture show twice a day, though that would never be allowed. I would be advised to save, save, save.

This was my first trip to Cotton City alone. The Trailways was huge. It was fun riding on something as big as a bus. You could see farther than you could see in a car, and it seemed like all the other traffic was puny. The only bus trip, besides the city buses I had taken, was the year before on a school field trip. Our whole class had gone to Vicksburg, to spend a day at the Vicksburg Battlefield, visit the museum and learn about the courage of the Confederates and their battle against the invading Union Army.

It was then and there that we learned that two battles a thousand miles apart, twenty-four hours apart—Vicksburg and Gettysburg—had determined the fate of the Confederacy. We got to stay out of school the whole day and take dinners our mothers had made for us. It was like a day-long picnic. The trip there and back was over a hundred miles. It was the only world travel I had had.

The bus reached the city limits and moved northwest picking up speed. The huge red and silver cruiser was in its highest gear headed toward Cotton City, and to a strange adventure.

I stuck my arm out of the window and let the air rush

between my fingers. It felt good, the air flowing and blowing at high speed.

Just then a gravel-garbled announcement came over the bus intercom: "Do not extend your arms out of the windows, please."

Of course everyone on the bus turned and looked at me. If the driver had known my name, he probably would have used the opportunity to yell it out, "Jake Conner, get your arm inside. Now!" I felt an early twinge of fear. Was the FBI on the phone to my mother and daddy? I tried to forget about it. Anyway, that was just something Farley had made up—about the FBI informing our parents.

CHAPTER 2

Flora, Mississippi was the first stop, but I didn't count it as a real stop because no one actually got off. There were only a couple of passengers getting on at the bus stop, which was just a grocery store with a Trailways sign stuck on it.

Some seedy-looking man got on and sat across the aisle. He wore a straw Stetson and a blue work shirt with the sleeves rolled up above his elbows. He wadded his sport coat up and put it behind his head for a pillow. The shirt was too small for his fat stomach, and you could see his undershirt between the buttons which were stretching his shirt open between them. He had a tattoo of an eagle on his arm and underneath it was written, YEAH BOY. It didn't look like he had shaved in a while, and I would make a guess that he was about fifty or sixty. A pretty old guy anyway.

But the bad thing was, the thing that I had been most afraid of, was that some old lady with straw-looking hair got on, and stopped next to my seat. After staring at my sandwich bag for about five minutes, she said, "Anybody settin' here, Hon'?"

I started to say something smart like, "Oh yeah, a little bitty guy is in that sack." I didn't though. The FBI might find out that I had smarted off. There'd be a black mark on my conduct, plus the wrath of my mother and daddy if they found out.

"No, ma'am."

She sat down. Fortunately, I was able to swoop up my bag before she made mush out of it.

"Well now, that feels better," she said. "I feel like I been on my feet forever and ever." She plopped a big round-ish bag down in her lap.

I couldn't tell if it was a huge purse or a clothes bag of some kind, but it had a bunch of stuff in it, and it was really round and big, like she had her own toilet in it or something. She hugged it like it was a prize she had won. "Well, now I guess we're gonna be fellow travelers for a while," she said. She smiled yellow.

"Yes, ma'am, I guess so." I didn't know what that meant for sure. I heard my daddy talk a lot about communists and their fellow travelers, so maybe she thought I was some kind of a communist or something.

"And where're you goin' this fine day?"

"Cotton City."

"You got family there?"

"Hope you ain't kin to that dead guy they found in the river," blurted the man with the Yeah Boy tattoo.

"Dead guy? In the river?" My lips almost quivered when I said it.

Her glare brought him up without a word. "Now you just keep your mouth shut. This young gentleman don't need your comments. Now go ahead, young man." Yeah Boy frowned and slumped more in his seat.

"Yes, ma'am. I have a bunch of cousins up there. None of my parents or grand people or regular family though. They're mostly all in Jackson. Except for a' uncle in Meridian."

I hated talking to grownups. I never knew the right thing to say to them. She was kind of beat-up looking, and her hair was scraggly, and she had on about a hundred pounds of rouge, like she'd been smacked with a ripe pomegranate on each cheek. It made her yellow teeth look more yellow. It was hard enough to talk to regular grownups like teachers or baseball coaches, or even Sunday School teachers, but old ones that were, as my daddy would say, 'haggard -looking,' were even harder to talk to for some reason.

"Oh, why cousins are regular family, too," she said. "Jus' a bit more distant."

"Yes, ma'am, that's right. They live way up in Cotton City."

"No, no," she said. "I meant distant, like they don't have as strong a blood tie as yo' momma and daddy and such."

"Yes, ma'am, I guess."

She pulled out some little papers and some kind of little pouch from her bag. I didn't know what she was doing until she started sprinkling tobacco onto some little papers. What they called 'the makings' was what she had. I had seen it in a Red Ryder picture show. This bad guy was always asking somebody for the makings so he could have a cigarette.

She drew the length of the paper across her lips, rolled it into a cigarette, then poked it into her mouth. "Well, my young fellow traveler, I don't suppose you have a match do you?" She smiled, as if she didn't really expect me to have one.

"No, ma'am." It did sound kind of funny asking me, and I laughed a little. That brought on another yellow smile.

She rooted around some more in her bag, pushing and twisting whatever was in there, so she could find some matches. She finally found a pack, pulled one out and struck it. She leaned against the headrest and sucked on the wrinkled-looking cigarette, then exhaled a cloud of smoke through her mouth and nostrils, her eyes closed. I waved my hand at the cloud of smoke.

The bus moved up the two-lane highway, seldom passing anyone, except an occasional pickup truck driven by a farmer, who seemed in no particular hurry. Other than that, most of the cars passed the bus.

The woman smoked two or three cigarettes within an hour and asked me about a million questions, often blowing smoke in my face. How old was I? How long was I going to be in Cotton City? How big was my family?

I had been taught not to be nosey, but since she was asking me so many questions I decided it would be okay to ask her one or two, just to be friendly.

"How much stuff do you have in your bag? Sure is big." I kind of leaned over trying to peek in.

She started rummaging around as if she were taking some kind of account for me.

"Well, let's see now. What all do I…" She paused while she pulled out an old scarf. "…well look a' here. How many years have I had this? My late husband give me this. I can't hardly believe I still have it."

It looked faded and I was sure I saw a cigarette hole.

"What was he late for?" I asked.

"No, no Hon, I mean he's no longer with us. He's dead, Hon'. Deceased." She pointed her hands up and wiggled her fingers, trying to gesture some kind of ghostly shape going upward, I think.

"Oh," I said. So, that's how I learned that being late meant the same thing as being dead. That's why talking to grownups was so hard; you were always in danger of learning something that didn't make sense.

"Yes indeedy. I've had it for some time—some time. But let's see what else we have. Looka here, a pack of bobbie pins. I thought I'd lost those." She kept reaching and pulling different things out to show me. It was like a little treasure chest.

It reminded me of one of those magic acts where the guy keeps pulling a string of scarves out of his mouth. You finally realize that there've been more pulled out than there should have been room for in the first place. Then I saw a little pistol, like one of those derringers.

"Is that a gun?"

She pushed it down under some of the other stuff in the bag. "Not a real one. Just a cigarette lighter—outta flint."

"Oh. Sure looks real." Not that I had ever seen a real one. The ones in the picture show were the only ones I'd ever seen.

"Oh I jus' carry it mostly outta sentiment. My late husband give it to me one Christmas."

Just then she pulled up a Barq's Root Beer bottle that had a wad of cloth wedged in the top.

She pulled out the wadding and announced, "I'm jus' gonna have a little medicine now." She tilted her head back and took a big slug.

I think I caught a sniff. It smelled like the lighter fluid my daddy used in his cigarette lighter.

Yeah Boy stirred. He looked like a bloodhound that had picked up a scent in the wind.

"Excoose me, ma'am."

It sounded funny the way he said 'excuse.'

He gently tipped the front of his hat. "I don't mean to pry but is that a good cough medicine?" He put his hand over his mouth and coughed.

The woman looked at him, then me, then back to him. "Well, it helps with gentle coughs. It won't he'p if you got something big, like TB or somethin."

He took his hat off and leaned across the aisle a bit so he could lower his voice. "Oh, no ma'am. I got none of that consumption. Not me. But I got me this cough that wuz caused by a piece of shrapnel I got in the First War. Some German chunked a grenade at me and blew a hole in my lung. Been coughin' gently ever since. Ever since, jus' been coughin gently." He covered his mouth and coughed again.

"Well, I suppose I could spare a little for some gentleman that hep'ed defeat the dreaded Hun," she said. She handed him the bottle and he took a big slug without wiping the mouth of the bottle.

I thought that was pretty putrid—drinking out of the same bottle as someone else—someone you had just met; someone with tattoos and a fat exposed stomach. I wouldn't even drink after my brother. I couldn't stand the thought of someone's cooties in my mouth. He could have had cooties from anywhere—Bombay, China, even Biloxi.

She continued talking to him. "Well, my late husband offered to fight them but he was turned down for flat feet—also had a bad case of athlete's foot. He always had feet problems." She took a small drink then offered him the bottle again. "But he found work in the carnival. Flat feet don't matter, I guess, if ya got sawdust in yo' veins."

I thought the two of them were pretty funny the way they told stories. I'm not sure my mother would've approved though. She and my daddy had always told me to respect grownups but to be careful of strangers. Some would tell exaggerated stories to impress young children; stories about who they knew or where they'd been or what they'd done. It was, my mother had said, just a function of poor conduct to begin with. My daddy said they were sorry trash.

"How'd he die?" He held the bottle up to the light as if he were looking for life forms in it. "Is that what ya said, he's dead? Fall off the high-wire or summin'? A lion kill him?"

She had begun rolling another cigarette and was concentrating on her makings. "He was hit by lightning. Sad. Not only killed him but knocked one of his eyeballs out. Never did find it, so we couldn't stick it back in. We wanted an open casket, so we put a patch on his eye. And he did look natural except for the patch. And one of his ears was almost burnt off." She licked the papers and put the cigarette in her mouth.

He took another drink and handed her the Barq's bottle. He tucked his chin down close to his chest, then lifted it back up a bit and let out with a belch louder than Farley had ever made after drinking a hot Coca-Cola. I think half the people on the bus must've turned and stared at him. I noticed the driver gave a long look into his mirror and glared.

The woman turned and whispered in my ear as if she were my mother, "Prob'ly from Arkansas."

"Well, golly. I guess that cough of mine got busted some." He looked around as if he expected everyone to laugh or something. None did. He reached behind his head and pulled his wadded coat down. He pulled out a pack of Pall Mall cigarettes and lit one. He inhaled deeply then exhaled a stream of smoke. He coughed gently once or twice.

The bus pulled into Yazoo City. My daddy always said that Yazoo City was the 'Gateway to the Delta.' Once when I was little I asked him where the gate was, but he said that it was just an expression. I hated things like that, the way grownups said the gateway or other expressions that I later learned weren't really that at all. I guess I didn't really hate them. I was just disappointed not to find them. I was always on the lookout for things like that, like a giant gate, things that I thought were real. There were bumper stickers on cars that said, 'Rock City, Tennessee: See Seven States.' I later found out that all you could really see was a long way off. How were you supposed to know what you were looking at? There weren't any state lines in colors or anything, like on our maps in school. As it turned out, I wasted a lot of time looking for things that were never there.

"Yazoo City, Ladies and Gentlemen. We'll be here about fifteen minutes, if you want to stretch your legs or get something to drink," the intercom squawked.

Yazoo City was about fifty miles from Jackson. It had taken us over an hour to get here, and though I didn't really need to stretch my legs, I wanted to see if there were any pinball machines for me not to play. I figured I'd at least watch somebody else play. Watching somebody play pinball is like watching somebody fish, it's not a spectator sport. But every once in a while you'd run across a world-class player that could really rack up some points. It gave you something to tell your friends about when you got back home.

I didn't get full use of the fifteen minute layover because I had to wait on the straw-haired lady to get out. Then the fat-stomached belcher squeezed in behind her. He waddled down the aisle, winding like a fat trout in a stream, bumping a seat on one side then the other. She was carrying her giant bag. It seemed like it took almost five minutes for them to get off. I left my sandwich bag on my seat to save my window space.

Sure enough there were two pinball machines backed up against the wall which reminded me of something else my daddy had told Farley. "Son, anything that can back up against the wall and take on the world can't be beat."

Farley knew Daddy made sense, but he still wanted to play them. I think a lot of things are like that. You hear things from your parents that make sense, but you want to see for yourself why they are bad.

I decided to get a Coca-Cola, so when I got back on the bus I could have it with my sandwich. The waitress at the counter was about as old as my mother and very pretty. She was wearing a white dress kind of like a nurse's.

"And what'll you have, Darlin'?"

"May I have a Co-Cola please, ma'am?"

"Why, you surely may." She had a pretty smile.

"And will you put it in a cup for me, please. I'm gonna take it with me on the bus, and I don't want to pay the deposit on the bottle."

"I surely will. Anything for a nice little gentleman like yourself. Would you like some ice in it, too?"

"Yes, ma'am. Thank you." She turned and walked the length of the counter to get my Coca-Cola. By the time she got back, the straw-haired lady and the belcher had plopped down on the stools to either side of me.

"Well, now did ya ever see such a right smart whisker of a boy as this one?" the straw-haired lady said to the waitress.

"Well, he certainly is a sweet little man. Here's your Co-Cola, Darlin'. That'll be a nickel."

"What can I get y'all," she said politely to the other two, offering no smile.

"Lemme have a cup of coffee, Sweetheart," Yeah Boy ordered. He roared like she was a half a mile away.

"Me too, Dearie," the straw-haired woman said.

I wanted to watch the pinball machine players so I got up. "Thank you for the Co-Cola."

The smile lit up again. "Well, you're jus' more than welcome, Darlin'. You come back to see us, ya hear?"

I stood next to the pinball machine and watched as some teenager and his friend, both about Farley's age, played it. There was a guy in an Army uniform playing the other machine. I decided to watch the teenager.

There was an excitement watching the balls bounce, hitting one stob, then another, lights going on and off, sounds like a cash register made: ca-ching, gong, ching, ching. He was really playing great—ca ching, gong, ching, ching, body English, ca-ching, body English, too much—tilt!

He swore with all the anger of a guy who'd just lost a nickel.

"Now you just watch your mouth over there!" It was the pretty waitress. "There're ladies and children in here. If you don't watch your mouth I'll have a policeman here in two shakes."

The teenager slumped and mumbled, "Yes, ma'am."

I backed away and decided to get back on the bus, since the

fifteen minutes were almost up. But, mostly, I didn't want the pretty waitress to think I was friends with the cussing teenager. When I looked back I saw the straw-haired lady in the back of the station closing the door on one of those lockers they have in bus stations.

Before I got to the door, I heard that familiar sound from the belcher, still at the counter. Everyone else heard it, too.

"I think your bus is about to leave," the pretty waitress said to him.

Yeah Boy and the straw-haired lady got back on the bus behind me and took their same seats. The bus pulled out and made its way through downtown Yazoo City, which wasn't as big as Jackson but bigger than Flora for sure, and soon we were on Highway 49.

I had finished my sandwiches before we reached the city limits when I noticed she didn't have her big round bag. She had a brown grocery sack rolled down from the top. I had been taught that it wasn't polite to pry, but I didn't want her to forget something important to her. "Ma'am, did you forget your bag in the bus station?"

"No, no," she whispered. She leaned her head back and closed her eyes.

Yeah Boy had pulled his hat down over his eyes. In a way I wanted to ask him about the dead guy he had mentioned earlier. But I didn't. I was afraid she would wake up and shush him again.

She slept, grunting, snorting like she was having a dream. Somehow the family book my mother had given me had gotten wedged slightly under the straw-haired woman's butt. She was a little bit wide and I guess when she sat down she sat partially on the book, which was beside me. I had to get it before she smashed it completely. It was just a spiral notebook and wouldn't survive her load long. I had been admonished to be very careful with it. I very carefully tugged at the edge of it. She gave a quick snort. I pulled some more. Another short snort. Gave a quick yank. It was free.

Since my companions were asleep I opened it to the middle

just to see what my grandmother had written. She had often read some of her writing to Farley and me.

Our farm was a broadly covered area of green stalks, blanketing the ground for hundreds of acres all around. In a slow-motion explosion, day-by-day, week-by-week, the land revealed the white birth of cotton, the king crop of the Mississippi Delta. There were great vines of honeysuckle on one side of the house. The aroma seemed more noticeable in the open country, too. It occupied your nostrils like a natural perfume; a fragrance of home. Also, large, fifty-year-old sweet gums, magnolias and four giant oaks fortified the house and yard, forming a canopy of shade, from the hot dusty summers. There was no Bermuda grass or St. Augustine, just yard grass, crab grass, lush and green from the rich soil. We cut it with mower and sling blade.

The house was apropos to the Mayfields and their lives. But it was almost home to all of us. And each of us was in many ways like the other.

The rooms seemed bare, though wallpapered: browned by age and time and dust and humidity. Various prints of artwork: The Blue Boy; a ship sailing an unknown sea presenting dark sails against a moonlit night; a lake in the mountains somewhere, unknown but to the artist. A clock rested on the mantle in the living room, the hourly chime spilling throughout the house, somehow more wistful after bedtime.

The ceilings were high, and the furniture was dark mahogany, firm and sturdy and had a look of dominance. Though it could be scarred, it would hold its ground when bumped by an elbow, or a toe without a slipper; though it shared its masculine power with a feminine gentleness: No drink touched its skin absent a coaster.

The wall along the stairway was festooned with photographs of the Mayfield tree: great and grand uncles and fathers, many deceased; the depictions clearly etched, fading with age. One, a former Confederate soldier, an empty sleeve pinned to his chest.

I got sleepy as I read. I closed my eyes for just a bit.

CHAPTER 3

The Trailways bus had taken us up Highway 49 into the Delta, winding around bends and curves, as the rivers and streams set the course for the highway. As we passed through towns I could see the reflection of the bus in the store windows, a distortion waving up and down like a silver and red ship. The ride from Yazoo City had taken over an hour. Riding the big bus became tiresome as we got closer to Greenville. I still had more than an hour before Cotton City.

The straw-haired lady and Yeah Boy remained on the bus. He had been asleep since Yazoo City, and she slept on and off. She told me, in one of her awake moments, that she was going to Clarksdale. That wasn't too far above Cotton City, so I knew she'd be with me until I got off.

"Greenville, Misissippi," the driver's voice squawked over the intercom. "We'll be here about thirty minutes. Get out if you want and stretch your legs."

"Have a couple of belches," I said under my breath.

"What's that, hon?" asked the straw-haired lady.

"Oh, nothin'," I said. I didn't realize she was awake. Her eyes were closed and her head had been on the headrest.

Yeah Boy didn't budge. I guessed the medicine bottle must have had some sleeping stuff in it.

"Are you gonna get off, ma'am?" If she wasn't, I was gonna have to crawl over her or get her to move.

"Well, I believe I will. I think I'll just giv' this ol' body some movement. Maybe get the circulation goin'. Whadayathink, Mister Jake?"

I kind of wished I'd never told her my name, because every once in a while she called me Mister Jake. It would've been pretty hard not to tell her my name though, since she'd asked. My parents had always told me to be careful about giving information to strangers, but it was pretty hard not to when trapped on a bus with someone who kept asking.

"Yes, ma'am. Circulation would be good, I guess." I waited while she uprooted herself from her seat. She put the brown sack under her arm and shuffled down the aisle with me right behind her. A few others got off, too, but the belcher remained asleep, or unconscious, or whatever he was. I figured the driver would know if he was supposed to get off; or if he was dead.

I had thought about watching pinball again, but nobody was playing either machine. I thought about trying one nickel, but I was afraid there might be some FBI guy hanging around waiting for me to scrub the pooch or whatever it was Farley had said. I went to the counter for another Coca-Cola instead.

Greenville was bigger than Yazoo City. The bus station had a bigger counter, and there were more people milling around. It surprised me that there was nobody playing the pinball machine. There were more of those bus lockers too. I didn't understand why. I thought lockers were something that you only needed at the Y.M.C.A. to keep clean underwear in and stuff like that.

The straw-haired lady had already plopped down at the counter. Although I didn't want to sit next to her, I didn't want to hurt her feelings and sit a hundred miles away. She already had her coffee and had finished some makings when I walked up. I sat down in time for a great cloud of smoke.

"And what can I get you, my handsome little man?" said the lady behind the counter.

They were always saying nice things to me, and I didn't really mind except I hated feeling cute all the time. "I'll have a Co-Cola in the bottle, please, ma'am."

"One Co-Cola comin' up."

"I believe you drink as many Cokes as I drink coffee."

"I guess." I didn't know what else to say. I had no way of knowing how much coffee she drank.

"I must be addicted to this ol' coffee."

"Yes, ma'am."

She put about three big spoonfuls of sugar in her cup and began stirring it. My mother and daddy never let me have coffee, so I didn't know if sugar made it taste better or not. They had started letting Farley have coffee about a year ago, and he put five spoonfuls in the first time. My mother told him that was way too much. She told him he could have two at most, and if he wanted, he could have a little milk or cream in it. My daddy told him that only sissies put milk and sugar in their coffee.

"Here's your Co-Cola, Sugar. That'll be a nickel."

I had seven pennies and gave her five. My daddy had always told me not to hold onto anything with Lincoln's face any longer than you had to. He had told me that if I ever got a five dollar bill, to get change for five ones. George Washington was a fine Southern gentleman. Abraham Lincoln was a skunk.

"Thank you, Sugar." She turned and put my Lincoln discards in the cash register.

"Afternoon, ma'am." The big deputy sheriff sat down on the other side of the straw-haired lady. At the same time, a Mississippi highway patrolman sat down next to him. The deputy spoke and tipped his cap to her. "Two coffees, Rachel, if ya please," he said.

"Two coffees comin' up." She turned back and put two cups and saucers down in front of them, then poured. "Y'all find out anymore 'bout that dead fellow in the river?"

I froze.

"Not much. Not much to work with. Just a dead white man. Older fellow." He reached for the sugar. One teaspoon. "Two colored fellows found him while they were fishin'. He'd been shot twice it looked like." He glanced at me and stopped talking.

"Trailways Scenic Cruiser now departing from dock six for Jackson, Magee, Mendenhall, Hattiesburg, Gulfport and Biloxi."

The blaring intercom broke my trance. The deputy's story was as exciting as any I ever read. Except this story was true, and there was a real dead man.

The straw-haired lady paid less attention to the story than to her coffee, dipping her finger in the cup and stirring it and licking her finger. She didn't seem to care, or maybe her medicine made her sleepy. But the others at the counter seemed to hang on every word. The waitress stood and listened to the deputy, the coffee pot in her hand, chewing what smelled to me like Dentyne.

It was different when you heard something coming from a policeman standing right beside you. Someone who knew the real truth instead of your friends in school talking about what they heard somebody say, or what they'd bet had happened. And it was a little scarier listening when you were by yourself instead of with your mother and daddy. I wondered if my cousins in Cotton City had heard about the dead man. I could hardly wait to tell them.

Another blare: "Trailways Scenic Cruiser leaving in five minutes from dock number two, for Cotton City, Cleveland and Clarksdale. Please board now."

"Well, Hon, we better get back on. That old bus's liable to leave us. You wouldn't want to walk to Cotton City, would you?" The straw-haired lady pushed her cup away, a giant lipstick smudge on it.

"No, ma'am, I guess not."

"I can tell you one thing—I'm too wore out to walk to Clarksdale." She laughed.

"Goodbye, sweetheart. You come see me again, you hear?" The waitress gave me a small wave, and the highway patrolman flipped a two-fingered salute from the bill of his cap.

The straw-haired lady and I walked through the back exit to the bus docks and were about to climb aboard when we saw Yeah Boy descending the bus steps. The driver waited by the door for passengers to board.

"Excuse me, sir. Aren't you continuing?"

"Better believe it. Jus' gonna git a coffee here."

"I'm sorry but we're fixin' to leave, sir."

"Leave, I thought we wuz gonna be here half an hour or so?" He had put his rumpled up sport coat on and was rubbing one of his eyes.

"We've been here for jus' about that now, sir. Now we're fixin' to leave."

"What? Leave?"

I think it jus' then dawned on him that he had slept through the entire layover.

"Damn!"

"Excuse me, sir," the driver said. "But there's a lady here."

Yeah Boy glanced at the straw-haired lady as if he was still asleep. "Oh, well…"

She gave a broad smile, exposing her familiar teeth again. We got back on the bus. Yeah Boy went back to sleep. At least I knew he wasn't dead.

The trip was almost over. I could see the familiar outskirts as the bus approached and slowed, then stopped. The town was the same as I remembered. The sign read: 'Cotton City, Heart of the Delta, Pop. 909'.

There was a water tank, painted 'Cotton City, Home of the Mustangs'; the First Baptist Church; the one and only picture show, the Majestic; a few small businesses; two filling stations; and two grocery stores, though not either as big as a Jitney Jungle. Everything was close to the town square.

The square was a patch of grass in the middle, big enough to play chase and roughhouse football. There was a line of pecan trees along one side. It had swings for little children, criss-crossing sidewalks, and a gazebo in the middle where old men played checkers all day.

Dr. Henry had been city champion of the world-class checker championships for about the last twenty years. There was a story that some very old dentist had driven all the way from Shelby to play him. Supposedly the dentist left town crushed, having lost twelve straight games to Dr. Henry. Dr. Henry was ninety-three when he died last year.

There had only been one man in the county who could come close to matching him—a lawyer named Mr. Bainbridge. But he had died some years before I was born. Shot to death when he got caught cheating at cards in Vicksburg one night, Farley told me.

He lived in another town in the county, a lawyer who had a bad reputation for not accounting to his clients regarding their bills. This is something that I overheard my daddy and cousin say one time when they didn't know I was listening. He was a gambler who would try to win money at anything, whether dominoes, cards, checkers or anything you could bet money on.

Now Dr. Henry wasn't a gambler but a reliable man of great character, my cousin had said. But when he played checkers, he was fierce. One Saturday afternoon Dr. Henry and Mr. Bainbridge sat down for twenty-one game match where the man who won eleven was the winner. The gazebo had a crowd of over fifty people watching as Dr. Henry took the match, 11-7.

It was only a week later that Mr. Bainbridge went gambling in Vicksburg. Some say he was trying to recover his checkers losses.

No passengers got on or off during the brief stop, but the driver dropped off some deliveries. The bus station in Cotton City wasn't much bigger than the one in Flora.

I thought maybe I should ask the bus driver if I should get my suitcase out, since I would be getting off soon. My mother had said that I should ask him as soon as I got to Cotton City to let me off at Trek Mayfield's mailbox. But I had forgotten about getting the luggage until I saw him pull out a package. Now he would have to get less than two miles down the road and open that big side compartment again.

"Excuse me, ma'am." She didn't say anything, just grunted some. "Excuse me, ma'am." I nudged her shoulder and she just grunted some more. Just then the Yeah Boy reached across the aisle and whacked her arm with the back of his hand. A big whack, too. The straw-haired lady lunged forward in her seat like she had been hit with a mallet.

"Wha—whas goin'—are we there? We in Clarksdale?"

Yeah Boy looked at me and said, "That cough medicine made her a little drowsy, I imagine." He stuck his finger inside his shirt and scratched his stomach.

"I'm sorry, ma'am, but I got to tell the driver something. I'm sorry I got you up," I said.

"Oh, don't you worry a nickel's worth, hon'. You jus' go right ahead." She got up and stood in the aisle rubbing her arm. She gave Yeah Boy a nasty stare.

"Thank you," I said.

I scooted down the steps and was able to get to the driver before he had closed the compartment. "Excuse me, Mr. Riley." His name was printed on his nametag. "My mother and daddy said to ask you if I could get off at Trek Mayfield's mailbox just outta town."

"Well, I think that'll be okay, son."

"The reason I'm tellin' you now is because I thought you might want to get my suitcase out now. So you wouldn't have to do it two times in jus' a few minutes."

"Well, that's a good idea. I appreciate that, little buddy. Let's see, you gotta a claim check? You haven't lost it, have you?"

I dug down in my pocket and found it among my pocket knife and the change I had gotten from breaking one of my dollar bills. It was pretty crushed and rumpled, but you could still read the numbers.

He pulled out the big suitcase that my mother had packed. It was one of the really big ones that our family used for long trips. I mean really big. Daddy had said that it was big enough to put me in, and if we did, we could save the bus fare.

"Think you can handle that, son?"

Although I wasn't sure how much my mother had packed, I was sure there were three or four tons in the suitcase at least. If I could have wrapped both my hands around the handle I might've been able to drag it to the door, but I don't believe I could ever lift it up the steps.

"Here, better let me get that," Mr. Riley said. "We'll jus' put it up front. You can ride up there, too. Jus' hang onto the safety bar til we get to Mr. Mayfield's mailbox. Jus' about a mile. We'll only be a couple of minutes gettin' there."

It was quarter past four as we pulled up at the mailbox. I saw Cousin Trek, and Taylor and Casey standing by the farm pickup, waiting for me. Mr. Riley lowered my suitcase for me and Cousin Trek put it in the bed of the truck. Cousin Carol had stayed at home, probably working on a big-meal welcome.

After the big greeting and a grownup, finger-breaking, handshake with Cousin Trek, Taylor, Casey and I all piled into the bed of the truck. The truck was only two or three years old, a brown Ford, but it looked like all farm trucks. It had dents on each side and a rusty bumper. There were bits of wire and various tools scattered in the bed. The spare tire lay on its side, useful as a seat.

Casey and Taylor had on their denim overalls. I wore my nice trousers and a clean shirt, so we couldn't horse around in the back of the truck. We talked mostly about who was going to beat the Yankees for the American League Pennant. It looked like the Dodgers would win the National League. The cloud of dust from the gravel road descended on us as we approached the house. By the time we got there, we had the next three weeks all planned.

As we pulled up in the front yard, it dawned on me that I hadn't told the straw-haired lady goodbye. I hoped it hadn't hurt her feelings. Anyway, I supposed I would never see her again.

CHAPTER 4

Farley and I called Cousin Trek's father Big Trek. He had been a farmer all his life and had hoped one of his boys would take over the family farm and continue growing his beloved cotton. He owned eight hundred and ten acres; more than a section. About seven hundred were on the home place and the rest were out in the county. He worked some of it, rented some of it, and hired sharecroppers to work the rest. Some families had been there forever it seemed like, and most would live out their lives in the Delta. My daddy had once said that some lives were tragic, some were brilliant, and all were held together by the stretch of Mississippi sinew.

I once asked Daddy if Big Trek ever grew anything but cotton. He told me only during crop rotation did he grow anything else. The Delta soil was rich and could grow whatever a farmer had a mind to grow, he said, but cotton had always been king. And as far as Big Trek was concerned, it always would be.

Cousin Trek was the only one of the four brothers who didn't go to Ole Miss. He had gone to Mississippi State College and become a farmer. Farley said it was the cow college; something I didn't understand. Cousin Trek didn't have any cows, just cotton. Why hadn't they called it the cotton college? Something else over my head.

Cousin Trek's wife, who I called Cousin Carol even though she wasn't blood-kin, was from Bastrop, Louisiana. Trek had met her when he traveled there for a meeting of some kind about farm equipment. I think her daddy was the manager of John Deere over in Monroe.

"Well, my goodness, look how you've grown, Jake," said Cousin Carol.

Cousin Carol always acted excited to see me. She had always been special to Farley and me. She had treated us almost like we were her own children because she and my mother had become good friends after she married Cousin Trek. She wasn't really a cousin, but we called her one because she had married our cousin. And she did seem to give us special attention.

She had those polite habits that most grownups I knew had, where they would say things like, 'look how you've grown.' If a grownup hadn't seen you in fifteen minutes they were liable to say, 'look how you've grown.' But it was okay. They were just being nice. After she squeezed me in one of those hadn't-seen-you-in-forever bear hugs, she gently pushed me away, keeping me at arm's-length. She stared at me and said, "Yes, indeed you sure have grown."

"Your daddy must be workin' you, huh, Jake?" Cousin Trek said. "That makes a boy grow. Hard work and rain."

"Yes, sir, a little."

He and my daddy had some of the same way of thinking. When it looked like rain my mother would worry and say, 'Now get your raincoat and hat.' My daddy would say, 'Oh, Leslie, nothing to worry about. Rain'll make 'em grow.'

Farley and I had to work at whatever jobs our daddy could find for us. We were responsible for cutting the grass and helping my mother water her flowers around the house. My daddy would often have stuff for us to do on weekends at his lumber and supply business

But the worst job of all was painting. House, garage, anything that had to be painted, we painted. Never did we hire anybody to paint. I hated it. I would rather be stung by a million yellow jackets than paint.

My country cousins worked like men, and it built into them toughness. They chopped cotton, clipped cotton, cut cotton, hoed cotton, and worst of all, they bore the back-breakin' duty of picking cotton. If you could have peeled and canned cotton they would have done that, too. Their school year started three weeks later than mine, so they could help get the cotton in.

Always before we had visited earlier in the summer when

there was less to do, so Farley and I had never been to the fields. But now, late in the summer the cotton was getting high. This visit I would get a sense of where that toughness came from. I was going to hoe cotton.

Farley had found out about tough farm boys a couple of years earlier when he got into a fight in the park downtown. Farley was thirteen and the guy was barely twelve, but the guy had bloodied Farley's nose and split his lip before a couple of men came over and broke it up. I think Farley was glad they had. Every time Farley knocked the farm boy down he got up. That boy kept fighting like the rest of his life depended on it, when all they were fighting about was who had a better football team, Jackson or Greenville. Farley was ahead on points, but his opponent had taken everything thrown at him.

"I hope you're ready for some good fried chicken, Jake," Cousin Carol said. She started back to the kitchen. Her apron, tied behind her back, had a sunflower printed on it.

"Oh, yes, ma'am. I am. That's my favorite."

"Did you have any dinner?"

"Yes, ma'am. Tuna fish, and some bologna sandwiches, and three marshmallows. I ate them on the bus." Actually, I had given one of the marshmallows to the straw-haired woman, and I remember her talking while she chewed it. It looked like she was rolling taffy with her tongue, but I didn't say that to Cousin Carol.

"Well, that's been a while ago, so you'll be good and hungry by suppertime. We'll eat about six."

"Oh, by the way, Mother told me to give you this. It's for y'all." I handed her the notebook. "It's some things Granny wrote about y'all and the home up here. I read some of it on the bus."

She took it and thumbed through it, pausing in a couple of spots to read to herself. She smiled at one spot. "Well, thank you, Sweetheart. I guess I've got a thank-you note to write."

She kept flipping through the book, stopping after a few pages, looking a second, then thumbing some more. When she stopped at a particular page she would run her finger across the page and then smile. She seemed happy with it. It hadn't seemed such a fun thing to read to me. And it didn't have any pictures.

"Well, Granny has certainly a talent. We're going to really enjoy this. Now, y'all go on up stairs."

Cousin Trek had brought my suitcase inside. "Y'all take Jake to your room and help him put his grip up."

I grabbed the handle with both hands and tried to pull it. Casey and Taylor stepped over to help. Although Casey was just a little guy going into the third grade, he would tackle most anything. The three of us thrashed around with it until we finally maneuvered it off the floor and carried it like a coffin. Like pallbearers, Taylor held the front and I held the rear with Casey hanging onto one side. We trudged up the stairs.

Cousin Trek said, "How much did your momma pack? She got enough for the winter?"

Before I could answer, Cousin Carol called from the kitchen. "Now just don't be talking about Leslie. She put in what he'll need."

Cousin Trek put his finger to his lips, signaling for us to hush and just move it. He whispered, "She's got ears like an elephant."

The Mayfield house always seemed like another home to me. Even though I wasn't here but a couple of times a year, I never felt like I was walking in after a long time away. I once asked my grandmother why some places seemed this way. She told me it was because it was a family home. And to South-erners, family was the most important thing next to God. She said Yankees, though cordial, would when first meeting ask what the other did. Southerners meeting for the first time would ask where the other was from. Or, 'who are your people?'

"Momma said you get the top bunk or the bottom one," Taylor said.

"Okay, I'll take the top." I took the top since Farley and I didn't have bunk beds.

Casey and Taylor each had their own room, connected by

double doors which stayed open when somebody was sleeping-over. Both rooms had bunk beds.

There was a bedroom for their sister, Cousin Sally, but it had a regular bed and a big mirror and a bunch of pink things, and stuffed bears and kittens and other pretty useless stuff. We were not allowed in her room under any circumstances. Girls' rooms were like national monuments. You could know about them, even look at them from a distance. But if you trespassed on them, it was like a national crime.

Sally had won a scholarship to Vanderbilt in Nashville and had stayed in Nashville for some extra classes over the summer. I would sleep on the top bunk for the next three weeks and stay as far away from her room as possible.

"So are we goin' to the picture show tonight?" Casey asked. He was two years younger than Taylor and me, so a lot of the time when he wanted to do something, he made it a question.

"There's an Abbot and Costello one on tonight," Taylor answered.

"Yeah, whatever y'all wanna do," I said. Actually I wanted to go and had hoped they would bring it up. Friday night—picture show night.

"Daddy'll take us into town and pick us up after it's over. Better get your stuff out of the suitcase and stuff it in a drawer. Momma always wants things put away."

"Just shove it under the bed," Casey said.

"You better not listen to him," Taylor said.

Taylor had no sooner spoken than Cousin Carol walked in and began giving instructions, the kind that were about organizing clothes so you could find them, and that neatness kind of stuff. It was the same kind of thing my mother always said. And you had to do it.

"Now y'all help Jake put up his clothes. He can use the bottom drawer of your chest-of-drawers, Taylor. Be sure and fold them. Don't just dump them in. And hang your Sunday clothes on a hanger in the closet. What do y'all have planned for tonight?"

"Picture show, if it's okay."

"It's okay with me if it's okay with your daddy. He's the one that's got to drive you back and forth. Now Jake can wear what he's got on if he wants, but you boys are going to have to put on something nicer than those overalls. And you both have to bathe. You're filthy."

"Where is Big Trek?" It wasn't considered rude if you called a relative by a family nickname.

"Oh, that's right," Carol said. "You didn't know. Well, he's in Clarksdale 'til Wednesday. Just a little business." She tried to hide a smile. "Or so he says. Probably just swapping old stories, mostly. But you'll see him Wednesday. He's sure looking forward to seeing you." She turned back to Casey and Taylor. "Let's see now, what time does the picture show start—about seven fifteen. Now y'all get to moving, if you're going to bathe. It's almost five and we're going to eat around six."

Suppertime was a big event at my cousins', just like at our house in Jackson. It seemed like the biggest part of the day. Everybody was at the table, and there was plenty to eat. You had to keep track of your manners, all the knife and fork stuff. No talking with your mouth full, and absolutely no playing with your Jello, like at school. But you got to relax and listen to every-body's stories from the day. We ate in the kitchen, one of the few rooms without a ceiling fan. It had one of those fans that swung back and forth and hummed like my mother's sewing machine.

Cousin Carol was a good cook, just like my mother. She always had something you liked, and she didn't overkill with stuff like squash and beets. At least she didn't have them at the same time. That was thoughtful. That night we had fried chicken, mashed potatoes, crowder peas, turnip greens, a giant fruit salad and dessert.

Cousin Carol also made terrific pies. She had even won prizes at the fair. She and my mother often traded recipes and the two of them were co-champions of the world when it came to making pies, as far as I was concerned.

Cousin Carol's best, no doubt, was her cherry pie while my mother's was apple. Their only point of disagreement was coconut. My mother made them and loved them. Cousin Carol hated them. She called them hair pies. They were okay as far as I cared. I would eat any pie, any time. That night, we had cherry.

"Now I'll pick you boys up in front of the picture show," Cousin Trek said. "Y'all oughta be out by nine-thirty. The movie, news, cartoon and serial all last about two hours—maybe a little more—right?"

"Yes, sir," Taylor said. "But can't we go o'er to the square 'til you get here?"

"Well, I don't see why not, but be on the lookout for me."

"Now, Trek, you tell them I don't want them playing around in their good clothes," Cousin Carol said.

No playing in our good clothes. I think she and my mother had some long distant mental communication or something, the way they always had the same things to say.

"Okay, I'll pick you up, and you can go to the park. But you heard your mother. No rasslin' or rollin' around in your good clothes."

"Yes, sir."

"Yes, sir."

"Casey, did you hear me?"

"Yes, sir."

"Now who wants cherry pie?" Cousin Carol asked.

After dessert we helped clear the table. On my first night, Cousin Carol didn't make us wash and dry the dishes. We also could have gone to town on our bikes since it wasn't too far. Although I didn't have my own, there were at least six bikes around the farm—old ones, new ones and Sally's girl bike. But Cousin Trek was going to take us that night because I had just gotten there in the afternoon. Cousin Carol said she wanted us home as soon as possible since it was my first night, but Taylor and Casey had told me once that, really, she was a little nervous about crossing Highway 49 after dark.

Like most places in the South, summer time in Mississippi meant two things—baseball and swimming. If you lived in the country there was a third, fishing. City boys fished, too, but it took more planning, since you had to get past the city limits to find a creek or pond. In the country you could usually just walk out the back door.

"You wanna go fishin' tomorrow?" Taylor asked. We were waiting on the bunk bed while Casey finished brushing his teeth following supper.

"Where to? The branch along ol' Cottonseed Road?" I asked.

We had been there before. It was only about forty feet wide at the widest point but deep enough and had some pretty big catfish and some bream. There was a bridge over it that was a pretty good place to get underneath and fish. We sometimes walked up or down stream if they weren't biting under the bridge.

"Yeah, might as well. Say, what's Farley doin' now that he's got his driver's license?"

"Aw, he's always talking about driving all over the country. But he doesn't even have his own car. Even if he did I don't think Daddy would let him jus' drive anywhere he wants to. But he talks about it all the time. You know, he's got that teenager big-shot status."

"Is he playin' football still?"

"Yeah. That's one reason he didn't come. They have summer practice. But I think Daddy'll make him come the weekend they pick me up. I think their first game is about the middle of September."

"Is he gonna play in college?"

"Maybe. He wants to go to Ole Miss though. I don't know if he could play there. You have to be very good to play there, what with all the good players they have. Daddy said he might be able to play at Mississippi College or Millsaps. Anyway, he's got two years left in high school after this year."

"Why does he want to go to Ole Miss—Johnny Vaught?"

"Dixie Daniels."

"You mean our Dixie Daniels? From Cotton City?"

"Yeah, same one."

"She's already at Ole Miss. Has been for the last three years."

"Yeah, I know. But there's something about a guy when he

starts gettin' close to drivin' and havin' a driver's license."

"What's that?"

"Well, they start payin' close attention to girls for some reason. And two years ago, when we were here at Christmas, I noticed he was noticin' her down at the park. And that was jus' about the time Daddy started teachin' him to drive. I'm tellin' y'all—it's weird."

"Why good grief, she's old enough to be his mother. She's gotta be over nineteen or twenty. Besides, I notice girls," Taylor said.

"Yeah, but not like guys that have drivers licenses do. I asked him what it was about them. I asked if was because they started using lipstick or something."

"What'd he say?"

"He said that was part of it. But also when girls got older… well, their… you know…" I held my hands to the front of my chest, palms up and slightly curved, "…well, these get bigger. You know… their…their—"

"Their bosoms." Taylor said the magic word.

"Yeah," I said, "those. Now we've been comin' up here since I was too little to remember, and Farley has been seeing Dixie Daniels since she was ten or eleven. So he's watched them progress, you might say."

Casey walked in. He was wiping the remaining spit and toothpaste from his mouth with his hand.

"What are y'all talkin' 'bout. I heard y'all say fishin' and bosoms."

"Not so loud, Casey. You wanna get us killed, talkin' about stuff like that?"

"Talkin' 'bout fishin'?"

"No! 'Bout bosoms."

"I jus' wanna know if y'all decided to go fishin' tomorrow. Whada I care 'bout bosoms?"

"Jus' a minute, we're talkin' about something else right now." Taylor turned back to me. "Well, 'progress' sounds funny."

"Well, they have…progressed. I wonder why ours don't progress," I said.

"They jus' don't. It's jus' a law or something. Ours don't change. I think they're jus' there for balance or something. I mean it's not like they're a couple of hamsters and you can feed 'em and train 'em to make 'em bigger."

We both laughed.

Casey didn't laugh. He just looked at us like we were crazy. "When y'all get through with your bosom talk, will y'all tell me one thing?"

"What?" Taylor said.

"Are we gonna go fishin' tomorrow?"

Taylor and I looked at one another. Then Taylor put his hand on his little brother's shoulder for reassurance. "Definitely."

CHAPTER 5

"Now I'm gonna give you boys twenty cents apiece. That's a dime for the movie and a dime for popcorn." We were parked in front of the Majestic, the pickup idling while Cousin Trek dropped us off. He dug into his pocket for change.

"Thank you, Cousin Trek, but Daddy gave me some money." I knew my daddy would want me to try to pay for myself, and anyway I felt important saying I had my own money.

"That's fine, Jake, but save your money. I'm treatin' tonight. Y'all are gonna get a chance to earn a little hoeing cotton next week."

I thought of that extra money and smiled. Taylor and Casey didn't smile. The thought of doing anything with cotton wasn't special to them—money or not.

"BB's helpin' work that hundred acres across the road for me and Big Trek, and he needs to get some of the weeds out. They been gettin' ahead of him, and his daddy and the share-croppers got more'n they can handle this year. Anyhow, the picture show's gonna start in a minute or two, now git goin'."

The three of us turned and bolted to the ticket window. Cousin Trek shouted a final instruction. "I'll be back by nine-thirty. Don't wander away from the square—y'all hear—I don't wanna have to look around for y'all!"

There were few things in my life as exciting as a Friday night picture show. The marquee put the titles up in big block letters so they almost shouted. Every picture show, I thought of in these gigantic titles: ABBOTT AND COSTELLO MEET THE INVISIBLE MAN. On top of that they were showing a serial, RADAR MEN FROM THE MOON, starring Commando Cody. He had this great rocket suit and could fly all over the

Earth just by turning on his power and jumping in the air, and flipping the up and down buttons.

Tonight they had a Bugs Bunny and Yosemite Sam cartoon. You got all this with popcorn, and you could yell and holler as much as you wanted since no grownups were in the way. It was hard for me to believe Farley was no longer interested in watching Commando Cody falling from the sky, unable to get his up-down buttons fixed. Now all he cared about was watching girls and their progression. I guessed that when you got older, life had less meaning for you—although you did get a driver's license.

The show ran a second time starting at nine-fifteen. And though we wanted to watch it again—Farley and I had watched Red River five times one weekend a couple of years ago—we had to get outside to meet Cousin Trek at the park.

We raced across the street right in front of Mr. Siler, the slowest driver in the entire State of Mississippi. I don't think he could hurt you, even if he hit you. He never drove more than two miles an hour probably, but if you ran across the street before he passed you, he would honk and yell, "You boys are gonna get killed!" Then he always turned to look at you, nearly running up on the sidewalk in the process.

About twenty other kids had gotten out of the picture show and there was already a roughhouse football game going on in the square. Nobody had brought any kind of a ball to the show, but a bunch of wadded up popcorn boxes were shaped into something you could throw. It worked fine. Most of the kids were in their good clothes, and probably had been told to not get their clothes dirty. If they had, they were just hoping they didn't fall down and leave evidence of grass stains or ripped knees.

"There's Mr. Hightower." Casey pointed.

"Don't point, Casey," Taylor told him.

"Cousin Trek and Cousin Carol don't go for that pointin' stuff neither, huh?" I asked, knowing the answer. It was funny the way every set of grownups had the same bunch of rules.

"Oh yeah. Pointin' at people or scratchin' your behind in

public is a major crime," Taylor said. Casey started scratching his behind like he had lice. We both laughed at him.

"Okay, somebody's gonna tell on you and you'll get a switchin'. Wait and see," Taylor said.

"What's a' matter, Casey? Got ants in ya pants?" Earl Hightower, a man who rented from Cousin Trek had been watching from across the street, and walked over.

Renters were men who rented certain pieces of land from farmers, planted their own seed, then kept the difference between what they owed in rent and what the cotton brought at the gin. Mr. Hightower was one of these. He also worked for some of the farmers by the hour or by the pound during picking season. I always heard Cousin Trek say Earl was a hard working fellow. Calling a man hard working was a compliment.

Mr. Hightower didn't look much older than Farley, but I had been told he was at Guadalcanal in the War, so he had to be a lot older than he looked. In any event we didn't call him Earl. He was Mister Hightower to us.

"Hope they ain't them fire ants. You'll really be in trouble then." He didn't wait for an answer. "Well, boys, was the movie good?" He stood with us at the gazebo where we were watching the ball game.

"Yes, sir. Did you see it?" Taylor knew he probably hadn't but asked anyway. Taylor had told me that only once in a while did the Majestic have a picture show that anyone older than us liked. If there was a real special picture show, like the ones I had heard Mother and Daddy talk about, like Gone With the Wind or All the King's Men, the grownups would go to Clarksdale where they didn't allow hollering.

"Naa, I been over at the café, havin' Friday-night coffee."

Once I heard Cousin Carol speak to my mother about the café in what my mother called dark tones. She said on Friday and Saturday night there was a high-stakes domino game going on in the back room. She said she had it on good authority that some of those men played for a penny a point. She couldn't understand as hard as a dollar was to earn, how some men could gamble it away. Whenever we went to that café, we had instructions from my mother never to go into the famous back room. Mr. Hightower was a nice man, but I'll bet he'd seen that back room.

I was sure that the gazebo checker games, played right out in front of everybody, were not played for money—at least not so we knew about it. Dr. Henry and the others played for the pride of being best. I figured that no amount of money in the world could have helped that old dentist from Shelby. His pride had been taken.

"Y'all waitin' for your daddy?"

"Yes, sir," Taylor said.

"Maybe he'll give me a ride home. Had to put my truck in the shop earlier today. Saw y'all, and thought I'd catch a ride back home, maybe."

"He's gonna be here any time Mr. Hightower, I 'magine," Taylor said.

"And who do we have here?" he said, looking at me.

Oh, this is our cousin Jake. From Jackson—"

"Earl Hightower, son. Nice meetin' ya." He extended his huge hand. It seemed as big as a catcher's mitt as he shook my hand.

"Nice to meet you, Mr. Hightower."

"What's your last name, Jake?"

"Conner." I didn't tell him I knew who he was. I had heard Cousin Trek and Cousin Carol talking about him lots of times. And they always seemed to be saying nice things about him. But I didn't say that. I just pretended not to know him.

"Jake likes hoeing cotton. Prob'ly likes pickin' it too," Taylor said.

Casey laughed. "He's kind of stupid," he said.

I punched him on the arm. I knew they were just playing with me, but it made me kind of mad—made me feel like a city slicker. "I didn't say I liked it. I said I like to make the money."

I wasn't about to let it get out that I liked hoeing or picking cotton. Nobody in his right mind liked that, and I could be the laughing stock of the county if such a rumor got out.

"Well, don't worry, Jake. I'll keep your secret." Mr. Hightower smiled and rubbed the top of my head, while reaching and grabbing Casey by the nose with two fingers, making him squeal like a piglet. "And if there's any stupid goin' round, this one's got his share." He laughed at Casey, then let go of his nose, giving him a little push backwards.

Casey faked great pain: "Ouch, ouch, ouch!" then laughed.

Daddy told me that hoeing cotton meant hoeing out the weeds during the growing season—usually from about April to the end of September. Cotton has a long growing season, which is one reason why it grows mostly in the South; that and the need for plenty of rain, which the Delta gets. Too many late freezes in the spring or early freezes in the fall are bad for cotton farmers. He said that cotton requires a certain amount of heat, and if it gets too cold when it is young in the ground, or when it is coming out almost ready to be picked, it can be damaged. In both cases the farmer's yield is cut back a whole lot.

I knew that hoeing cotton wasn't nearly as awful as picking it. Picking was brutal back-breaking work. But hoeing was slow, boring and hot. Not long after the sun rose, the temperature rose quickly to the mid eighties. By late-morning it could reach one hundred degrees.

If you had been picking every year since about an hour after you were born, you could get tired of cotton fast. But since I hadn't I could at least make some money while on vacation.

"Your daddy says you're gonna be helpin' me and BB next week," Mr. Hightower said.

"Yes, sir," Taylor said.

"Who's BB?" I asked.

Mr. Hightower said, "That's Big Black Julius. We jus' call him BB. His daddy jus' calls him Julius. His football coach gave him the nickname Big Black Julius. You don't know him, Mr. Jake?"

"No, sir. But Cousin Trek told us we were gonna be helpin' him on Monday. Said he played football pretty good—"

"That's what they say. Supposedly he could have got some kind of scholarship at Florida A&M. Jake Gathier wanted him—pretty good coach. That's what the colored folks say. But he went in the army right outta high school. Said he didn't care much 'bout college right then."

"Where's Florida A&M?" Casey asked no one in particular.

"In Florida, dopey," Taylor said.

I laughed. So did Mr. Hightower, but not as loud. It wasn't that funny to him, I guess. "Well, I think it's in Tallahassee. It's a colored school. Usually have a pretty good football team. I know that."

"And y'all know Big Black Julius pretty good?" I asked. I couldn't remember if I'd ever heard the name when I'd come up here before.

"He's a colored friend of ours," Casey said.

"Yeah. A big guy, too," Taylor added.

"Just got back from Korea," Mr. Hightower said. "Big, strong boy; a hard worker, too. Julius Samuels is his whole name. His daddy is Ben Samuels. He says he might want to go to that new school for colored students at Itta Bena. Mississippi Valley State or something like that. Probably can't play ball now though. His wound in Korea might not allow it. Least, that's what I heard."

Mr. Hightower took a toothpick from behind his ear and put it in his mouth. Lots of men did that—put a toothpick in their mouths for no reason. Just something to do, I guess. "Y'all got a big Saturday lined up? Or your daddy got y'all workin' all day?"

"We're goin' fishin'. We don't have any work 'til Monday; at least none in the fields. Momma and Daddy always got summin' to do around the house," Taylor said. "We're goin' down to the branch at Cottonseed Road. Bet you anything we'll pull in some big cats."

"Y'all oughta get your daddy to take you over to the river, down at the bridge at Greenville. If y'all want big cats."

"I don't think he's gonna have time while Jake's here. He'll be pretty busy gettin' ready for pickin'."

"Well, maybe I can take y'all after church next Sunday. I got a friend or two with boats down there. We could really do some catfishin'. Blues, channels--they catch some giant spoonbills on trotlines down there, too."

Just then Cousin Trek pulled up in the pickup. He stuck his head out of the window and held out his hand to shake Mr. Hightower's. "Hello, Earl. Whadaya say? Makin' a night on the town?"

"Not really. Jus' havin' coffee over at the café."

Before Mr. Hightower could finish, Taylor piped up. "Can we give Mr. Hightower a ride, Daddy? His truck's broke down."

"Well, sure nuff. Jump up here in the front, Earl. You boys climb in the back."

Viewing the rows of cotton in the daytime, it seemed they stretched for miles, and almost like a long straight highway in the distance, seemed to come to a point on the horizon. At night they disappeared into the darkness only a few yards away. Each row seemed to make me blink in the headlights as we drove by, a reminder that they would be there in the morning.

At night before the moon was up, there seemed to be a jillion stars. To me they looked like eyes that had come out to look at the land while the sun rested. It was much different out here in the country than it was in Jackson. As we passed the rows of cotton, I thought of the cottonseed plant in Jackson. When we drove downtown, Farley and I would always plead with Daddy to drive close to the cottonseed plant so that we could smell the cottonseed oil cooking. But out in the country there were things to smell that the city didn't have.

It was an extra three or four miles out of the way to Mr. Hightower's house, but that was fine with us. At night, the air felt good blowing on you. Riding in the back of the truck gave us a kind of free feeling that felt especially good as a change from the daytime heat. We had to shout to hear one another over the rush of the wind and the noise from the Firestones against the pavement.

"Did y'all hear about that dead guy they found in Greenville?"

"What dead guy?" said Taylor.

"What dead guy?" said Casey.

"A dead man they found in the river. He got shot two times. Then he was chunked in the river." I guess in all the excitement of my arrival I'd forgotten to mention it. But when Mr. Hightower mentioned the bridge at Greenville, I remembered it.

"Aw, c'mon. Where'd you hear that?" Taylor asked.

"You mean y'all haven't heard about it?"

"Aww you're jus' makin this up," Taylor said.

"No, I'm not. The deputy sheriff told me."

"A deputy told you?" Casey asked.

"Well, not really jus' me. I was sittin' at the counter at the bus station in Greenville and he kinda told everybody—at least everybody sittin' there."

"And you're not makin' this up?" Taylor asked.

"No, really. Some colored man and his son found the body."

CHAPTER 6

We had a glass of milk when we got home. Then we were off to bed, well before eleven.

"Do y'all have to sleep in pajamas, still?" I asked. By a certain age, most boys were of the opinion that pajamas were a little sissy.

"Not really, but Momma would rather we did. Daddy said it wasn't a big thing on his mind. Besides farm boys have to get up early and quick. Ain't got time to fool with pajamas."

I put mine back in the drawer. Mother had made me pack them, but she didn't say I had to wear them.

Cousin Trek came in and told us to get to sleep and not lie down and talk all night, not if we expected to get up and go fishing. These were mostly standard instructions, and we went to sleep as soon as we could. We were excited about the three weeks ahead.

Cousin Carol let us sleep late, until seven. But we were still tired. We had whispered until after one.

"Hey, let's eat and get on out," Taylor said. He stood on the edge of the lower bunk and was holding on to the top edge while he poked me with his finger.

"I'm up. Have been for a while. Is Casey up?"

"I doubt it. He sleeps like a drunken sailor." That must have been something he heard in a picture show, or maybe one of the men playing checkers had said it. I was pretty sure he had never seen a drunken sailor, sleeping or not.

"Get up. I'll go get him," Taylor said. He went through the open double doors into the adjoining room.

I threw back my sheet and swung my legs over the edge of the bed. There was a ladder at the end. That was for cowards, since real men jumped out of their beds like firemen or paratroopers. After jumping, I went through my assigned drawer looking for my most worn blue jeans. I was standing there in my underwear when Casey walked in.

He rubbed his eyes for a moment then stared at me. "Hey! You gotta hole in your underwear. Booty, booty, booty. I—see—your—booty," he hollered.

Casey was only eight and he was always doing stuff you'd expect from a guy in the third grade. I dropped my underwear and mooned him.

"Ahh!" He put his hands over his eyes.

Taylor broke up laughing.

From downstairs I heard Cousin Carol. "Y'all better get dressed and get down here before I throw these pancakes out and make you paint the chicken house instead of goin' fishin'."

Painting—the curse of mankind. "C'mon, y'all, let's get goin'."

Cousin Carol made pancakes like she made pies. They were great. Or maybe it was easy to make pancakes. I don't know. Anyway, my mother made good ones, too. I couldn't remember if that was a family trait my grandmother had mentioned in her book or not. But we ate as many as she fixed, and almost all the Aunt Jemima in the large bottle was gone by the end of the meal. We probably could have eaten more, but we wanted to get on down to the branch.

Cousin Trek had already left. He and Big Trek went downtown most Saturday mornings and drank coffee at the café, waiting for the seed and feed store to open, or to talk with other planters before they made their rounds in the fields. Today he had gone alone since Big Trek was still in Clarksdale.

"Y'all got your poles and everything you need?"

"Yes, ma'am." Taylor said.

"Finish your milk, Casey. Now wipe your mouth, and not on your sleeve. Use your napkin." Too late. "Casey!"

Trying to recover, Casey wiped his sleeve with his napkin. Awkwardly, he murmured, "May I be excused?"

Cousin Carol didn't answer. She stared at him with one

corner of her mouth up, one corner down. There was a brief silence. "Get out of here. All of you." A slight smile materialized.

"The pancakes were good, Cousin Carol. I sure enjoyed 'em," I said.

"Well, I'm glad you did, Jake."

"Me, too. Thanks, Mama." Taylor said.

"Me, too, Mama," Casey uttered, licking his lips.

"Y'all get upstairs quick and brush your teeth. And be back here for dinner. I didn't have time to make you any sandwiches."

We walked through the back yard, past the garage and the chicken house, toward the field of ripening cotton. We walked our bikes down one of the rows that led to Cottonseed Road, then followed it to the bridge.

It was about a mile and a half to where the branch passed under the bridge. We left our bikes and walked along the branch. It was eight o'clock or thereabouts, since none of us had a watch. And we'd have to guess about what time noon came so we'd not be late for dinner.

We carried our cane poles over our shoulders. Casey carried the can of worms. Cousin Trek had also scooped up a few roaches out of the barn and put them in a jar for us, careful to poke some ice pick holes in the top so they wouldn't die before we killed them. I carried the roaches while Taylor had a cigar box under his arm full of extra hooks, sinkers and some extra line.

Roaches, crickets and worms were the best bait for bream, although they would even bite on white bread if it stayed on the hook long enough. All of these were also terrific for catfish, because catfish were scavengers and would eat most anything.

I started with a worm and began sticking it head-first, though I was never sure which end was the head, over the point and past the barb and bend, crushing the life out of it. Taylor put a roach on, its squirming little feet wiggling just like anybody's would, I thought. He ordered Casey to do the same. Taylor said that worms were a sure thing, but we needed to see if they were biting roaches this early in the morning. I had my line in the water first and soon heard Taylor hollering at Casey.

"Casey, don't do that. That's dumb. You wanna have 'em alive for a little bit."

"What difference does it make? They're gonna die anyhow when they drown."

Casey was shaking a roach out of the can and then squashing it with his tennis shoe. Then he scraped it onto his hook.

"I don't like 'em wiggling in my hand. It tickles. Besides, roaches'll put a hex on ya."

Taylor shook his head. "You dope," he said. "That's jus' some ol' story you heard."

"It's true. Humphrey Turnipseed told me."

"Aw squat! Humphrey Turnipseed is dumber than a baked cow pattie."

"He is not. You're dumb."

"He failed the third grade twice."

"He did not. He failed it jus' once. And that was because he had mumps and measles in the same year."

"Well, he's still dumb," Taylor said. "There ain't no such thing as a roach hex."

"Well, jus' the same, I'm not lettin' 'em wiggle in my hand."

"You're jus' chicken," Taylor said. When he turned back to the water Casey distorted his face and stuck his tongue out at Taylor's back, then cast his dead roach into the branch.

We sat on the bank under the bridge and watched our corks. Fishing made me think about the dead guy, and about the colored men who found him while they were fishing. Last night while we whispered after bedtime the three of us wondered if it was BB who had been with his daddy and found the body. Taylor said it might have been since a lot of the time BB and his daddy did go fishing at the river bridge down at Greenville. It could have been anybody, but I think we wanted it to be somebody we knew so we could ask questions about the big crime.

"Y'all think we can ask BB or Julius, or whatever his name is about that dead guy?" I asked. "I mean, when we see him."

"Sure," Taylor said. "Might be the first thing I'm gonna ask him."

"He won't mind?"

"Naaa. BB's a nice guy." Taylor pulled his line up to check his bait, then flipped it back in. "I guess you've never met him, huh? In all the times you been here? You never have?"

"Never have," I said. "Guess he was never around, or something. How come he didn't want to play football in college?"

"Don't know. I think he jus' wanted to go fight Communists," Taylor said.

I held up my hand. "Shhh. I got a bite. Watch my cork." My cork was moving around and bobbing just a little bit. Just enough to make some small ripples before it would stop. Then the whole thing would be repeated: bob—ripples—bob—ripples.

"Ahhh, that's a turtle after your bait," Taylor said. "Better check it. Bait might be gone."

I pulled my line in and the worm had been mangled some—a pretty good sign of a turtle attack. Turtles would swim under the water and jus' nibble around on your bait, never getting' their mouths on the hook, just teasing you. I reset my worm and flipped the line upstream some.

"He could have gone to college and then to war, it looks like to me," I said.

"I don't know. Why don't you ask him that? I'll ask him if he saw the dead guy, too."

"I wonder who killed that guy?" I asked.

"I wonder, why?" Taylor asked.

"Will y'all shut up talkin' about dead guys? You'll scare the fish away. Hey! I got one," Casey screeched.

His cork darted below the brown water. His line pulled hard. His pole bowed and shimmied in his hands. He tugged, both hands on the pole. He yanked hard and up on the bank a big blue catfish sailed, landing in the grass in a flopping frenzy.

We caught three more. Taylor caught a cat, a hand-sized bream, and I caught a cat almost as big as Casey's. After about an hour or so they stopped biting under the bridge, and we decided to move up the branch. It was probably after ten we figured, but we had time to try a couple more spots before going home for dinner.

We followed the branch, sometimes staying close to it, sometimes getting back a ways. There were some cattails close to the bank and some willow trees so close to the branch that you couldn't get around without slipping into the water. Besides, we were more likely to step on a water moccasin walking through cattails and drooping willow branches. Casey said there was danger stalking us every step of the way.

"There's a good spot jus' up here," Taylor said. "We'll try it for a few minutes. If they don't bite we'll try one other spot before we go home for dinner."

We reached a big cottonwood tree and an old weeping willow, both about ten feet back from the bank. They were old and full and gave shade; as much as the bridge had, anyway. It was over ninety degrees by then. There was plenty of room for all three of us to sit and throw our lines.

At first they didn't bite, but just as we were about to move, they did. I caught three bream and Taylor and Casey each caught a cat and a bream.

Taylor looked at the sun, almost directly overhead. "We better go eat," he said. "Prob'ly gettin' close to noon. We'll come back after dinner."

I started pulling the fish stringer out of the water.

"Aww, jus' leave 'em there. Nobody's likely to come by here anyway. Let's take our poles, though," Taylor said.

Taylor had a good sense of sun time. It was just before noon when we parked our bikes and walked in the back door.

"Catch any?" Cousin Carol was looking in the refrigerator, her chin cradled between her thumb and forefinger. She spent a lot of time looking in the refrigerator. Like my mother, she had to engineer a food plan for meals, making sure all the leftovers got used, and the diet was all balanced and everything.

"I caught a bunch," Casey blurted. "Maybe four, I think."

"Well put them in the sink on the back porch, and I'll clean them for y'all later. Maybe y'all can eat them for supper. Or maybe I'll freeze them. We'll see."

Taylor sat down at the kitchen table. "We jus' left them in the water, 'cause we're goin' back after we eat."

"Okay." She took a bowl of something out, then closed the refrigerator door. She looked at Taylor, sitting at the table. I was about to sit, myself.

"Now y'all don't sit down until you wash your hands."

"Yes, ma'am," Taylor said.

"I washed mine in the branch," Casey said. His attempt to dodge a rule flopped. Cousin Carol pointed the way. We went to the backdoor sink and washed.

Cousin Trek walked in the back door. He rubbed each of our heads while we were washing. "Catch any? Don't forget the soap, Casey." He kept walking into the kitchen. "Hi Hon'," he said to Cousin Carol.

I was pretty sure that it would be hard for me to ever get married if I had to use names like "Hon" and "Sugar" and "Dear." I guess they sounded okay on the radio programs or in the picture show, but if you had to say them yourself it sounded terrible. One time I told my mother that if I got married I'd call my wife Jake Jr. She gave me the look she sometimes gave Daddy.

We dried our hands and walked into the kitchen. I said, "We caught seven or eight, I guess, Cousin Trek."

"Let me see…" Taylor started counting on his fingers, and mumbled some numbers. "You know what? I think twelve."

"Good for you. You got 'em in a bucket? Lemme see."

Cousin Carol put some bread on the table and answered for us. "They left them in the branch. Said they're going back."

"Well, they'll be okay I imagine, as long as they are in the water so they keep fresh. And there ain' a lot of fish thieves in the county." He smiled. "I'm hungry. Let's eat."

Some leftover chicken and ham and some butter beans and tomatoes made up most of our dinner. Cousin Carol even gave us a piece of pie for dessert, a treat at dinnertime. I'm sure she did it just because I was there. Company was king in our whole family.

After eating we went upstairs for a few minutes to rest our stomachs, and just sit around and talk about nothing special. Casey kept counting to himself how many fish he had caught. One count he would remember four, one count five, another count back to four. And he kept saying, "All on squashed roaches."

"Whaday'all wanna do when we get back from fishin' this afternoon?" Taylor asked, ignoring Casey's squashed roaches comments.

"Maybe we can go to the picture show again," Casey said.

That sounded good to me, even if it was the same show. Taylor sat on the bed, his back against the wall, his hands clasped behind his head. "Naaa, I don't think we can go tonight. That'd be two nights in a row. Even havin' company, that isn't likely. You know, Daddy'll say that's too much money for something you already saw. Momma will agree with him like she always does."

"I know, I know," Casey said, lying on his bed, punching his naval with his finger.

"Anyway, I think we might be havin' homemade ice cream. I noticed the bucket was out of the closet. It was sittin' on the back porch when we came in," Taylor said.

"I wish we didn't have to crank so much," Casey said. "That's a lotta work."

"Whadayamean 'we'? I do all the work anyway. You always start whinin' that your arm hurts."

"Well, it does! Crankin' that thing is hard."

"Aww baloney! You're jus' lazy."

"So? Lazy's okay, if you're a gentleman about it. That's what momma says: 'Anything you do, do it like a gentleman.' "

Taylor just shook his head.

Eating homemade ice cream sounded good, and just sitting around the porch was always kind of fun. Maybe swinging in the big swing; maybe playing Chinese Checkers or something; even climbing the windmill and looking at the sunset—not because it was pretty like Mother and Cousin Carol would say, but just because you could see it longer from high up. It was stuff we didn't do at home.

A full stomach and a warm room had made us sleepy. We were lying on our beds when Cousin Carol called out, "Y'all better come on down and get back to your fishin' spot, before something happens to your fish."

She gave us a thermos full of lemonade and put it in a brown paper sack with three small jelly glasses. She admonished us to not get back too late. Supper was at six and maybe we should get back by five. She might have a surprise. That told us for sure we were going to have homemade ice cream.

We left our bikes at the house since we had worked our way up the branch close enough to the house to walk. And it was easier to carry everything walking. It was hotter now, and we kicked up dust between the rows of cotton. In the morning the dew hadn't dried, and the rich soil was still matted and would stick to your Keds. The stalks of green with their white bolls were dry and taking in the sunrays. I almost felt sorry for the little white bolls facing the sun. We picked up little clods of dirt to throw at the dragon flies circling. You had to be pretty accurate to hit one. To my knowledge, no one had ever hit a dragonfly with a dirt clod in midair.

Taylor tried to tell a joke while we walked. He said he hadn't heard all of it, but it was one that he had overheard in the seed and feed one day. It was something about a farmer's daughter and a salesman, and how they ended up in her daddy's barn one night and fell out of the loft. Taylor said maybe when we were older we would know what it meant, and then maybe it would be funny. I told him if he had heard all of it, maybe it would be funny. He had heard Cousin Carol say one time that some of those men at the seed and feed store were lazy and had nothing better to do than play dominoes at the café and tell dirty jokes. She had said they ought to be careful when children were around—telling some of the jokes they told—and they were the same men you never saw in Sunday School, either. The farmer story must have been a dirty joke.

We passed through the field, then turned through the trees toward the spot where we had been earlier. We sat under the cottonwood tree and put down our poles and our sack with the thermos. The first thing we wanted to check was our fish. Casey screamed when he saw the snake; a great high-pitched scream, like a girl.

"Oh, man alive, look at that," Taylor said. Casey had retreated almost all the way up the bank. "Is it dead?"

I was about five feet away and didn't want to get any closer. I leaned forward and squinted at the dark colored snake. "He doesn't look like he's movin'. Y'all think he's dead?"

"Hand me a stick," Taylor said.

Casey started poking through the weeds, trying to find a tree limb. Finally he picked one up about three feet long. He pitched it to Taylor, who was closer to the snake.

"I think he's dead," I said.

Taylor poked the snake. It didn't move. He poked it again. Finally he slipped the stick underneath it and lifted it. It didn't move until Taylor lifted the stick high and the snake started sliding down toward his hand. He dropped the stick and jumped back. It just lay on the ground. Finally, satisfied it was dead, we closed in.

"Cottonmouth," Taylor said. "Sure death if you get attacked by one of those."

"My daddy said they'll make you sicker than a dog with mange," I said.

"Shoot! They'll kill you too, Jake. I've heard lotsa guys say so," Taylor said.

Casey had gathered courage at the discovery that it was dead and moved in a little. "I wonder how it died?" The three of us stood directly over it.

"You think somebody came along here and killed it, Taylor?" Casey asked.

"Beats me. Say! Look it's kinda got a bloody spot on its head." Taylor put his foot on it just below the head, and pointed with the stick. "Look at that. Looks like little holes in its head. Maybe somebody shot it. Hey, Jake, see if the fish are still on the stringer."

I looked at the stringer. I imagined a giant cottonmouth attached to the fish.

I tugged the stringer then pulled it up. "Yep, looks like they're all here."

"Hey, what's this shiny thing?" Casey said. He was pushing something with his toe, just beyond the snake. "Look, Taylor," he said, holding up the small object in the sunlight. Its reflection sparkled.

"Look, another one," I said.

Before I picked it up Taylor took Casey's, held it in the air and said, "That's a bullet shell…you know, a casing. A .22." He looked at Casey.

"I'll bet it's Looty," Casey said.

I looked at both of them. "Who is Looty?"

"He's a guy we know," Taylor said.

"Yeah," Casey said. "He lives across the cotton field over yonder." He pointed toward the field. "All by his-self."

CHAPTER 7

Sunday morning seemed to come earlier. Maybe it was because you knew you were going to have to get all dressed up, and you felt tired before you even got out of bed. We had bathed the night before, and after we ate breakfast we were instructed to get a move on. Get dressed so we could get to Sunday School by nine-thirty. I had my sport coat and necktie with a picture of the Lone Ranger and Silver. Even if it did scratch my throat, I liked the way it looked. My Sunday shoes had a nice shine, something I had done before I left home.

"Now don't get up there and play in them and scuff them up. You've worked hard to get a nice shine on them. Try and keep it for at least one day," my mother had said. It seemed to me un-shined shoes could keep your feet covered as much as shined ones.

Taylor and Casey had to make the same sacrifice, getting dressed in Sunday clothes. Cousin Trek had the same attitude my daddy did. Why would you dress like going to church was just anything else? You went to school casually, but you went to Sunday School like you were going to see God, dressed your best. Besides, if you went to see the governor would you go like you were going just anywhere?

"Let's go, boys," Cousin Trek hollered up the stairway. We had already started before he called and almost ran into his voice as we flew down the stairs. We didn't go in the pickup on Sunday, but instead all climbed into the '49 brown Ford sedan. No sitting in the bed of the truck and getting our Wildroot Cream Oil-combed and parted hair blown into an urchin look. No dust coating us from the gravel road. But nothing could stop us from sweating. It was still hot.

We turned off the highway and as we slowed, approaching downtown, you could hear through the open windows from The New Glory Baptist Church:

"Oh Victory in Jesus,

My Savior forever..."

The colored people, dressed in their Sunday best, were already lifting their voices. Trek blew his horn and waved at one of the late arrivals approaching the front door of the one room church. The man turned and returned the wave.

"Who was that?" I asked.

"That was BB. As hard a workin' man as you'll ever see, black or white. But he don't miss church much."

Cousin Trek and Cousin Carol went to the First Baptist Church of Cotton City and rarely missed. Farley and I had visited before, and we both knew a lot of Taylor and Casey's friends. We were a few minutes early, and I got to see some of them. We talked about what we might do the next two weeks before we were told by the director to take our seats, and to please remember that we weren't outside on the playground.

Church service began thirty minutes after Sunday School, eleven o'clock. Like most Southern Baptists we started with the Doxology:

"Praise God from Whom all Blessings Flow,

Praise Him all ye creatures here below,

Praise Him above ye heavenly host,

Praise Father, Son and Holy Ghost."

I'll bet you could have heard us for miles.

The service would last about an hour, then Cousin Trek would shake a few hands, talk about the sermon and the cotton crop, and Cousin Carol would chat with several friends before we piled in the brown Ford and went back to the farm. Cousin Carol had cooked a big roast, and she would need to get back home to the business of Sunday dinner.

Cousin Trek moved off to the side with Mr. Hightower and a couple of other men and began to have a conversation, less public, though Casey had gotten within earshot before he was shooed away. He came back over and told Taylor and me what he thought he heard them talking about.

"I heard one of 'em say something about Greenville and the body, before they made me leave."

"They're talkin' about the dead man, I'll bet you," Taylor said.

I wished we were old enough to have gone over and listened, because grownups always had some good stuff to hear that they wouldn't share. Cousin Carol walked over and put her hand on Taylor's shoulder. "Go tell your daddy we need to get on home so I can get dinner on the table."

We sat down at the table, not having wasted any time on peeling our Sunday clothes; exchanging them for the uniform of the day as my daddy would say—white tee shirts, blue jeans and high-top Keds—at least for me. Casey and Taylor were back into their denim overalls. My Lone Ranger tie was stored for another Sunday.

"What time're we supposed to meet BB tomorrow?" Taylor asked. The food was still being passed and Cousin Carol was handing me a large bowl of creamed corn. I peered over it at Cousin Trek, waiting for him to answer Taylor.

"I'm not sure yet. I'll prob'ly drive over there this afternoon though." He was carving the roast and his answer came slowly.

"Can we go?" Casey asked.

"May we," Cousin Carol corrected.

"Yes, ma'am. May we?" Casey said it like he was choking and mockingly put his hands to his throat.

"You want to leave the table?" Cousin Trek stopped carving and stared straight at Casey. Smart-aleck behavior could be a problem if you didn't correct it in a hurry.

There was a long silence—the period when it would be determined if Casey got to stay at the table or sent to his room and wait. Finally, Cousin Trek went back to carving. Cousin Carol offered Casey a tender look. He lifted his eyes at her. A relieved look appeared over his face. He would live another day.

"Here you go, Jake." Cousin Trek lifted a large portion of roast beef between a carving knife and a big fork and reached toward me, an indication I should hold out my plate. "Well, maybe we can all drive over there. A Sunday afternoon drive'll be good for all of us. Whadaya think, Hon?"

"Oh, that sounds nice," she said. "Here, Casey, have some peas."

The food was passed, and for a brief period there was no sound other than the clink of dishes and glasses and the scraping of bowls with spoons, along with the polite and soft-spoken "thank you" and "please pass…"

"Cousin Trek," I said. "You know we found a dead water moccasin yesterday? It'd been shot."

"Oh yeah, Daddy—"

"Okay, Taylor, one at a time," Cousin Trek said. "Now Jake, where'd you find the snake?"

I don't think the dead snake caught his attention as much as the 'been shot' part. "Down at the branch. We found it down there after we went back from dinner."

"Yeah, been shot twice in the head. I'll bet it's Looty," Taylor said.

"Taylor. Jus' a second, I said. I can only hear one at a time." Cousin Trek wiped his mouth with his napkin and, in clear violation of a cardinal rule that had been pounded into me over the years, leaned forward, his elbows on the table. "Now, Jake, how do y'all know it was shot?" He clasped his hands together under his chin, almost like he was going to pray.

"Well." I pointed to Taylor. "Taylor poked it with a stick and we could see blood and holes in his head…and Casey found two bulletshells." Casey seemed happy I had brought his name up for something important.

"Y'all found bullets?" Cousin Carol asked at the mention of bullets.

"No, Dear, they jus' found the casins. The bullets were in the snake… they think." First Hon, then the Dear name. Lord, I don't know how he could do it. He leaned back from the table. He had one of those looks that only grownups got. The ones where they didn't get excited, at least not where you could tell, but they seemed interested. "Well, people are always shootin' those things."

"It was a .22," Taylor said. "I'm tellin' you, it's prob'ly Looty."

Cousin Trek scooped a spoonful of peas from the bowl. "Well, lots of people have .22s. I don't think there's more to this, boys, than jus' someone shootin' a poisonous snake. What part of the branch were y'all on when y'all found it? And, anyway, you don't know whether it was Looty or not, so don't you go repeatin' that."

"It was at our fishin' spot—the spot where we left our fish before we came home for dinner," I said.

Cousin Carol got up from the table and turned the gas burner on low under the corn. The bowl on the table was empty.

"Well, I guess somebody jus' came along and saw it and shot it. Y'all be careful when y'all are fishin' or even jus' playin' around that branch—lots of snakes down there. Pass the corn, Carol, please." He used her regular name. She passed the peas and looked at him. She didn't smile, she didn't frown. She jus' looked and passed.

Another dinner, and I had been filled. Cousin Carol was a monster of a cook. For dessert we had the rest of the cherry pie, then got up from the table as soon as we were excused and began clearing the table for her. Casey put a little extra into his efforts.

Most Sunday afternoons were passed doing whatever seemed fun or just doing something other than work. Often a ride through the countryside, or maybe to stop and visit somebody you hadn't seen in a while. I think Cousin Trek liked to get out and go somewhere without having to do something when he got there. And I know Cousin Carol liked to get out and get away from the house for a while, because I had heard my mother say the same thing.

It was always good to have a reason to start out, and a visit to BB's would be Cousin Trek's reason. Taylor and Casey and I were going to be helping BB and Mr. Hightower tomorrow, and we could stop by and make sure of the time we were to meet.

Besides he wanted me to meet BB, I guess, since I had never met him.

We drove out and turned onto the highway toward a section of Big Trek's land about two miles away. BB and his daddy lived about a mile past it on a hundred and twenty acres they farmed. That was in addition to sharecropping part of Big Trek's. Taylor told me that BB's momma died when he was a young man, and BB and his daddy also hired out to Mr. Hightower, sometimes on his rented property.

Ben Samuels, BB's daddy, had gotten his land from Elizabeth Nash. She had gotten it from Ben Samuels' parents. It was a twist to a strange story, or maybe I was just too young to keep it straight. Cousin Trek was telling us about the Samuels' land as we drove. It was mostly for my benefit, I think, since everyone else probably knew about it.

He told us that Ben's place was once owned by Jackson McComb's family. McComb was a Confederate officer whose war ended at Vicksburg when he was seriously wounded in 1863. Unfortunately, some of the Yankees moved northward to the Delta, and McComb's entire family was killed along with two of three Negro servants, all murdered by Grant's Yankee marauders. The only survivor was a boy, four years old.

After the war the carpetbaggers came, swarming like maggots on a wounded carcass. Taxes were pushed up by the occupiers, and many landowners lost their land. McComb somehow kept his. Reconstruction worked a hardship, but he saw his way through it with the help of the young boy who worked from childhood to save the Mississippi farm. Mr. McComb died in 1899. In his will he left the entire one hundred and twenty acres to the young boy, now grown and married with an eleven-year old son, Ben Samuels. But McComb's will had stipulated that should the former servant have children, the property would go to someone who would hold it for them until they were grown, in the event the parents died. Ben was the only child and McComb had chosen Elizabeth Nash—Looty Nash's grandmother.

There wasn't a cloud in the sky and the sun bore down like

a torch. The wind blowing against us in the bed of the truck offered some relief, but tomorrow in the field, hoeing, there would be no wind. No relief. It would just be Mississippi Hot.

We turned off the highway and onto another gravel road, winding, a curve, then straight, a curve: the road bordered another stream. It was easier to allow the roads to wind than to build a lot of bridges.

Cousin Trek slowed at the first house we came to. The mailbox had a rural route number hand painted on it and the name, B. Samuels. Cousin Trek pulled into the driveway, a grass-less path scoured by the constant movement of vehicles. I could see a big John Deere tractor on the side of the house. It had a tool box balanced on one of the huge tires, as if someone had just been working on it. When we stopped, the dust cloud flowed over the truck and gradually settled like a brown mist. Cousin Carol waved her hand in front of her face and coughed.

An old colored man stood on the porch, a curved-stem pipe squeezed between his lips. He took it out and waved with it in his hand. "Hello there, Mr. Trek. How y'all doin'?" Chickens pecked and scratched around in the yard, their heads bobbing as if in competition for the last morsel of food.

"Hot as usual, Ben. How're you doin'?" Cousin Trek had gotten out, a signal that we could, too, and we piled over the side of the truck. Casey picked up a rock and threw it at a blackbird perched on a fencepost. It stretched its wide wings and lifted itself, flying low and slow across the cornfields.

"I need to hire dis young fella to watch my corn. Dem birds's after it all day long." Ben pointed at a stick cross, adorned with a hat and ragged shirt drooping on it. "Dat scarecrow don't scare nobody—at least no birds." He laughed. We laughed with him, looking at the pitiful looking scarecrow.

"Well, Casey's a good chunker. I can tell you that," Cousin Trek said. Casey smiled. I think he liked being called a good anything.

"Hello, Ben," Cousin Carol spoke her first words.

"Hello, Mrs. Mayfield. Looks like you gittin' an afternoon off."

"Well, jus' a little bit," she said. Cousin Carol was wearing a broad-brimmed straw hat, but she put her hand under the brim at her forehead to block the glare, anyway. "Watch where you step, Casey." She pointed at a spot on the ground.

Casey lifted his foot and looked at it. "I am," he said. He scraped the bottom of his shoe against the side of the other.

The original McComb house had been burned to the ground by the Yankees, as well as all outlying houses on the place. The small wooden house Ben Samuels lived in was built many years later as a temporary living place. Gray weathered boards lined its structure from front to back. It was what I had heard my daddy say was a shotgun house. That meant if you walked inside, you could walk all the way to the back without turning a corner. The living room was up front, then down the hall, doors opening into bedrooms, then to the kitchen and out the back door.

There was a porch on the front with an overhanging roof. An old sofa and a straw-back chair sat where you could watch the sun set. The yard was not cluttered with various articles of junk that many of the houses in the county had. Many country folks often had an assortment of old worn-out and unusable items scattered around their yards: tires; old cars; bits of furniture, appliances, etc. But the Samuels place had nothing unusable. Just a John Deere tractor and some rolled chicken wire.

"Maybe I ought to hire Looty to come shoot 'em," Ben said.

"Looty, huh? What's he up to," Cousin Trek said.

"I tells you, I don't really know. He was by here the other day. Said he'd shoot any bird in the corn for ten cents a bird."

Ben and Cousin Trek both laughed. I wasn't sure what part was funny so I didn't laugh. Cousin Carol didn't laugh either. I wondered how much more she knew about Looty than I knew. And I wondered what they meant about shooting birds. All I knew was what Taylor and Casey had told me yesterday at the branch.

Just then a big, muscular colored man walked out on the porch. He had a peach in his hand with what looked like about two good bites gone. He was taller than Cousin Trek who was exactly six feet tall himself. The man was as black a man as I had ever seen, except for those in the Tarzan picture shows. The ones Tarzan always called the Jaconi Tribe. I knew without anyone telling me that this was Big Black Julius, BB.

"How ya doin'?" Cousin Trek called.

"Doin' fine, Mr. Trek. You're lookin' fit. Good to see y'all." He nodded at Cousin Carol. "Mrs. Mayfield, how are you doing?"

"Fine, BB, jus' fine. Thank you. Good to see you looking so well." An obvious reference to his war wound. "Been working on the tractor?" She pointed to the side of the house.

"Yes, ma'am. At least I'm fixin' to. It's been missin' some. Jus' changed my clothes from church." He stepped down off the porch. "These boys are lookin' fit, too. They'll be off to Ole Miss before you know it."

Cousin Trek gave him one of those looks that was supposed to be friendly in a nasty way. Ben smiled then laughed. BB laughed, too.

"Well, if they do, they're gonna pay their own way. They're bound for the cow college if I pay for it. They gonna be farmers, not no sissy doctor or lawyer."

"We'll see," Cousin Carol said.

Taylor and Casey and I jus' listened. We weren't sure what was funny and what wasn't. Anyway, Cousin Trek changed the subject.

"How's the leg, BB?"

Cousin Trek said he never was sure why BB didn't go off to Florida A&M on that scholarship, but by October BB was in Korea. Later, he was in a famous Battle up near China, called the Chosin Reservoir. Cousin Trek said the men called it the Frozen-Chosin. He said there were almost as many casualties from the cold as from the fighting.

BB got shrapnel in his legs and frostbite in his toes. He was discharged due to his wounds, but he got a Purple Heart and a Bronze Star for helping some other men. Little pieces of shrapnel were still in his leg. The doctors said his leg would be stiff for a while, and that he was lucky he hadn't lost any toes.

"Leg's fine, Mr. Trek. Gettin' better every day. I'll be up to snuff all the way pretty soon. But now who's this new fella you got here?" BB looked straight at me and smiled. It was a big pleasant smile. His huge white teeth contrasted against his pure black face. I knew right away why Taylor and Casey called him their friend.

Cousin Trek put his hand on top of my head. "Jake Conner. He's our cousin. And the hardest workin' city boy you ever saw."

BB laughed big. I was kind of embarrassed being called a city boy, but something in his laugh told me he was going to be my friend, too.

The subject of the dead guy at the river hadn't come up. And I figured I'd better not bring it up now. And despite Taylor's big talk about asking BB as soon as he saw him, Taylor didn't mention it.

We had piled back in the truck and Cousin Trek was taking us on the rest of the Sunday afternoon drive. I had met BB and we had gotten set for meeting him in the morning at seven. After seven, Taylor told me, we'd just work "until we were dead."

I wasn't sure what part of the county we were driving through. Cousin Trek had made too many turns for me to keep track. I was just happy being in the open bed of the truck joking and fooling around with Taylor and Casey.

I wanted to talk more about Looty, and I wondered what else there was to know. After we found the dead snake yesterday, Taylor and Casey told me about him. Taylor said he was kind of a crazy man who lived by himself. His house was not far from theirs, and his grandparents had once had a lot of land and a lot of money. They had lost most of their money a long time ago, and no one seemed to know much about Looty's momma or daddy, or whatever became of them. He lived with his grandmother from the time he was about five until a few years ago, when she died.

That's when the story got a little stranger. Taylor said he had it on good authority that after Looty's grandmother had died, Looty cremated her in the bar-b-que pit. It was a big brick one, and certainly could handle a little old lady about a hundred years old, or whatever she was. Casey swore that Looty kept her ashes in a mayonnaise jar on the mantle in the living room.

Once Looty started living alone, he started using his .22 rifle to shoot crows and blue jays that got in the vegetable garden. His grandmother never would let him use it, even after he was grown. But after she died, he got to be such a good shot that he had to spend ninety days on the county farm for shooting somebody's chickens. While Looty was on the county farm, Cousin Carol and Cousin Trek helped take care of his place. They felt sorry for him.

I scooted over next to Taylor so he could hear. "I said, how come you never told me and Farley about Looty before?" Casey scooted over next to me so he didn't miss anything.

"Well, we aren't supposed to talk about him much. Daddy says he's jus' an unfortunate guy, and we were too little to be swappin' stories anyway. But when we found that snake shot, Casey jus' shot his mouth off."

"Well, I still say it's a good guess," Casey said.

I missed some of what Taylor said and he had to say it again. "Maybe I shouldn't have said anything about the snake to Cousin Trek," I said.

"Naaa, it's okay. We jus' aren't supposed to be blabbin' lots of stuff about him. I mean about Looty. But I guess it's okay now. We were jus' kids when that rule was first passed," Taylor said.

"Did your momma and daddy see the ashes in the mayonnaise jar when they went inside the house? You know, when he was in jail?"

"Oh, yeah. But Daddy said that it was a jar full of sand most prob'ly."

Cousin Trek turned the truck for downtown. "I'll bet Daddy's gonna buy us a Co-Cola," Taylor said.

Casey mumbled something.

"What?" Taylor asked him.

"I said, I don't think it is."

"Is what?"

"Just sand."

CHAPTER 8

The next morning came quick. It started getting daylight early, and I wasn't ready to start anything, even at twenty cents an hour. I thought maybe no one would notice me tucked away on the top bunk buried under the sheet. Maybe they'd think I was dead and leave me alone until my parents came. Maybe they'd just forget I was here. I would have rather painted the state capitol building than get up.

"Let's go, boys," called Cousin Carol. "Time to get to work." The gentle voice that I had heard all weekend had a sharp edge. Maybe it's just that anybody's voice would have a sharp edge at five-thirty in the morning.

We had stayed up late last night talking about BB and Looty, and us going to Clarksdale on Wednesday. I don't know what time it was when I finally fell asleep, but it was late. I could tell that now.

I swung my legs over the edge and was greeted by the tickling fingers of Taylor. "Stop it, you idiot!"

"Now stop that, Taylor," Cousin Carol said. "You're just going to start something."

Casey walked into Taylor's room. He was rubbing his eyes. "It can't be time to get up yet. I'm sure this is a dream. I'm goin' back to bed."

Cousin Carol grabbed him by his ear and pulled him back. "Do I sound like a dream?"

"Ow, ow, ow! It sure don't feel like one."

"Doesn't."

"That's what I said."

"No, it was not."

"I mean it's what I meant to say."

"I think tonight maybe y'all won't stay up half the night talking." She glared at all of us. "Will you?"

"No, ma'am."

"Well, y'all wash the sleep out and hurry on downstairs. Breakfast is almost ready."

We dressed and made our way downstairs. Cousin Carol was busy in the kitchen. Cousin Trek was having a cup of coffee and whistling his favorite tune, The Bonnie Blue Flag. I looked out of the kitchen window; it looked like the pink eastern sky was about to build into another hot day.

"Have a seat, Mr. Jake," Cousin Trek said. "You too, boys." Casey was still rubbing his eyes.

A large glass of milk and a glass of orange juice marked our places at the round table, a red and white checkered tablecloth draping off around the edge about six inches. The tablecloth was on for every meal but seemed to stand out more at breakfast for some reason.

Breakfast was eggs, toast, bacon, grits with lots of butter, plenty of milk and orange juice. The sustenance began to bring us back to life. Back from the peace of deep sleep and soft beds—just in time for Mr. Hightower.

He drove up about six-thirty. He was like family, the way he knocked on the screen door and with a quick "Good mornin'," walked right in.

"Good morning, Earl," Cousin Carol said. "Pour yourself a cup and sit down."

Earl put his brown hat in the chair next to him. In his work clothes, he looked tanned and strong—a real cotton farmer. His blue cotton shirt sleeves rolled up revealed big hairy forearms, with hard-looking muscle that came from farm work. He had a gentle way about him, but a mannerism that made you know he was definitely no softy. One of his big hands swept around the cup, not using the crook, and took a big swallow. Black. No sissy coffee for Earl Hightower.

"BB is gonna meet us at seven over on that twenty acres on the far side. That right, Trek?"

"Yep. We saw him yesterday afternoon. Drove by there.

He'll be there at seven. Prob'ly already there."

Cousin Carol poured some milk out of the bottle into my empty glass. She refilled Casey's and Taylor's. "Want some eggs, Earl?"

"No thanks, Carol. I ate an hour ago." He winked at Casey. "I had two rattlesnakes and a panther's haunch. I'm full and ready to work. Ready to get burned up in this hot Delta sun of ours."

Casey yawned. I could tell he had heard these kinds of stories before. I wished Mr. Hightower had left out the part about the hot Delta sun.

"I think there'll be enough to do for these young fellows for most of the day in that twenty acres alone. If it's not, I've got some other things, if it's alright with you, Trek."

"Yeah, that'll be fine. They're all ready to go," Cousin Trek said. Casey yawned again. Cousin Trek picked up the newspaper.

"What'd the Browns do?" Mr. Hightower asked.

"They lost. Nine to one."

"Maybe you ought to sign up with them, Earl," Cousin Carol said.

"Oh, yeah. Ya think so?"

Probably the favorite baseball team in Mississippi next to the Jackson Senators was the St. Louis Cardinals. But some followed the pitiful St. Louis Browns, the American League team in St. Louis. The Cardinals mostly had pretty good teams, but the Browns stunk up the place.

She poured some more coffee in his cup. "Anybody that eats rattlesnakes and panthers for breakfast oughta be able to hit a curveball."

We had to get all the equipment into Mr. Hightower's pickup. Since he rented from Cousin Trek, who supplied the hardware, Earl provided the labor. Mr. Hightower did use his own truck, but then most everybody did. We loaded hoes, rakes, shovels and a big corrugated tin barrel of water. It had a single dipper hooked to a small chain clipped to the top. That made me a little nervous, not having your own cup. I hoped the hot Delta sun would kill the cooties.

"Want 'em back here at noon to eat?" Mr. Hightower asked. He had just slammed the hood on his truck. I think he was checking his oil because I saw him wipe something with a piece of paper.

"No, I gave them some sandwiches. Just find them a shady spot to eat. If they don't die, then have them back in time for supper."

After we loaded the truck, the three of us piled in the back. I was wearing my worn blue jeans, white tee shirt and baseball cap. Casey and Taylor had their denim overalls, no shirts, and straw hats. It would be hot. It would be dirty. But I would get almost two dollars when the day was over.

All Farley would get would be to drive around town with his friends and talk about Dixie Daniels and her progressive bosoms. I almost felt sorry for him.

My back was about to break and it wasn't even ten. In order to hoe you had to bend, and staying in a bent position while moving nothing but your arms back and forth and shuffling your feet along the long rows left you with a backache. The sweatband on my baseball cap had absorbed all it could, and the salt was being carried by the sweat upward around the sides and out to the bill.

If a cow got near me she would lick my head off. I waited as long as I could, to avoid the water can, the one with the common dipper. But I finally surrendered after over two hours and sucked down two dippers, scoured with everybody else's spit and cooties.

BB was in fact the relentless worker Cousin Trek had talked about. I believe behind a mule he could have turned more ground than a tractor driven by a stock car driver. Taylor and Casey worked hard, too. They sweated and got dirty and drank spit-water, but they didn't seem as worn as I did. Casey was two years younger than me but fifteen yards ahead of me in his row, and I was glad Cousin Trek was paying me by the hour instead of by the yard. As I watched my country cousins, I knew why Farley had had such a fight on his hands with that little guy a couple of years ago.

"Well, Mr. Jake, I can tell you ain't a lazy boy." BB smiled that big bright smile I had seen yesterday. "Your momma and daddy make you work at home, I can tell." He hoed a couple of shallow weeds in my row that I had missed. "Don't worry if you stay a little behind. This work in the fields is as hard a work as there is. And this Mississippi cotton makes you work hardest. That's one reason it's the best cotton—it's the hardest to get. But the best kind of work is hard work. And the best crop's the one hardest to get."

I don't know if what he said was a riddle, or if I was just too tired and dizzy to understand.

I took my cap off and ran my hands through my hair just to shake off the sweat. BB's talking to me gave me a chance to straighten my back, take a break. Maybe he knew that. "I never heard that—that hard work is the best work. I thought you only worked hard so someday you didn't have to work hard."

BB pulled out a red and white bandana from his back pocket and wiped his face. He smiled that big black and white smile again.

"Well, lots of folks think that I reckon. But I think they're wrong. Yes, I do. I think they're wrong."

He looked at the sun, holding his head at a sharp angle, and I don't think he even blinked. The sweat reappeared almost as soon as he had wiped it. He seemed strange to me in a way, but it was like he had a special wisdom, too. Sort of like my daddy or Cousin Trek. It was kind of like he knew just what to say at the right time. I wondered why he had joined the army and gone off to war when he had had a chance to go to college and play football.

"Well, we'll be eatin' dinner in a bit. You'll get your second wind by then."

Second wind, I thought. Any wind would be nice.

"Hey look!" Taylor yelled across the long rows. "A king

snake. Who wants him?"

"You can have him for dinner," BB yelled back. "If he don't have you." He laughed. "Don't forget it's August. Only time you gotta be careful of king snakes."

"Why is that?" I asked.

"Not sure," BB said. "Just in August, for some reason they'll latch onto you and squeeze you, they say."

I would have taken my shirt off, but it was so wet that it felt cool clinging to my body, like standing in front of a fan after getting out of the tub. I felt almost cold in the shade by comparison to the fields, and nearly five hours of dust settling on me had turned to mud. I was just glad to sit down for a while; out of the sun; away from bugs; away from spiders; away from snakes; and away from the cotton.

We had plopped down in front of a large shade tree close to the road, and filled the jelly glasses from the thermos of iced tea Cousin Carol had put in Taylor's bag. As soon as I poured mine I gulped it down before I even looked to see what kind of sandwiches I had.

In the distance I saw the old pickup that had been parked at BB's house yesterday. It was approaching at a pace that made it look hot and tired, struggling with its own life. A plume of white smoke trailed from the exhaust. The rattles made distinct sounds, like a jazz percussion on the rough road. Smoke, Farley had told me, was a sign that a car was burning oil. Ben Samuels pulled off the road and onto the grassy shoulder.

"Hey, Daddy. What're are you doin' here? I thought you'd be workin' all day at home."

Ben walked up slowly, limping. Yesterday when I had met him I guessed he was about sixty something, although I hadn't noticed a limp. I figured it was one of those old people things I had heard my mother and daddy talk about, like arthritis or lumbago or something. Old people tended to limp and get bent with age. It was kind of sad. Both Ben and his son had to limp around the fields.

"Well, I figured you boys would like summin' with yo dinner—summin' cool and sweet."

I knew before he said it—watermelon. Sugar cane and watermelon both were sweet, but only watermelon was cool and sweet, because you could keep it iced down.

"Julius, I'll let you tote it outta the truck. Been keepin' it in a wash bucket of ice water."

Taylor and Casey and I lay back against the trunk and relaxed like a trio of hoboes traveling through the county. I was tired, but happy as a pig in slop that I had made about a dollar so far. I began to struggle with a tuna fish sandwich, pulling at the corner of it with my teeth, which were exhausted just like the rest of me. I couldn't understand how even your teeth could get tired. Another slug of iced tea. It was a nice dinnertime. Iced tea from my own glass and now a piece of watermelon—my own germs, my own cooties. And shade.

"Looka here, boys," BB said. "Cold watermelon." He had it hoisted on his shoulder and carried it as effortlessly as if it were a jar of honey. He put it down beside Ben who had brought a lunch pail from his truck, then took a seat in the shade.

"Thanks," we all said.

"Well, you boys are mighty welcome. You deserve it, workin' hard as y'all have." He opened his lunch pail and pulled out a hard-boiled egg. He took out a small salt shaker, sprinkled then chomped more than half the egg in one bite. "Is Mr. Earl comin' by 'fore quittin' time?"

"He might, Daddy," BB said. "Said he was goin' into town, then he was goin' to check on his field hands over on that place down across the road. What you need him for?"

"Well, the sheriff come by wantin' to ask some questions 'bout that man o'er at the river."

I couldn't help asking, "Are you talkin' about that dead man they found in Greenville?"

Ben looked surprised. He finished his egg and took out his pocket knife and began to scrape the bowl of his pipe.

"Why, Mr. Jake, whadda you know 'bout dat bidness?" He chuckled, a light kind of curious laughter that made me laugh a little bit too, though I wasn't sure why.

Taylor and Casey looked at me. They wanted to know too if it had been Ben, and was the "Julius" I had heard about at the bus station our BB?

Cousin Trek and Cousin Carol hadn't said anything about the dead man since I got to their house Friday. I didn't know if they even knew about it, but they were just like my mother and daddy when it came to stuff like that. They had probably read about it in the paper or somebody had told them, but it just wasn't the thing to do, talk about such things in front of us boys.

"I jus' heard some deputy or somebody talkin' about it. The waitress had asked out loud about it. I jus' heard them talkin'."

BB had taken a large butcher knife from Ben's lunch pail. He cut the watermelon right down the middle then cut the two halves in half. It was dark red, ripe red, and sweet.

"Well, we jus' found dis man in the river. He was dead. Dat's all we really know. He was dead. An' you really couldn't tell who he was. Looked like the fish'd been gnawin' on him a little, maybe," Ben said.

He took a box of wooden matches from his overalls and struck one. He let the flame burn almost down to his fingers—like his thoughts had momentarily drifted—before he rested it in the bowl and puffed up a cloud of sweet, cherry-smelling smoke.

"Daddy, now don't scare these boys," BB said.

"Aw, dey gonna hear 'bout it sometime. It's all over da county by now." He turned toward BB. "Don't ya think?"

"Well, what's Mr. Hightower got to do with it?" Casey asked.

Taylor slapped him on top of the head with two fingers. "Shut up, dope. That's none of your business." The truth was, Taylor probably wanted to know as bad as Casey did, as bad as I did.

Ben spoke again. "Well, I jus' wanted to ask him if he knew why the sheriff was askin' 'bout Looty."

"Looty?" I asked.

"Yessir, Mr. Jake—Looty. The sheriff was askin' 'bout Looty and if I'd seen him around lately and what he was doin' and things like that. I don't know what he thinks it got to do with dat dead man."

"Well, maybe because he was shot with a .22," I said. Everybody turned and looked at me. I hadn't even mentioned to Casey and Taylor that I had heard it was a .22.

"How do you know that?" BB asked. "That he was shot with a .22?"

"That's what the deputy said at the bus station," I said. "They were talkin' about it and about a man and his son 'Julius' who had found him while they were fishin'."

"Well, I'll be. So you already know 'bout this business," BB said. "And you're sure he said it was a .22?"

"Pretty sure."

"Well, well, Julius, maybe that s'plains it—the sheriff askin' 'bout ol' Looty, I mean. I wonder if they's thinkin' old Looty is doin' more'n shootin' chickens now."

"Well, let's jus' forget about it, Daddy. It's nothing we need to be talking about anymore; none of our business, now."

I felt important, like I knew something that only the police knew. I took a big bite of watermelon and leaned back against the tree. Taylor and Casey looked at me with a jealous look. I guess because I knew something they didn't.

"What did you tell the sheriff, Daddy?" BB propped himself up with one arm on the ground, holding a slice of watermelon with the other. He took a small bite then spit a seed.

"I jus' told him Looty was Looty. He come 'round from time to time. Came by jus' de other day offerin' to shoot birds in my corn." Ben put his pipe on the ground and began scraping the remainder of his watermelon from the rind with his knife.

"Well, I don't think you need to see Mr. Hightower about it. I think we know what the sheriff is thinkin' now," BB said. "They know Looty spent time on the county farm for shootin' what he wasn't supposed to be shootin', and they gonna see what he was up to before they found that man. I'll bet you a nickel that's what it is. Jus' makes sense to me."

Just then, we saw Mr. Hightower coming. His pickup rattled about as much as Ben's but didn't show the trail of smoke. He pulled up behind Ben's truck and got out, his back and under-arms soaked in sweat. He walked briskly as if he had all the energy in the world. His Stetson was pulled down shading his face, the crown soaked with sweat, like my cap.

"Well, BB, Ben. How we doin'?"

"Fine, fine, Mr. Earl. Jus' brought these hard workin' boys some watermelon for dinner."

"Waste of good melon, Ben. They ain't worked but half a day."

Ben and BB laughed. Casey and Taylor and I sort of laughed.

"Y'all gonna be on these weeds the rest of the day, BB?"

"Yes, sir. I thought we might get through a little early, but it looks like it'll take the rest of the afternoon."

I couldn't help but wonder if I was holding them back. After all, I was the sissy city slicker being out-hoed by a cousin two years younger than me. Then BB said something that made me know we were friends.

"This here fellow from the big city of Jackson is 'bout as good a field hand as I ever seen. I'll take him as a workin' man any day of the week." He reached over and patted me on the head.

It made me feel especially good when Taylor and Casey smiled at me and didn't say anything, although they knew they had covered much more ground than I had. I looked up at BB. I liked him.

"Well, that's good," Mr. Hightower said. "I'll jus' leave y'all here with your work and come back and get you later—after five prob'ly."

He took off his hat and wiped the sweat from his forehead. He replaced his hat, then stooped down and picked up some dirt and squeezed it with his hand. Farmers were always picking up dirt and rubbing it and studying it, it seemed like. My daddy had told me once that the soil was almost a part of a farmer's soul.

"Say, Ben, you know anything about what Looty's been up to lately? Sheriff's been askin' about him." Mr. Hightower resumed his full height and rubbed his hands together, shaking the dirt from his hands.

Ben rubbed his chin, like he had anticipated the question. "Well, to tell you de truth I was gonna ask you the same thing, Mr. Earl. De sheriff done ask me 'bout him. I guess he tol' you dat me and BB found a body down at the Greenville bridge. Ugly, ugly sight, I tell you." His eyes darted toward BB.

BB leaned on his rake and just listened. We remained on the ground, getting every bit of shade time we could, our eyes and ears glued to Ben and Mr. Hightower and their conversation.

"Yeah, he told me it was y'all that found him. I had read about a man being found dead. It was in the paper, Wednesday or Thursday, I think. But they didn't say who found him. Jus' said two unidentified Nigra men who had been fishin'. But the way he's talkin', he might even bring Looty in for questioning. Maybe hold him for a while. Anyhow, that's 'bout all I know."

"Sheriff say how the man was killed?" asked BB. "Never did tell us. We thought maybe he was drowned." He glanced over at me.

"Said he was killed with a .22 bullet. Shot two or three times. I forget jus' how many. Didn' y'all read it in the paper the next day?"

"Oh, yeah," BB said. "I do remember that now."

There was quiet for a minute. It seemed like everybody was thinking—probably the same thing, Looty and his .22 rifle. Taylor and Casey would be thinking the same thing I was—that business about the snake and about the shells.

Both Mr. Hightower and Ben drove off, back to whatever they had been doing.

BB announced that it was almost one, and we needed to get back to the field. Casey pretended not to hear—pretended that he was asleep, lying in the shade. Taylor didn't pretend anything, he just said he would rather go fishing or be dead.

BB laughed and announced that we had better get back to it or Mr. Hightower would be back, or even worse Cousin Trek would come out and we'd really have the devil to pay. After considerable effort, the three of us struggled to our feet and made one last delay, a drink of water. The ice tea was gone, so even I was willing to drink from the diseased dipper.

I looked out over the long rows of cotton. They looked like they were laid out by a surveyor with a plumb bob and tripod. Perfect. These same fields would be ready for picking in just five or six weeks, then again in October. Taylor and Casey said that picking was the closest thing to dying that there was without actually doing it. Hoeing was close enough for me.

About the only thing hoeing had in common with picking cotton was that it was hot. During picking season, in addition to the heat you had to bend and stoop a lot more, and there wasn't a hoe to lean on either. In order to get the cotton out you had to pull it out of the boll by hand, grabbing the entire boll with its needle sharp, dried petals wherein your fingers would get stuck until they bled. And for some reason, big red wasps like to hunker down in some of the bolls, unknown to the picker until he got stung. Cotton fields were also a paradise for the large yellow cotton spiders and their webs.

BB caught me in my daydream. "What ya thinking' about, Mr. Jake? You lookin' at that cotton like it's a cloud or something. Maybe you're tryin' to make a picture out of it. Maybe make it into something it's not. Or maybe you're hopin' it'll blow away." He laughed at his own wit.

"I was jus' thinkin' about y'all havin' to pick it after I leave. Cousin Trek says that's the hardest work."

BB pushed his rake out into the dirt, drawing it back and forth making a bunch of lines in the dirt. Just back and forth, lines and more lines, like he was trying to design something. "Let me ask you, Mr. Jake, have you ever read about Booker T. Washington? You know who he was?"

I wasn't for sure what BB wanted to know, if anything. He might have been just testing me to see how much I knew about Booker T. Washington. But I was glad for the conversation because it gave me more rest time.

"A little bit. We learned about him some in school. I think he used to be a slave, and when the War Between the States was over he started a school or something for Negroes. I think it was in Alabama."

"Well, that mostly right. And maybe I'll tell you more about him sometime. But mostly you should remember something he said: 'Nobody can prosper 'til they realize that there is as much dignity in hoeing a field as there is in writing a poem.' Now, pickin' cotton may be hard work, but it's not bad work. There's no such thing. Don't you ever believe somebody when they say that some work's not good enough for them. You avoid that kind of fellow like a plague."

I looked at him as he looked out over the field. The sweat was already breaking out on his face again. He seemed happy in what he was doing, but also had a look of adventure—like he might do more with his life if his Mississippi cotton days ever ended.

"I guess I never heard that exactly before. My mother always says, 'Any job worth doing is worth doing well.'"

"Well, your momma is right. But I guess what it should mean to you—I mean right now while you're learnin', is that all work is worthy. Every bit of it. Mr. Truman's job in Washington and this job you and me are doin'. Both just as important, one to the other. Hard work can only make a better man out of you. In fact, it is the main thing that'll make a man out of you. And I'll tell you something else. If work is bad, then the Lord is bad, 'cause He gave it to us."

"Well, He must really like us, 'cause He gave us plenty of it," I said.

He tilted his head back and gave a big laugh. "Well, I s'pose you're right 'bout that."

As hot as it was, and as tired as I was, I almost wanted to race out into the cotton inferno and start weeding. BB had somehow excited me about hard work. I wanted to ask and couldn't hold back. "BB, how come you went to war instead of goin' to college?"

He turned and smiled the BB smile—big, broad, happy and genuine. "For the University Grays."

"Huh?"

"Let's get back to work, Mr. Jake."

CHAPTER 9

Tuesday afternoon and my second day of work was over. I had earned almost four dollars for the two days, and I had the blisters to show for it. But relief was on the horizon. Tomorrow we would be going to Clarksdale to pick up Big Trek, and I was looking forward to the long drive. About forty miles, Cousin Trek had said. It would be fun riding in the open bed of the pickup watching as we passed the fields, not having to be in them. On a long trip like that, Cousin Trek might even stop at a filling station and buy us a Coca-Cola. A day off.

The rest of the week looked good, too. We told Cousin Carol we might go fishing again on Thursday, if we could get out of work part of the day. I had only worked Monday and Tuesday, but I still had Friday and Saturday morning of this week; then all through Friday of next week, before my final week.

But what we really wanted to do Thursday afternoon was go skinny-dipping in some old private pond. There were regular places to swim like the old Highway 49 county pond. It was pretty big, and everybody could go there; nevertheless we liked our own private place. But if Cousin Carol knew what we were going to do one of her laws would be laid down: No naked swimming.

"It is not only sinful but in poor taste," she had once said. Cousin Trek had offered no opinion other than when we brought up the subject of swimming at all, he just told us to be careful at the county pond because it's pretty deep in some places.

And Friday was picture show night again. THE MAN FROM PLANET X was coming Friday and Saturday. Yep, the rest of the week would allow me some rest from BB's world of hard work, and as motivated as I had gotten, loafing was a narcotic. I had once heard Daddy say that. I could believe that hard work would make a man out of you. I just didn't want to grow all the way up in one week.

"Y'all get cleaned up, supper will be ready about six," Cousin Carol said. She was working over the stove and hollering instructions over her shoulder. "Take a bath. And if y'all want to sleep on the screened porch tonight, y'all will have to pull those old pallets down from the attic."

"Yes, ma'am," Taylor answered all questions.

We planned on sleeping on the porch—after we went to Looty's house.

"Well, you fellows don't look any the worse for wear, for two days of work," Cousin Trek said. He took a platter of country fried steak from Cousin Carol, stabbed a nice one, and passed it to Casey. "Don't forget we're gonna leave about nine in the mornin'. That means y'all can sleep in a little, but I don't want y'all stayin' in bed all mornin'."

Casey tried to flip a steak with his fork like he was using a spatula. It missed and he had to drop his fork and grab the steak and juggle it while he held on to the platter for what seemed an interminable period. I couldn't believe it didn't flop on the floor. As soon as he rescued the steak, he placed it gently on his plate, leaned over and picked his fork from the floor. There was a silence.

Cousin Trek stared a white-hot stare at Casey for about five minutes it seemed like. He didn't say a word, just stared. I personally thought Casey's life was about to end and Taylor and I would be going to Looty's by ourselves. Playing around at the table was one of the major no-no's. Of course one thing in Casey's favor was neither the steak nor the platter had hit the floor. It was a technicality that I'm sure he was praying would save him.

After the long pause, I guess Cousin Carol realized that Cousin Trek wasn't going to dismiss Casey or kill him so she said, "Now just march into the kitchen and get a clean fork. And don't play with it."

Cousin Trek finally broke his silence. "If you ever do that again, you'll wish you had never heard the word switch."

"Yes, sir," Casey said. He got a clean fork.

"Now, Jake, would you like some corn?" Cousin Carol asked.

"Yes, ma'am. Thank you." She passed it to Taylor, who passed it to me. He looked at me, trying not to smile. We were both thinking how funny it was, Casey juggling the steak. It took everything we had not to break out laughing.

We helped with the dishes and got the pallets down from the attic before we announced we were going to play outside for a while. It was almost seven and was getting close to dark. Playing outside after dark was something everybody did as far as I knew. In Jackson we played outdoors after dark in the summer all the time. After June, and the great lightning bug chases had passed, we played games like kick the can, red light green light, may-I and others. For some reason, after dark had its own excitement and was a time when you were without your parents' supervision for a little bit. There were no cars to run over you unless you were downtown, as most people had only one car, and it wasn't routinely used for driving around at night for pleasure. And it was as cool outside at night as it was inside.

But this night we had a special mission, for what we had begun to think of as a murder case. We decided that the place to begin our investigation was at Looty's house. Naturally our plan had to be kept secret because we couldn't just say, "Oh, by the way we are going to spy on Looty's and see if we can find out if he's a murderer. We'll be back by bedtime."

Looty lived about two miles from Cousin Trek's farm. We rode our bikes, a jostled ride down a gravel road and across rowed and hoed fields. By the time we got close enough to go on foot, it was past dark. We got off our bikes and laid them down behind a clump of trees.

From the edge of the trees we could see his house. It appeared a single light was on inside. There wasn't a porch light on, front or back, and the moon was high and full tonight so we could see pretty good. There was enough light for me to see the barbecue—the big brick one around back. At first, it made me nervous just to look at it. I hoped I'd get a chance to peek in the window and see the famous jar.

We crept out of the trees, staying in the shadows before sprinting to the back of the house. We moved down the side of the house until we got close to the front porch. A single cloud floated over the moon, and for a brief moment we lost our night vision. It was scary, and almost felt as if someone was watching in the darkness. We paused, waiting for the moonlight to refocus its beacon on the house. Even the crickets seemed subdued tonight, as if they were aware of something sinister. Taylor motioned with the flat of his hand for us to move slowly and signaled with his finger to his lips. He turned around and put his arms around us as if we were in a little football huddle and he was about to call a big play.

"Okay, jus' whispers from now on," Taylor said. "We got to be careful. Be quiet, absolutely quiet. Don't make a sound. I mean not a sound. We can't be sure if anybody's out here. So just keep very quiet. Very quiet."

Casey farted.

"Will you quit that, you little dope!" A loud, airy shush from Taylor. Casey and I both had to put our hands over our mouths to keep from laughing.

Taylor got a little mad. Some of it was because he thought we weren't being serious, and some of it was because he really was scared. "Now, I'm tellin' y'all, we could get killed out here."

Casey and I both nodded. We had gotten control over our laughter, but not enough to risk an audible answer.

"Now come on," Taylor said.

We dropped to our hands and knees and crawled the short distance toward the front porch. Taylor was leading and by the time we got to the corner we could see there was another light on in the front of the house. Without a word, we understood Taylor's goal. It was to get on the porch and look through the front window. He started up the first of three steps which were on all three sides of the wooden porch. There was a creak from the old boards, and we all froze for a split second.

Although Casey and I heard the creak, Taylor motioned in

a downward movement with his hand for us to crawl, and in the moonlight I could see him mouth the words, "Be careful, some of these boards are loose."

Taylor moved to one side of the window. Casey and I raised ourselves just enough to peak in the other side. There was a floor lamp, the single light in the room. There was no one in the front room, but I could see directly across it. The mantle, the jar.

"Is that the body?" Although I whispered so low that I wasn't sure they could hear me, Taylor pressed his fingers to his lips.

We could see inside the house. My throat felt dry, and I was scared. I was afraid that any minute somebody inside was going to push his face against the window from the inside and give me a heart attack.

The furniture looked old and broken. A cushion chair was leaning to one side, a leg missing. The sofa had been covered with a sheet, but most of the sheet had fallen off so that over half of the sofa was showing. There was a Philco radio on the table by the lamp. If it was on, it was not turned loud enough for us to hear. I thought that it must've been about time for Fibber Magee and Molly. Just as the three of us peeked through the window, our fingers gripping the lower edge, all on our knees, we saw it.

We dropped below the window with exchanged looks of panic. What we had seen was racing across the front room, pounding the wooden floor. We heard the jiggling of the front latch. Someone was at the front door trying to get out to us. We dived off the porch and scrambled underneath it just before the front door opened and the screen door swung out.

We lay in the darkness under the porch with the roly-polies and spiders and roaches and moldy, soft ground that had been hidden from the sun all day. I felt my heart beating, I was terrified. Casey was next to me squeezing my arm like he was on the edge of a cliff, his fingernails cutting into my arm. What if it had seen us crawl under the porch? I was too scared to run away, I would have to die here. I tried to hold my breath, fearing my breathing would move the ground like a small tremor and give away our hiding place.

Above we heard footsteps, first toward one end of the porch, then the other. Whoever was there must not have seen us scramble under the porch. I wondered if it was Looty. Casey was squeezed between Taylor and me and was still holding my arm. Our bodies were touching, and I wasn't sure whose heart was beating fastest because I could feel all three.

We had to get home before we were late. But all we could do was wait. We were in total darkness, the moonlight making a sharp shadow-line at the edge of the porch. But I couldn't get the image out of my mind. What we had seen... .

It stopped pacing. We heard the creak of the boards as it leaned on one foot, then the other. We waited for the sound of the door. We waited for it to go back inside, we hoped. Then steps: one, two, three; the spring creak of the screen door and the shutting, then clicking of the front door latch.

Taylor whispered, "Let's get out of here."

We crawled the length of the porch to one end, then up and ran for the trees. Under the full moon we made our escape and found our bikes. In the hurry, I had bumped my head on the edge of the porch. It hurt like crazy, and I would have yelled under any other circumstances. My fear strangled my pain and we wasted no time in getting home.

We got up early, no sleeping in, no prodding from Cousin Carol was needed. We had not slept much on the porch, and the excitement had kept us talking most of the night, so we were awake by the time it was time to get up. My head still hurt a little. It had a small knot under my hair. We weren't sure if we had discovered anything or not. Just because somebody was at Looty's didn't mean anything, except that whoever it was scared us. For all we knew it was Looty.

We had had only a brief look through the window and jumped under the porch as soon as we saw him. But why would he dress like that? What we had seen was a black silhouette, but the dark outline revealed a caped figure, the cape draped to the knees and a hood over the head.

We put up the pallets and washed up, then gathered for breakfast about seven o'clock. Cousin Trek had eaten earlier and already left the house. Cousin Carol said he would be back before nine, and then we would leave for Clarksdale. She had laid out the schedule and wanted to talk about who we might see and who she hoped we didn't see. She had no idea we were paying little attention. She seemed excited for different reasons than we were.

Casey ate heartily, a sign he had come out of his mental shock from last night. Cousin Carol shrieked, "Casey! Stop that!" He was about to scratch the inside of his ear with his cereal spoon. He was definitely back to normal.

Taylor ate and once or twice glanced at me but said nothing. Course there wasn't much we could say in front of Cousin Carol.

Cousin Carol had dressed for the trip. She puttered around the house waiting for Cousin Trek while Casey and Taylor and I hung around the couch, whispering when we could about last night. Course we had talked about it last night on the porch about a hundred times so that we were about to get bored with our own talk.

It seemed like a real big event last night. In the daytime, and having talked about it over and over, we began to think maybe what we saw was just Looty after all, and we had just got scared in the dark.

"Everybody ready?" Cousin Trek said. It was jus' before nine. He had walked in and announced that the truck was gassed up and anytime we were ready, he was. What that meant, was that he was ready and we should be. "By the way, when I stopped by the feed store they were talking about how Looty had been taken in for questioning early yesterday afternoon. Word down there was he was held all night."

Cousin Carol said, "Yes, well let's not talk about it in front of the boys."

Too late. We had heard. If Looty wasn't at his house, who was? Who had walked out on the porch? Who would dress like… like a…vampire?

CHAPTER 10

We piled in the truck. Jostling down the gravel road to the highway, we began talking again about last night at Looty's house. Each of us said he wasn't scared as much as the others. And now his being taken in for questioning renewed our interest. I really didn't think Looty would kill anybody, but I didn't know him. They were probably questioning him just because he had been in jail before. And maybe because he was kind of simple, I guess. People who were a little slow got picked on more than others.

Soon, the long trip to Clarksdale took our full attention. No cotton to hoe. No work. Nothing to do but ride and let the wind blow in our faces.

"Wish I had a gun," Taylor hollered. "I'd like to shoot some of them crows up there."

Crows perched on the telephone wires along the highway. The long rows of crossed poles with wires strung from pole to pole made inviting places for birds in search of rodents or insects in the fields, or even crops. Mississippi cotton was still king, but there was a lot of corn and other food crops. Birds were eaters, especially crows.

"Aw, yeah," Casey said, "like you could hit something outta the back of this truck goin' 'bout a hundred miles an hour."

"Aw shutup, nitwit. I can shoot anything I can see. And, anyhow we ain't goin' no hundred miles an hour."

I held my hand up and over the side of the truck. The wind rushed hard against it as I forced it into the airstream. "I'd say that's about fifty miles an hour."

Taylor and Casey did the same thing. Through some magical calculation known only to us, we were able to determine the speed of the truck by the rush of wind against our hands.

"About fifty-two," Taylor said.

"A hundred," Casey said.

A rapid tap, tap, tap, on the window of the cab from Cousin Carol.

"Don't put your hands out like that! You want some car to knock them off?" She yelled loud enough to hear through the glass. She probably broke Cousin Trek's eardrums. Sometimes it wasn't easy to have fun.

"I hope we get to eat dinner at Pete and Buger's café," Casey said. The subject of shooting birds had passed.

"Yeah, me, too," Taylor said. "Better'n any café around here. Better hamburgers anyway."

"Yeah, I think we ate there back when Farley and I were here about five years ago or something. I was only five or six. I remember they got a pinball machine."

"Yeah, but Daddy'll have a heart attack if we ask him if we can play it."

"Yeah, same with mine," I said.

"Our daddy'll say, 'put your own money in it if you want, but not mine,'" Casey said. He tried talking in a low voice like a man. We all laughed. Pinball machine warnings were legendary.

"Big Trek likes to eat there. And he'll tell Daddy we oughta eat there because we don't know when we'll be back," Taylor said. "Mostly Big Trek'll jus' wanna eat there, but that's what he'll say."

I tried to lie back against the side of the truck and just rest and enjoy the ride. It was kind of hard to keep yelling over the rush of wind and road noise. I had heard Daddy and Uncle Trek and other men talk often about the land we were driving through.

The soil across the land was rich because floods from the river had washed over it many times from long ago, and from not too long ago. Just a few years before I was born there was one of the greatest floods of all time anywhere, right here where we were driving. It was called the Great Flood of 1927. It was like all the water in all the United States had come from other rivers and streams and flushed into the Mississippi. Nobody had ever seen a flood like it, except maybe Noah.

The Mississippi Delta had the richest soil in the world. Over and over during hundreds of years the Mississippi River had dumped sediments and nutrients into this area in northwest Mississippi. Some of my most memorable stories were of the Great Flood. The river stories were so much closer to us, and we knew they were true, and we knew the people. We were part of these stories. They were part of us.

One family of six got into a small boat about twelve feet long. They put as much of their stuff into the boat as they could and tried to paddle away while the water was only knee deep. But one of the temporary levees broke, and a huge rush of water hit the overloaded boat and all were washed away. Only a small three-year-old boy's body was recovered—his tiny body found tangled in the roots of a large, washed-away magnolia tree.

The flood was the greatest disaster in the history of the United States. It had rained and rained during the spring of the year all over the Mississippi River basin, which covered almost half of the United States, and finally all tributaries had been filled and the levees couldn't hold anymore. So the water spread everywhere.

I had heard grown men talk about it with a respect for the river as a wild force of nature. Some of them appeared to believe that if they didn't speak reverently of the river, it could act on its own and return at will. "If you didn't have any other reason to believe it, the Mississippi River would be reason enough to believe there was a God of creation," my uncle in Meridian had once said.

Clarksdale had 16,235 residents, so the sign said. It was probably as big as Cleveland and Yazoo City put together. Once my daddy brought Farley and me up here. Every now and then Daddy would talk about getting a farm and getting back to the land and being a farmer, because, like a lot of people in Jackson, he was reared on one. So when we were visiting Cousin Trek and Cousin Carol one time he brought us up here to look at some hogs and stuff for sale at an auction. The hogs pretty much just waddled around making oink and snort noises. Daddy asked some questions, but he didn't buy any since we didn't have a farm; and I don't think my mother would have allowed them at home. She had said that Farley and I already ate enough for one household budget. Daddy's farm idea would come and go. After I'd hoed cotton for two days, I'm glad it went. I hoped it stayed gone, especially if our crops were going to be cotton.

Cousin Trek had slowed down to about thirty, I figured. Big Trek was at the Clarksdale Hotel, Taylor said, and that's where we'd go first. Then probably go by a couple seed and feed stores, a hardware store, maybe the John Deere dealer. Those could be pretty interesting, especially if there were some old men telling stories and stuff. Sometimes they would spin tales that were probably half made up, but they were almost always fun to hear. Old men had a special way of telling stories that my mother called "delightful" unless they got crude.

At some point we'd probably have to wait while Cousin Carol went to some dress shop, or something equally useless. There was nothing as wasteful as hanging around waiting at a dress shop. Hat shops were none too exciting either, although they could be good for laughs. If you laughed too much, they'd ask if you wanted to leave. But you couldn't say yes even though you wanted to, because then you would get punished for talking back. So you were trapped there, wasting time.

We turned the corner onto Main Street and saw the hotel. The streets were crowded and there was a lot of traffic. Clarksdale had a lot more stores and picture shows and cafés. In the small towns the crowds and traffic usually didn't come until Saturday. But in Clarksdale even Wednesday was busy. There was a policeman directing traffic at an intersection. I thought about Mr. Siler driving here. He'd probably hit the policeman, or just yell at him. Of course it would probably take fifty years for Mr. Siler to drive this far from Cotton City.

We saw Big Trek standing in front of the hotel talking to a couple of guys who were wearing straw hats and denim overalls. Big Trek was poking the air with his finger. My guess, he was informing them of some weather that he was speculating about—probably rain. Big Trek was like a walking, talking Farmer's Almanac. He just seemed to know when it was going to rain, or be dry, or when tornadoes were about to drop from the sky. No one knew how he did it. He mostly was right about his predictions and people listened. Casey had said they should send his name into *Ripley's Believe It or Not.*

Big Trek waved at us as we parked in front of the hotel. All of us climbed out and went to greet him. Hugs and more hugs. You'd think he had been in Alaska or someplace digging for gold for about ten years. Big Trek told me how much I had grown, which couldn't have been much since last Christmas. But he said it anyway.

"Well, now, I trust the farm ain't burnt down," he said. He always joked with Cousin Trek, and Casey and Taylor, that they'd let the place burn down or get destroyed. They laughed and Cousin Trek said something like, "Not when we left, but you can never tell."

Big Trek laughed and rubbed the top of Casey's head. "Well, I've still got some errands to do. Maybe by the time I'm finished, we can get some dinner at Pete and Buger's before we head back."

"Where you goin' now, Daddy?" Cousin Trek asked.

"First, I gotta go to the hardware store. I gotta get some nails and paint. Then I wanna go to the tractor dealer."

"Okay, we can jus' leave the car parked here for now. Come back in an hour and stick another nickel in the meter," Cousin Trek said.

"Well y'all can go the hardware store, but I'm not spending part of my day off listening to those hair-brained, seedy stories y'all be telling," Cousin Carol said. She didn't consider them delightful today, I guess. "I'm going up the street to a shop I've wanted to visit for the longest time."

Cousin Trek said, "Well, that's fine, Honey. You go ahead." The 'honey' word meant he hoped she didn't ask him to go. I supposed those names did come in handy once in a while, if they got you out of something horrible like going to a dress shop. There was a brief silence. Casey and Taylor and I shuffled our feet, as if we hadn't heard her.

"Well, doesn't someone want to come with me?" she asked.

Now, she had to know we would rather have an eye gouged out with a hot poker and a wasp stuck up our nose than go to some woman's shop. "How about my baby? Casey, you wanna go with your mother?"

"Well…maybe…I guess…"

She reached over and pulled his head toward her and kissed him right on the forehead, right there in broad daylight. Then she laughed and said, "Y'all go on, I'll meet y'all back at the car about a quarter 'til twelve. Okay?"

The hardware store was filled with everything you could imagine that had something to do with work. Nails, plenty of evil cans of paint, tools of all kinds, rope, chains, insecticides, even fishing tackle and hunting supplies, with rifles and shotguns lined up in racks behind the counter. It had a cement floor and smelled like a hardware store—rough, greasy, a hemp smell and the always great fertilizer aroma. A small group of men at the counter were talking, most likely about the baseball standings and the price of cotton.

Casey and Taylor and I stood in front of the counter looking at the rifles and shotguns, talking about which one we would buy if we had the money. "You could kill a bear with that one," Casey said.

"Aww, there ain't any bears around here," I said.

"Yeah, there are," Taylor said. "Back a long time ago there were lots of bears up here."

"Aw, c'mon."

"Really, Big Trek says about two hundred years ago there were lots and lots of bears in the Delta. Panthers, too. Before farmers started growing cotton and stuff like that. It used to be like a jungle almost, around here."

"Really. Panthers, too?" I asked.

"Yeah, and there are still some—panthers and bears, I'm pretty sure."

Big Trek and Cousin Trek walked toward us, each with a

can of paint. "See anything you boys want?" Big Trek winked at Cousin Trek when he asked.

"Casey wants a bear gun, Big Trek." We laughed.

"Well, sounds good to me. Picked one out yet?"

"Yes, sir. That one on the end," Casey said.

"That's a .22, Casey," Cousin Trek said. "You can't kill a bear with that, unless maybe you beat him over the head with it." He put his free arm around Casey's shoulder and squeezed him.

"Why not? You can kill people with one."

"Well, people are different than bears—and what makes you say that anyway? Whada you know 'bout killin' people?"

I broke in for Casey. "I told him about some dead man they found in the river the other day, Cousin Trek. I heard it from a deputy and a highway patrolman at the bus station when I was ridin' up the other day."

He and Big Trek looked at each other.

"Really? Well, it was in the newspaper the other day. Didn't know you boys were reading anything but the funny papers. But I don't think they know yet who the dead man is. They sure don't know who shot him. Not as far as I know, anyhow. Y'all jus' forget about it for now. Y'all don't need to be worrying about such things."

"That's right," someone behind me said. I turned around and saw a man, I think was the owner. He seemed to know Cousin Trek and Big Trek, because as soon as we walked in they started shaking hands and talking and laughing.

"What's right, Jimmy?" Big Trek asked.

"Sheriff was in here today. Said they still ain't identified that guy they fished out down there. Jus' said he had been shot and dumped in the river."

"Well, I guess he could be from anywhere," Cousin Trek said. "I mean he could have been dumped in at St Louis for all we know."

Jimmy walked behind the counter to get an ashtray. He had just lit a Camel cigarette. "Well, now I wouldn't say that." He blew smoke up toward the ceiling. "They figured out 'bout how long he'd been in the water, I imagine."

"Is that right, Jimmy?"

"Yep, and so now they think he was dumped in somewhere maybe not more'n a little bit upriver from the Greenville Bridge."

"Are you sure? Or are you jus' guessin'?"

"Well, I'm jus' guessin', but my guess is as good as the sheriff's, I'll bet you."

"Well, enough of this for me," Big Trek said. "I need some nails to go with this paint, Jimmy. I'm a payin' customer here, don't forget. Then we got to get o'er to the John Deere dealer."

"Hey Daddy, maybe he was dumped in at Rosedale," Taylor said. Rosedale was close to the river and Cotton City.

"Well, we don't have any idea where he was put in. He could have been put in right there at Greenville for all we know. Now, no more discussion. Y'all hear me."

"That's right," Big Trek said. "We got to get o'er to the John Deere place. Then we eat." The look in his eyes said he was ready for Pete 'n Buger's.

The door had just been slammed on the subject of murder for now. It was just as well since it was almost dinner time.

It was exactly a quarter to twelve by the big English-looking clock on the People's Bank of Clarksdale when we arrived at Pete and Buger's. We had timed it just right because Cousin Carol walked up the street toward us.

"I see y'all must've got all your hardware chores done," she said. She gave a little sarcastic punch to the word chores.

"Well, you don't have an armful of packages, so I guess we won't have to mortgage the back forty." Big Trek laughed at his own joke.

"Very funny, Bob Hope. Let's eat," she said.

Pete and Buger's was filling fast since it was almost noon. Ceiling fans whirled above the single room while three waitresses moved around the tables. Two more were behind the counter. They all wore white dresses, like nurses, but with aprons tied in back, green ticket pads in their pockets and yellow pencils stuck in their hair. Our waitress' nametag said Lucy. She was kind of fat and chewing gum. She also had a gold tooth that you could see when she chewed and smiled at the same time.

"How are y'all today?" She chewed and smiled, her tooth sparkling as she put five menus on our table with five glasses of ice water. I was always amazed at how waitresses could carry so much at one time.

"Fine, fine," Cousin Trek said. "And how are you, Lucy?" I don't think he knew her, but just saw her name tag.

"I'm just fine. How'r y'all today?"

The rest of us all said "fine."

"Hot, hot, hot," Cousin Carol said. "Mercy, it is hot."

"Oh, Honey, I am jus' so glad to be inside workin'," Lucy said. "At least I'm outta that sun. And these fans give me some breeze. Whooee!"

All the menus had a piece of paper clipped to the top describing the dinner special for Wednesday. Today it was meatloaf or catfish and a choice of two vegetables of green peas, beets, carrots or potatoes. Printed underneath the paper on the menu was the selection of steaks, chops, fried chicken and such. Taylor and Casey and I went for the hamburger side of the menu while Big Trek, Cousin Trek and Cousin Carol ordered the dinner special.

"Okay, and iced tea for everybody? 'Kay, I'll be back in a few minutes," Lucy said. She backed up—chewing, smiling, sparkling—then turned and waddled away.

Casey leaned over and whispered in my ear, "Nice hamsters."

Cousin Carol reached over and grabbed him by the nose. "Do *not* whisper in public like that."

"Yes, ma'am."

Cousin Trek gave him a stern look. Bad manners in public were like a thousand times worse than at home, for some reason. My greatest fear was Cousin Trek was going to ask him what he had said. That could have ruined dinner.

Big Trek came to the rescue and changed the subject. "Well, unless y'all need anything else in town, we can get on back after we finish. Trek, you prob'ly need to see Earl before it gets too late anyhow."

"We oughta be home before three. I'll have plenty of time to see him," Cousin Trek said.

Big Trek had been in Clarkdale for almost a week. He had caught the bus up here the day before I got to Cotton City. When I had mentioned to Cousin Carol one afternoon that he must have lots of business up here, she gave one of her 'hruummp's.

"Well, Daddy, you get a lot done this week? Find out who's planting what next spring?" Cousin Trek said.

I noticed Big Trek was looking at Cousin Carol kind of out of the corner of his eye. It looked a little bit the way Casey looked when he was about to say something goofy.

"Yeah. I been talking to some of the boys in the domino game about planting some corn."

"Corn, huh?" Cousin Trek said. "Are you serious?"

"How can somebody who deals with domino players be taken seriously?" Cousin Carol said.

Big Trek didn't answer. He just kept on talking. "We figure this new Sheriff Bibeau is gonna be honest since he's a Presbyterian and we'll have to make our own whiskey since all the bootleggers'll be out of business." He laughed so loud half the people in the café turned our way.

Cousin Carol just shook her head. "Big Trek, you ain't going to heaven if you don't quit your corruption. And these boys don't need to hear about such things."

The three of us looked at each other. We really didn't know what the corn talk had to do with anything, but everybody from first grade on knew that whiskey was illegal in Mississippi.

And I think she suspected that he participated in the domino game at the café in Cotton City sometimes, but didn't say it. But, if he played in the Cotton City café, what kind of wild games do they have in a big city like Clarksdale?

The place filled even faster now. Lucy had to weave through tables and new customers coming in. She got to our table with three plates riding up her right arm, two on her left wrist and the plate of rolls clamped in her fingers.

"Well, now, hamburger for you, hamburger for you and hamburger for you," she said as she unloaded her right arm. "And meatloaf, meatloaf and fried catfish." Big Trek got the fish. "Now I'll get y'all some more water and tea and y'all will be all set, I think."

She went to the counter and picked up two pitchers and returned. "Anything else?"

"I think we're okay for now," Cousin Trek said.

Taylor, Casey and I dug in. Pete and Buger's did have good hamburgers, big, and with big French fries. We had just started—shaking napkins for our laps, passing the salt and stuff like that, when Big Trek bellowed over his shoulder, "Hey, Lucy! Gonna need some catsup, please, ma'am!"

"My word, Big Trek," Cousin Carol said. "Why don't you use a bullhorn?"

"Well, she couldn't hear a bullhorn as noisy as it is in here," said Big Trek.

"Casey, don't eat so fast," Cousin Trek said.

Casey was eating like he hadn't been fed in three days. The burgers were good and he probably thought if he showed how hungry he was, he could get another.

"Jus' take your time," Cousin Trek said. "If you're still hungry, you can have another when you've finished." Cousin Trek was a mind reader, just like my daddy.

It was after twelve-thirty, and we would have finished sooner probably, but it seemed like every two minutes somebody who knew Big Trek or Cousin Trek would stop and talk. When we had finished and Lucy was clearing the table, Big Trek leaned back in his chair. He looked like he wanted to cut loose with a giant belch. Although that would have been the end of the world as far as Cousin Carol was concerned, it would have been funny.

"Oh, by the way. You know who I saw at the bus station when I got here?" said Big Trek. He paused, though nobody made a guess. "Looty Nash," he finally said.

"Looty?" Cousin Trek asked.

"Yeah. Said he was just visitin'."

"Visiting who? I didn't know he had any family left. And I don't think he has a lot of friends," Cousin Carol said. "He hardly ever goes anywhere."

"Beats me," Big Trek said. "Just said he was visitin'. Said he just caught a ride over to the highway, then caught the bus and came up to visit. I thought it was a little odd myself. I mean, he doesn't drive much. But then he doesn't go anywhere much either."

"Wonder what he was doing here?"

"Beats me," said Big Trek.

We loaded up the pickup with Big Trek's luggage, paint, nails and other stuff then drove over to the Lion Oil filling station. Taylor, Casey and I were in the bed of the truck, and sat up on the sides when we stopped. I heard Big Trek tell Cousin Trek, "I'm gonna get in the back with the boys."

"Are you sure?" Cousin Carol said. "There's plenty of room for the three of us in the cab."

"You boys want a Co-Cola?" Big Trek asked us. He really didn't have to ask. We did. "Gimme those empties and we'll trade 'em in for the deposit." He pointed to the empty bottles that had been rattling in between the jack and the spare tire.

"Thank you, Big Trek," I said. It had been a good day. Now an ice-cold Coca-Cola while we road back to Cotton City.

CHAPTER 11

I took a big slug, stifled a belch, and leaned back against the spare tire. "Big Trek, who were the University Grays?"

BB had said in the field yesterday that he was fighting for the University Grays. I hadn't understood it when he said it, because I thought he was fighting against the Communists.

I had forgotten about it until now. I guess sitting here watching Trek cupping his hands to light his pipe in the wind, his old gray hair blowing, made me think of it for some reason. The War Between the States always made me think about old men. All the stories we had been told in school were about young Confederates going off and fighting like crazy for their homes and land. Because they were so outnumbered they came back battered, beaten and old. They had aged, my grandmother had said, because they lost the cause.

We stood when Dixie was played—anywhere, anytime, and all of us fifth graders sometimes thought that we could win the cause back one day. My daddy said he wasn't sure that would ever happen. The way things were looking, we'd be lucky if we weren't ordered by somebody to stop singing Dixie. Anyway, I wanted to know what the University Grays were. I had heard about the Mississippi Grays, but not the University Grays.

Big Trek finally got his pipe going. It didn't blow out since we weren't going that fast, just driving in town past stores and filling stations. Going about twenty-five, I guessed.

"The University Grays were a group of young men at Ole Miss." He paused. "Actually it wasn't called Ole Miss back then. It was just the University of Mississippi. I'm not even sure it was a university then."

He stopped talking for a moment and sucked hard on his

pipe. I took a big slug of Coca-Cola.

"Well, back during the War of Independence—Southern independence," he began, "when we had one final chance to win, General Lee took his Army of Northern Virginia to a little town in Pennsylvania called Gettysburg. The battle took place over three days. And it came to be decided on the third day. You see, our boys had fought hard as anybody could fight those first two days, but it was the third day—and what came to be known as Pickett's Charge—when our Confederacy made its highest stand. The 'high water mark' they called it."

"What happened, Big Trek? We know about Pickett's charge, but what about the University Grays?"

Big Trek banged his pipe against the side of the truck, emptying it, the ashes blowing off to the cotton fields. "Well, General Lee and General Longstreet sent our boys charging right up the middle of Cemetery Ridge. But they were slow getting started and the artillery didn't work near 'bout as well as it should've. Anyway, our boys set out across that field, knowing they had to reach and hold the high ground at the top—to take Cemetery Ridge—and the War could've ended right there. They started trudging across that field and up that hill…" Big Trek spread his arms, making like he was showing a long line of men, "…and headed right for the middle…" he pointed straight ahead then paused, his eyes widened "…then the Yankees began firing everything they had—rifle shot, cannon balls, canister fire. They blew holes in our lines and the boys… the men, crumpled up shot, or were blown to bits and hundreds and hundreds and hundreds fell. They were bleedin' and busted and arms and legs were ripped away."

He paused and looked at each of us as if he was talking to each one of us alone. "And then, you know what?"

"What?" I said.

"When almost nine out of ten had been shot down, when there were only a handful left, they kept on charging. They wouldn't give up. And General Armistead from Virginia and a handful of what was left of our Mississippi boys crossed that stone wall and took that hill. Up and over that wall, General

Armistead was leading our boys, his hat held high on the tip of his sword." Big Trek paused again and eyed each of us.

"What then, Big Trek?" I said.

He took out his pocket knife and began digging into the bowl of his pipe, cleaning out the charred innards. "There were too few left to hold the hill, and they were pushed off. Armistead was killed and every one of our Mississippians was shot or killed. And those boys were the University Grays. They had made the greatest advance into the North out of the whole War—our boys. Our University Grays."

Cousin Trek had turned onto the highway now and we picked up speed. Big Trek again banged his pipe on the side of the truck, emptying it. He wasn't going to fight a sixty mile an hour wind huffing and puffing.

"What made you ask about them?" he said.

"Sir?" The wind seemed like it gobbled his words.

"I said, what made you ask that?"

Well, BB said he was fightin' for the University Grays—said that's why he went to Korea."

Big Trek scratched his ear with his pipe, grabbed his hat as the wind almost ripped it off. "BB is a fine young man. And I can tell you this—he's loves Mississippi. A lot of the young colored folks have gone off to Chicago and Detroit and New York. They think they'll like it better up there. But not BB. He is gonna be a Mississippi boy no matter what. He would love to play football at Ole Miss 'cause of the way Johnny Vaught's always talking about trying to get Mississippi boys to play up there."

He paused for a moment, drawing on his pipe. "But he can't play up there 'cause coloreds can't play at white schools. And to tell you the truth, not playin' football don't bother him as much, I don't believe, as not being thought of as a Mississippi boy."

"But what's it got to do with the University Grays, Big Trek?"

Big Trek stretched his legs out into the bed, crossed his feet and put his hands behind his head. "I think he sees himself as a fellow who's just as capable of sacrificin' as much as any man in Mississippi. And the Grays were about as fightin' and sacri-ficin' a bunch as you'd find. I think he believes he could've been one of 'em. But his time is now, 1951. Not 1861. So he went to Korea to fight for what all men fight for in a war."

"What's that?"

"For their family. And for the men next to 'em. Men don't go off to war for their freedom or their rights or any of that. That's what the government tries to tell you. Men go so they don't let their friends and family down. And to show them they are willing to sacrifice for those things and people around them. And that's what BB did. He was as willing to sacrifice for his Mississippi blood, whether at Gettysburg or Korea. Just like those University Grays and those five thousand colored Confed-erates at Gettysburg did."

"There were Negroes in the Confederate army?" I asked.

"Quite a few, yes. But you don't hear 'bout that much. History books don't put it in. They want it to...well, never mind that. There's things you boys don't need to know right now. Just enough to tell you that the Yankees weren't fightin' to free anyone. And old Abe Lincoln sure wasn't neither."

I scooted closer to Big Trek so I could hear better.

"I once gave BB a book written by Booker T. Washington, *Up From Slavery*. Like I said, BB's a readin' boy. The Lord put a lot of talent in that boy—reader, worker and a pretty dang good tailback. Booker T. was a former slave, but a real Southerner, too. That's what I hoped BB would learn. Some Negroes, mostly up North, said Booker T. was a white man's you-know-what. But I think he was a pretty decent fellow."

"We've talked 'bout him in school," I said.

"I remember one time when BB was about ten-years old—just after Pearl Harbor as a matter of fact—he said he would like to go off and fight. Said he and Mr. Looty would go because Mr. Looty was such a good shot and all. Said he could hit anything—man or beast. Said Mr. Looty could teach him. They'd be just like Silas and Andrew."

"Looty and BB are good friends, huh Big Trek," said Casey.

"Yeah. BB just always tried to watch out for Looty. At least since he was a boy. Maybe just felt sorry for him. Anyway, I do know this about BB. He's a hard worker. He attacks that cotton like a rabbit after cabbage."

Cousin Trek sped up as we passed a Trailways bus. The smell of diesel blew up my nose, and the wind noise roared. I looked up at the windows and thought about the straw-haired woman, and wondered if she was on it. Cousin Trek passed it at about seventy I figured, though I never got my hand up to be sure.

"Who were Silas and Andrew, Big Trek?" I asked. Looking at Casey and Taylor, I could tell they didn't know either.

I settled back and absorbed the story about Andrew and Silas Chandler that Big Trek told us. I pulled down my baseball cap hard, so the wind wouldn't blow it off.

Pretty soon Big Trek stopped talking and just sat there. I didn't know if he'd run out of things to say or if he just was tired of talking. But the wind felt good, and we were on our way back to Cotton City. No work again tomorrow. Taylor had asked him if we could have the afternoon off so we could go swimming. Big Trek said we might as well take the whole day off since I wasn't going to be here but a couple more weeks. He said we'd have to work this Saturday though, and all next week, too, if we were going to make any money.

"What are you boys gonna do when you get home?" Big Trek asked us.

"I don't know. Maybe we'll go downtown," Taylor said

"Gonna spend all that money y'all made?"

"Just look around," Taylor said.

"My mother and daddy don't like me to spend money much," I said. "They're always tellin' me to save it."

Big Trek smiled. "Well, sounds like good advice to me. Just don't get in a big domino game down at the café. You boys gonna work tomorrow?"

"Sir?" Taylor said, pretending he didn't hear.

"There's plenty y'all can do to make you some more money." He knew we heard.

"Well, we were gonna work with Mr. Hightower and BB

again, maybe Friday. Thought we'd go fishin,' maybe swimmin,' tomorrow."

"Hey!" Casey said. "Mr. Hightower said he would take us fishin' over at the river Sunday afternoon. We forgot about that. Don't forget, we gotta ask him."

Big Trek scraped the bowl of his pipe again. He banged it on the side of the truck. "You boys sure get off easy when you get company. Fishin', swimmin', picture shows. It's like Christmas in the summertime."

Casey spit as hard as he could out to the highway, and it blew back and almost hit Taylor.

"Will ya stop that, you little sh—" Taylor almost got the word out before Big Trek smacked his head. "Well make him stop, Big Trek. He's crazy!"

"You aren't supposed to be cussin'. And Casey, if you gotta spit, move to the other side."

"I was jus' tryin' to see if I had enough power to get it out far enough to not blow back."

We turned off the highway onto the gravel driveway. We were almost home. I leaned against the spare tire and thought about the stories Big Trek had told us—about the University Grays, and about Andrew and Silas.

CHAPTER 12

We took a back road into town on our bikes in order to stay off Highway 49. The shortcut led into the square and the gazebo. We parked there. There were some boys throwing a baseball around. There had been a guy from Cotton City named Bobby Taylor who was a pretty good pitcher and even signed a professional contract. But he hurt his arm and never got out of the minors. They had put up a sign that read 'Cotton City, Home of Bobby Taylor.' He lived in Atlanta now, but the sign was still there.

"Hey boys," Mr. Hightower called from across the street. "We goin' fishin Sunday after church?"

He had just come out of the barber shop. His hair was slicked back with some good barber shop stuff, not Vitalis or Wildroot Cream Oil, but some real professional stuff. He was scratching the back of his neck where the little clipped hairs clung. The barber always tried to dust them away but could never get them all. I had had a haircut the day before I left Jackson, so I was safe for a couple of weeks.

"Yes, sir," Taylor said. As soon as we got back from Clarksdale we had asked if we could go fishin' Sunday afternoon with Mr. Hightower.

"Okay, we'll take off right after church," said Mr. Hightower. "I got a boat and I got an old buddy who's got one. He wants to go, too. We'll go down to Greenville. Get some big catfish. Sound good?"

"Yes, sir," we replied in unison.

"Think we'll really get some big ones, Mr. Hightower?" Casey said.

"Well, I hope so. But we gotta be careful, cats been known

119

to eat boys under ten years old."

Taylor and I smiled and kind of did a half-laugh, but Mr. Hightower didn't smile. Taylor said, "Aww, c'mon."

"I'm serious. I took some Cub Scouts, eight and nine years old down there last year. I told 'em not to wade out. But they wouldn't listen. Four of 'em, whoosh! Gone. Catfish Cubbies."

"What happened then?" Casey asked. He knew he was being kidded. Mr. Hightower hadn't smiled yet, trying to keep up the front.

"Nothin'. We keep checkin' the trot lines. They'll prob'ly make Eagle Scout 'fore we find 'em."

"Aww, not really," Casey insisted.

Mr. Hightower very gently put his hat on so as not to mess up his nice, new slicked-down hair. He had coal black hair and although he wasn't as old as my daddy or Cousin Trek, he had some grey bits of hair around his ears. "Well, how was Clarkdale? Y'all get Mr. Mayfield back all right?"

"He's back, yes, sir. And it was fine. We ate dinner at Pete and Buger's and hung around the John Deere place and everything," Taylor said. "Daddy said he prob'ly needed to see you sometime today." Taylor felt big, passing information.

"Yeah, we got lots to do before pickin' time starts. I guess he's at the house."

"Yes, sir."

"Well, I'll see you boys later. I'll tell your momma and daddy that we're goin' fishin' Sunday afternoon for sure, Taylor."

You could run out of stores to go to in Cotton City pretty fast. It wasn't like Clarksdale or Greenville. Cotton City didn't have a Woolworth's, and for sure no Sears and Roebuck. We finally decided to go to the drugstore and look at some comic books. Maybe even get a Coke Cola.

We started across the street and got blown at by Mr. Siler from about three blocks away. We waved at him as we crossed just to let him know we had seen him. But he still stuck his head out of the window when he passed us about five minutes later. "You boys better watch out. You're gonna get killed."

Billy Joe O'Grady watched us cross the street. "Now,

boys, don't laugh at Mr. Siler. He don't go fast enough to hurt anybody."

"Yes, sir." We all waved at Mr. O'Grady. He was the town marshal. We hadn't noticed him standing on the sidewalk when we crossed.

He didn't have a lot to do in Cotton City. Just break up a few checker arguments from time to time. He had two deputies, just so there was always somebody on duty all the time. Whoever was on duty at midnight had to turn the two stoplights onto blinking-caution. There was a rumor that he was one of the best backroom café domino players in town. I wondered how there could possibly be any gambling with the town marshal being a player.

Inside the drugstore, we hovered around the magazine rack, away from the counter and behind one of the aisles where you couldn't be seen reading. It didn't matter. Mr. and Mrs. Marks, who owned the store, didn't seem to really care if we just read, as long as we didn't take anything to eat over to the rack. I think somebody had dropped a banana split on Lois Lane's face one time, and the chocolate syrup soaked in just right so it looked like Lex Luther had given her a black eye. That had brought an end to reading and eating.

"Look," Casey said. "This month's Captain Marvel is out." We sat down on the floor. "Billy Batson's about to get choked by a giant, weird-lookin' guy," said Casey. "He can't say Shazam with the thing's hands on his throat. He'll get killed if he don't say it so he can change to Captain Marvel."

"I never did understand how a guy could get hit by lightnin' and get help," I said. "How come it doesn't kill him?"

"Well, you're just gettin' what mother calls mature, Jake," Taylor said. "You don't go for that Captain Marvel kid stuff like Casey here."

"I think, when you start lookin' at girls the way Farley does, that's mature. My mother said that Farley was maturing. It didn't sound like she thought he didn't like comic books anymore."

Casey looked up. "You mean when you see progressed bosoms, you are maturing. So, progressed bosoms are more important than Captain Marvel? Now what kind of sense does that make?"

"You better not talk so loud about those things, or we're gonna get in trouble," Taylor said. "You jus' wait and see, Big Mouth."

The bell above the door rang and we heard Mr. O'Grady. He walked over to the counter where Mr. Marks and a couple of other men were.

"Well, Looty's back home now," Mr. O'Grady said.

"Did the sheriff find out anything?" asked Mr. Marks. "They have him there all night?"

"Yeah, most of it. Far as I know they didn't find out anything. I was gone for a little bit. I had to do a couple of things."

Casey stopped looking at Captain Marvel and looked at Taylor and me. We were all thinking the same thing, that maybe we weren't supposed to hear what we were hearing.

I started to say something to Taylor but he put his fingers up to his lips, like to shush me. I guess he thought they would stop talking if they realized we were there.

"He didn't act like he was worried or nothin'," one of the men said.

"How do you know," another said. "You weren't there."

"Well, that's what Billy Joe said. Didn't you, Billy Joe?"

"I just said he wasn't nervous. He said he didn't have his rifle anymore. He'd lost it, is what he said. But I told you I wasn't there the whole time they were talkin' to him."

"How come the sheriff didn't take him to the county jail?" someone asked.

"What for—can't prove anything. Just because he shoots a .22 don't necessarily mean anything. Lots of people have .22's. You'd have to bring in half the squirrel hunters in the state."

"He said he'd lost his rifle, huh?"

"That's what he said. You deaf?"

The bell on the door rang again. Another customer came in. Taylor and I peeked over the top of the rack. Casey wasn't quite tall enough. It was Mrs. Culpepper. She ran the beauty shop in town. The talk about Looty stopped.

"Well, good afternoon everybody. How are y'all doing? Sweatin' like the fires of hell, I imagine." I had heard my mother say one time that Mrs. Culpepper was as sweet as she could be, but a little rough around the edges. "I could use something cold like a Pabst Blue Ribbon Beer. But I'll just bet you ain't got none of them have you, Buleau," she said to Mr. Marks. "Awfully hot out there."

"Now, Eunice, don't start with me," Mr. Marks said. "If they ever legalize beer in Cotton City, you'll be the first to know. And anyhow, I ain't gonna sell it outta a drug store."

"Why not? It's a drug, ain't it?"

"Never mind, Eunice."

"Well, I need a bottle of Bayer Aspirin, and let's see, what else...?"

We walked from behind the rack and climbed up on stools at the counter. After we came out, Mr. Marks said, "Why, hello boys, I didn't notice y'all over there. What're y'all gonna have?"

"A cherry Coke, please," I said.

"Just water, please," Taylor said.

"Lend me a nickel, Taylor," Casey said.

"I ain't lendin' you a nickel. You got a nickel, I know."

"Yeah, but I wanna buy this new Captain Marvel and all I got is a dime."

"You got more than that. You made over a dollar just Tuesday."

"Yeah, but I got it locked up at home."

I was watching the grownups. They were silent and seemed to enjoy the negotiations between Taylor and Casey. Mr. Marks put my cherry Coke on the counter and leaned forward on his elbows, absorbed by my cousins.

"And a large bottle of hydrogen peroxide." Mrs. Culpepper had just recalled another of her items.

Mr. Marks came from behind the counter. She could get things for herself, but he wandered through the store picking up some Bayer and peroxide.

"And," she yelled at him across about three counters, "three boxes of bobbie pins!" He moved to another counter.

"Business must be good, Eunice," Mr. O'Grady said. "All that hair fixin' and stuff."

"Well, I guess, if I can keep my damn drier fixed. One of 'em keeps breakin' down. Have to send it down to Cleveland to get fixed. You'd think I could find somebody in Cotton City that could fix it. I'd get my husband to fix it if he wasn't dead."

"Now, Eunice, careful, these boys don't need to hear that kinda language," Mr. O'Grady said.

"Oh, my goodness. I wasn't payin' attention. I'm sorry, sweetheart." She looked at Casey. "I just got to blabbin' and forgot myself." She yelled to the back of the store, "Buleau! Give these boys a cherry Coke and put it on my bill."

I hadn't paid for my Coke yet, so I hoped she meant me, too. And I'd heard the word damn at least a million times mostly from some of Farley's friends. Also I had read it in the Bible, but it still wasn't to be said in front of children and ladies. Being rough around the edges may have disqualified Mrs. Culpepper as a lady, but I wasn't sure.

"Thank you, Mrs. Culpepper," Casey said. Taylor and I thanked her, too. I was still hoping she would notice I hadn't paid for my drink yet.

She sat down at the counter and lit an Old Gold. "Well, I might just as well have a cup of coffee, Buleau. I don't have no appointments 'til four o'clock."

"You know what, Mrs. Culpepper, I'll bet old BB could fix your drier," Taylor said. "He works pretty hard and he's smart, too. He was goin' to college if he hadn't gone to Korea. He still might go."

"Is that a fact," one of the men said.

"Where's he gonna go, young Mayfield? Is he gonna try and play football now?" Mr. O'Grady asked.

"Said he might go to that new Mississippi Vocational College in Itta Bena," Taylor said.

"I don't know if they have a football team," Mr. O'Grady said. "He could've played in Florida if he hadn't got shot and all. That Florida A&M got a dang good football program for colored boys. And that coach is like a Nigra Knute Rockne or something. What's his name—Jack or Jake somebody or another?"

"They ain't got a football team over at Itta Bena, I don't imagine. Jus' started the school last year," Mr. Marks said. "But they'll prob'ly git one up. It's like he only wants to stay in Mississippi."

"Well, let's jus' forget about the da—I mean, the football team for a minute. You think he can fix machinery?" Mrs. Culpepper said.

"I don't know for sure," Taylor said. "He jus' seems pretty smart and all. And he's always working on his tractor and stuff like that."

She smushed her cigarette out in the ashtray and took a sip of coffee. There was a big red blob on the cup and on her cigarette. She must've had about six pounds of lipstick on. At least she did before she started smoking and coffee-ing.

"He jus' got back from Korea, didn't he?"

"Yes, ma'am. That's where he got shot and all."

"Well, next time you see him, you ask him if he can fix something as big as a hair drier. Tell him I'll pay him a nice fee. Better'n sendin' the da… dang thing to Cleveland."

"I'll bet he can fix it," Casey said.

"Me, too," I said.

"How long are you gonna be up here visitin', Mr. Jake?" Mr. Marks asked.

"'Bout another week or two. Then my mother and daddy are comin' up to get me."

"Where's that brother of yours? Farley?"

"Oh, he's got his driver's license now, and he' stayin' in Jackson this time."

Casey started slurping the cherry Coke out of the bottom of the glass. Taylor smacked him on the head. "Stop! That's rude." Everyone smiled.

"Bet he's got a girlfriend now, doncha reckon, Mr. Pete?" someone said.

"Maybe, but I don't see why. Why would he want a girlfriend, jus' because he's got a driver's license?"

The grownups laughed, while Casey peered straight at Mrs. Culpepper. Not at her face either. Right at her chest. And when he did, he sort of blinked both his eyes at me, so it was all I could do to keep from laughing. Taylor, too.

After we left the drugstore we walked down to the Majestic to check the marquee. We knew The Man from Planet X was on. But we wanted to see the posters behind the glass. It had these artists' drawings of 'The Man' and a rocket ship headed to earth, and all these explosions going off on earth. And it listed the stars, and directors, and all that other stuff we didn't care about.

"Look," Casey said. "There's Looty." You could see him across the square, standing in front of the feed store.

"Let's go see him," Taylor said.

Looty was standing on the sidewalk like he was waiting for someone. I had never talked to him, but as we got closer he appeared like someone my mother and daddy might call simple. They didn't mean anything bad, but mentally quiet, as my mother said.

Looty was dressed in khaki trousers and a plaid sport shirt with the top button buttoned and wore a Cardinals baseball cap. I felt sorry for him because he had to go to the county prison farm and all. Then yesterday, everybody questioning him at the sheriff's office and everything.

"Hey, Looty, whadaya doin'?" Taylor asked.

Looty took his cap off to scratch his head. "Waitin' on the Trailways bus."

"Where're you goin'?" Casey asked.

"Greenville." He pointed south. "Down thar."

"This is our cousin Jake from Jackson, Looty."

"Hey, Jake."

"Hey, Looty, nice to meet you."

"Nice to meet you, too."

Looty looked younger to me than what I expected. And he wasn't shaved. Taylor said he thought he was about forty or so, although he wasn't positive. He spoke sort of slow, and he really seemed like he wanted to be a friend.

"Y'all know I saved y'all's fish?" Looty said.

"Oh yeah?" Taylor said. The three of us looked at each other.

"Thar was a water moccasin what was gonna get y'all's fish y'all left on the stringer. But I shot him. Shot him twice-d. I saw y'all when y'all left 'em to go home. He was crawlin' on the ground t'ward the spot where y'all put 'em, right whar y'all left 'em. They'll eat 'em, ya know."

"Well, we sure 'preciate it, Looty," Casey said.

"Whadaya goin' to Greenville for, Looty?" Taylor asked.

Looty sat down on the curb. He pulled a beat up old suitcase up beside his leg. It didn't seem like he heard Taylor's question the way he just stared. At last, he said, "Jus' goin'. I have some bi'ness to do."

He seemed younger in the mind than Casey, and it made him seem pitiful. I wanted to ask him what he was being questioned about last night. And what he had done with his rifle. And most of all, I wanted to ask him why he had shot those chickens that time. But I don't think I could ever ask him about the mayonnaise jar. I don't think I wanted to know now, for sure. But I didn't think I could ask him questions like Taylor and Casey. They had known him for a long time. I had just met him.

"And I have some friends thar, too," he said after a long pause.

"My granddaddy, Big Trek, said he saw you up in Clarksdale this week," Taylor said. "You're gettin' to travel lots, Looty. Mus' be fun."

Looty's face curled a weak smile, but he didn't reply.

"We went up to Clarksdale today. Went to Pete and Buger's and everything. We rode up in the pickup though. Prob'ly more fun on the bus, I'll bet," Taylor said.

"It's cool on the bus, if you open the winder. I don't drive my truck very far. I drive it downtown to catch the bus when I go somewhere far, like Greenville or Clarksdale. Sometimes I hitchhike," Looty said. His eyes seemed to wander.

I was sure Taylor and Casey were thinking the same thing I was—who had we seen in Looty's house that night? But I didn't think they were going to ask him. And I sure wasn't going to.

"Thanks for shootin' that snake," Taylor said.

"I told Ben Samuels I'd shoot crows for him, but he said he could do it. Anyways, I don't have my rifle now."

The big Scenic Cruiser turned the corner and pulled up in front of the feed store. The doors opened with a rush of compressed air. Looty stepped up. He stopped and turned around. "I'll see y'all. Nice ta seen ya, Jake."

"Nice to've met you too, Looty," I said again.

I finally got to meet Looty. He didn't seem as scary as I thought he would, and I felt sorry for him. He was grown-up and everything, but he was like us. And he seemed kind of lonely. But I liked him.

He had taken the back seat and looked at us through the window. He waved as the bus drove away. We waved, too.

CHAPTER 13

We were going swimming. We didn't want to go swimming in the public county lake because Taylor said everybody peed in it. He and Casey knew of a clean place. We took our fishing poles so it would look like we were going fishing. We planned to swim on private property. Whoever owned the land probably didn't care, but we weren't supposed to do something like that without permission.

Also, you didn't need a swimming suit since there weren't any girls around. If we brought home wet swimming suits, Cousin Carol would ask us where we had been swimming. Trespassing was like stealing. If we told her we had gone to the county lake, we would be lying. And if we got caught for lying, we really would be in trouble. If we told her we had trespassed we would be in as much trouble as for lying. So we took our fishing poles; this way we were only deceiving—which was lying without getting caught.

It was mid-morning. We didn't have to go home for dinner, so we could just swim and eat at the pond. Cousin Carol had made us sandwiches. It would be a good day to relax before we had to go back to work tomorrow. Cousin Trek had said we'd probably have to work some on Saturday, because BB and Mr. Hightower would be busy and need us. But he said he would pay for the movie again tomorrow night to help make up for the loss of work today.

"Hey, look!" Casey shouted. He was on the dam standing on an extended log, useful as a diving board. He had stripped naked and stood proudly perched on the end of the log overlooking the water. With one arm extended upward, the other grasping, he peed in a perfect arc into our clean private lake.

"You little creep!" Taylor shouted. He pulled off his socks

and slung them. "Now you ruined it for everybody."

"Yeah, like you aren't gonna do it when you get in."

"I wouldn't. I don't wanna ruin it."

"Oh, we'd be on the honor system, huh?"

I laughed at them. But Casey was right. Probably everybody did it in every lake from Atlanta to Dallas and in the oceans, too.

Casey splashed in while Taylor and I raced to undress. I beat him and ran in from the shallow end. The water was still cool because it was morning. Taylor and I were splashing around when Casey swam over to us. "Feels good. Kinda cold at first," he said.

"Yeah," I said. "It's great as soon as you get used to it."

Casey was treading water, not splashing, saying nothing, looking at Taylor.

"What's wrong with you?" Taylor asked.

Casey broke out with great effort. "Unnnngh, Ugnnnn, I gotta go! I can't help it, unnnngh, it's a number two!"

Taylor and I swam back to shore like Johnny Weismuller. Casey laughed. In the shallow water we stood naked, water just above our knees.

"I didn't really," Casey hollered.

"I'll bet you did," Taylor said.

I was laughing. It was funny whether he did or not.

Taylor was laughing, too. "C'mon, you did or didn't? Tell the truth."

"I was just playing," Casey said.

"You're crazy," said Taylor. "I hope you drown."

"I'll bet people do it in the county lake," I said. "You can do it and nobody would notice. In the city pools in Jackson, the water is clear and somebody would notice for sure. You prob'ly would get banned for life. Not to mention the whippin' you would get at home."

"Will y'all shut up about it? You're gonna ruin my dinner," Taylor said. "Already ruined my swim."

We swam some more but stayed away from Casey's spot.

It was almost noon, and we figured we had enough sun and fun for now. We got out, put on our underwear and lay on the soft Johnson grass beside the willow tree, waiting for the air to dry us. Lying in the grass with your shirt off made your back itch, but otherwise it was comfortable. Swimming made you almost as hungry as working. The sandwiches Cousin Carol had put in a large brown paper sack tasted great in our semi-exhausted condition. We drank out of a thermos filled with cherry Kool-Aid.

"Listen," Taylor said. "Hear that?" He jerked his head up and rested on his elbows. The low sound of an engine approached, out of sight, past the dam.

We scrambled like crazy to get our clothes on. We didn't want to get arrested and, for sure, not in our underwear. Casey got his tee shirt on backward.

The sound stopped. Maybe we were safe. We waited for what seemed like forever. Water was coming down my face, and I wasn't sure whether it was because my face was still wet or if I was sweating. It was probably close to a hundred now.

"Why, hello, boys. Y'all watchin' the pond to make sure nobody steals it?" BB walked up the slope of the dam.

We were relieved but still worried. What was BB doing here? Did he know we had been skinny dipping? Would he tell?

"Hey, BB," Taylor said. "We were just wonderin' if somebody would mind if we fished here—" He stammered some, "—but we ain't been fishin' here. Not without permission." He turned to Casey and me. "Have we, y'all?"

BB walked up and stopped under the tree. He wore work gloves and pulled at the fingers; got one off, then the other. "Oh, I know you ain't been fishin'. Whoever heard of skinny fishin'?"

We looked at each other. Even Casey knew what he meant.

"Now don't you boys know that you can see three little white butts from prob'ly a mile away? They look like big marshmallows, they stand out so much."

"You mean…you mean, you saw us? Are we in trouble?" asked Casey.

"Naw, Mr. Lipscomb owns this pond and the land around it for a long ways. He knows y'all been comin' here all along. He don't care as long as y'all don't do any damage to anything."

"So we aren't in trouble?"

"Not as far as I'm concerned. Course if your momma finds out, that might be something else." BB wiped the sweat from his brow. "But I'm not gonna be the one to tell. And I'm gonna guess Mr. Lipscomb never has, or y'all wouldn't be here."

Even if Mr. Lipscomb, whoever he was, didn't mind us being there, the point was we hadn't asked permission. That would be our crime with Cousin Carol and Cousin Trek. The skinny-dipping would be tacked on as a second count.

"What're you doing o'er here, BB?"

BB took a red bandanna out of his back pocket and wiped his face. "I'm just gradin' this old work road for Mr. Lipscomb with the tractor. It's a private road. The county don't keep it up. He pays me to keep it up, and since I use Mr. Hightower's tractor, he lets Mr. Hightower use the road for a shortcut when he wants. Me and Daddy, too. Wait, and I'll be right back."

He left and walked over the dam. We stayed under the willow tree and opened our sandwich sacks. In a minute he came back, bringing his dinner. "I might jus' as well have dinner with you boys. Nice shady tree here. 'Bout noontime anyway." He sat down beside the tree and took off his hat.

"Hey, BB," Casey said. "Can you fix Mrs. Culpepper's hair dryer? She has to send it all the way to New Orleans to get it fixed."

"Hair dryer?" BB opened his sack. "I don't know 'bout fixin' those things. I can fix a tractor. But I don't know 'bout a hair dryer."

"You know what they are, don't you?" Casey asked. "They're those things the ladies stick their heads in to dry their heads or somethin'. I think they spin their heads around and around to get 'em dry."

"Say, BB," I said, "Big Trek told us about the University Grays. 'Member, you said you went to war for the University Grays."

BB didn't respond. He just rooted around in his sack like maybe he hadn't heard me.

"But they've been dead for 'bout a hundred years, BB," Taylor said.

"Are you gonna tell us what you meant?" Casey asked.

BB found a hardboiled egg in his sack. He cracked it on a huge tree root crawling toward the pond. He still hadn't said anything. We just watched him. Usually he was friendly and talkative, but he was slow now.

"Well, fellows, I prob'ly shouldn't tell y'all a lot. Wouldn't want to get in trouble for talkin' too much of what they say is politics to young boys. Some folks don't care for it. I mean for a colored fellow to be sayin' too much."

I didn't know what he meant. From the looks on the faces of Taylor and Casey, they didn't either. For the most part what we had been taught in school and what my mother and daddy had told Farley and me about the War Between the States was that we had lost. And it was a shame, because we were right, they said. But if BB was talking about the University Grays and wanting to be fighting for them, what did he mean?

"I jus' got to readin' stories about Jefferson Davis and some of those old Confederates," said BB. "Jeff Davis' whole plantation system was about teachin' slaves what it meant to be free men."

"Huh?" I had never heard a colored man talk like BB. He talked about Jefferson Davis like we talked about baseball.

"Well, Mr. Davis taught 'em how to take charge of properties. He said that their best chance for freedom was in learnin' how to compete with whites in economic things." BB made it sound like President Davis was a football coach and he was one of his players or something.

He told us about the Confederate constitution and how it was the first one in America to stop slaves from being imported. He knew more than I had ever heard even from my school teachers. I wondered where he had learned all these economic things.

I knew that the War Between the States wasn't about slavery.

It was about things like tariffs and federalism and states' rights and stuff like that, my parent's told me. And that I would understand more when I got older. As far as I knew, colored people—well, they were just some very sad people who were slaves once. And after the War they weren't slaves anymore, mostly because Yankee soldiers took over everything in the South and told the slaves they were free. My daddy said that meant free to be used by the politicians.

"If you had been a slave, would you have run away, BB?" I asked.

"I don't know what I'd done a hundred ago, Mr. Jake. Nobody does. Lots of people talk about what they would've done a long time ago when things were different. They like to talk big, like they would have knowed as much about what everyone thought was right and wrong then as they do now. Maybe I'd run off, maybe not, can't really say."

"But you wouldn't wanna be a slave now, would you?" Taylor asked.

BB wiped his forehead then looked up at the sun. "Well, Mr. Taylor, I am a slave right now. So are you. We're slaves to this here cotton field. I got to work or I don't eat. You got to work or you'll get a whippin'." BB laughed, and we all laughed with him. "But I guess I wouldn't want to be tol' I couldn't come and go as I pleased," he added. "At least not by no mortal."

"Whadaya mean?" I asked.

He looked surprised. "I mean, I could be told by the Lord."

"No, no. I meant about being a slave to the cotton field," said Taylor.

He took off his hat and ran his hand over the top of his head. Then he wiped his brow with the back of his hand. "Well this here land's a gift. And the hard work that comes with it's a gift. And we are slaves, workin' for it to produce. We are helpin' it. It's kinda the way the Lord works. He gives you something so you can give back summin' of yourself. You see, slavery ain't summin' the Lord don't know about. It jus' summin' that He don't like when it's hard bondage like the Pharoah did in the Bible."

"Yeah, the Pharoah was bad on the slaves in Egypt," Casey blurted, quick to show he had listened in Sunday School.

"Is that why colored people sing Go Down Moses a lot?" Taylor asked.

"Well, I s'pose so."

"Why did you read books about Jefferson Davis?" I asked.

Taylor and Casey and I had started eating now. BB pulled a sandwich wrapped in wax paper out of his sack. He still seemed like he was hesitating—like he wanted to tell us, but something was holding him back.

"I met this fellow in the Army. An ol' master sergeant. He was from North Carolina and he was about as mean as he could be. He was mean to everybody. There were some boys from both North and South that didn't want colored people in the same outfits as whites. And they let us know it, too. You see, us colored people didn't mix in the Army 'til Mr. Truman put out an order to start doin' it. And lots of folks didn't like it. But this sergeant didn't put up with some of these boys, and more'n once he chewed on their backsides."

I knew that colored people sat in different places on the bus in Jackson, and they had their own picture shows, but I thought it was just the way things had always been and would always be. I never thought about the Army and colored people being in it. "What about the University Grays BB? You still haven't told us about them," I asked.

"I'm comin' to that." For another moment he said nothing, pausing to peel the shell from the soft white egg. Another pause, a sprinkle of salt.

"So this ol' sergeant knew I was havin' a hard time being the only colored man in the outfit. He called me aside one day wearing a bad look on his face. I was afraid I was about to get chewed out for something or other. But he started tellin' me about a man by the name of McElroy who had written a book about Jefferson Davis. Said if I had any guts I'd read it. It was in the library, and if I knew how to read and write I could prob'ly get a library card." BB paused to take a bite of egg. "That was the only time I believe I saw that man smile."

"You mean, he didn't think you could read and write?"

BB laughed.

"So you read the book?" Casey said.

"Yessir, Mr. Casey. I did indeed. The last time a man recommended a book to me was your granddaddy, and the book was written by Booker T. Washington. I never regretted readin' it either. I tried to get some other colored fellows to read it."

"Did they?" Taylor asked.

"Naaa. Maybe one or two. Not many," he said. "I thought maybe if more people read it, then colored and white people would have more to talk about than the price of cotton and where the fish were biting.

"When I read *Up From Slavery*, —that was the book he giv' me—I could tell that there was a difference between black folks as slaves before the War and black folks after they were freed after the War. You could tell that something had changed between colored people and white people after the War ended. So I started reading other books about the War and about what happened after it was over."

He leaned back against the trunk of the tree and took a big bite of his sandwich. "The colored people wanted to be free, but kinda like Mr. Booker T. said, it was one thing to be free, something else to know how to survive. So in their free condition, Yankee carpetbaggers and Southern scalawags used them, and it ended up with most whites in the South bein' real bitter against the colored people."

"Why were they bitter, BB?" Taylor asked.

"Well, the Southern people and the Yankee people, too, always thought that God had made the colored folks somewhat underneath them. But the Southern people saw it as kinda like a parent taking care of their children. So when the carpetbaggers and scalawags looted and stole and gave it to the free black men, the Southern white folks felt betrayed.

"And I thought that was pretty bad. I mean the Southern white people always treated the colored people better than the Yankees treated them; at least that's what I found out from being in the Army."

"Even though they'd been slaves?" Casey asked.

BB wadded up his wax paper and put it in his sack. He picked up the egg shells and put them in, too. "Well, the truth is, the Yankee slave traders was the ones that brought them over here in the first place. But they didn't see nothin' wrong with it. They were jus' buyin' people from Africa that had been made slaves by other colored people in Africa. Lots of them got sold to North and South at first, but pretty soon the North didn't have no more use for them and they sold most of them to South America and Cuba and other places way, way south. The South bought a lot of 'em for work in the fields. Better to have been a slave in the South than in Brazil or somewhere down there. Down there nobody cared, and they would jus' get worked to death."

"Why didn't the North have any use for them?" Casey asked.

"Well, they didn't have rich land that us Southerners did. And they saw themselves as traders and industry folks. Any farms they had were small and weren't goin' to have much future for them. So they sold them to Southern folks who needed the help."

"You learned all this after you got in the army, BB?" I asked.

"Well, mostly. I guess I found out in the army that it didn't matter whether white boys North or South wanted to be with me. I found out I was fightin' for my home. And my home was Mississippi. And I wanted to be with some Mississippi boys, Southern boys. And it made me think about Johnny Vaught and how he tried to get as many Mississippi boys as he could for his teams. His Rebel teams. His University Grays."

"But you said none of the white boys North or South wanted to be with you," Casey blurted.

"That's right, Mr. Casey. But white Southern boys didn't want to be with me cause their mommas and daddies had told them about how the scalawags and carpetbaggers had used black folk to beat down the white folks. Northern white boys didn't wanna be with me 'cause they just didn't like black folks."

Taylor handed me his and Casey's garbage, and I wadded it up and put it in my sack. "You've sure read a lot, BB," I said.

"You should've gone to college instead of war."

"Well, I jus' wanted the white folks to know I could fight for my land, too. And my land is Mississippi, my land is the South. I'm Southern and that's not black or white, that's gray. Robert E. Lee wore gray. And so did Stonewall Jackson. And both of those men prayed with colored folks, in church and out. And Jeff Davis sure didn't fight no war 'cause he hated blacks. He had an adopted black son." He winked at us. "Most folks don't know that."

"Well—" I started.

"I've prob'y said enough now. I need to get back to work anyway. You boys gonna keep swimmin'?" He looked at the sun, and smiled white.

The three of us were sitting Indian style. We were still caught up in BB's history lesson. We wanted to hear more. I had known colored people since I could remember, and I don't remember any of them ever being mean. They were just there, and if you knew them, you knew them, if you didn't, you didn't. Some were hard working and some were lazy, my daddy said. But I had heard him say that about white people, too.

I had once heard some man at my daddy's warehouse call a colored man a lazy nigger. I was shuffled along into the office while my daddy said something to the man. Daddy later told me that a lot of people used that word, but it was wrong to say it to a colored person. It was kind of a bullying thing, and the colored person would be hurt and could not really respond. He had said it was an unkindness to say it.

I wanted to ask BB if he had ever been called a nigger. But I didn't. I knew one thing—he'd never been called a lazy nigger—except maybe by a liar. He was what Cousin Trek had said—the hardest working man you ever saw, white or colored. And he was real smart.

CHAPTER 14

The week passed in a blink. We worked in the field Friday morning; it seemed like the hottest day of the summer. Cousin Trek said it was a hundred and three. We saw The Man from Planet X Friday night and the next chapter of Radar Men from the Moon.

As usual Commando Cody had been about to die and we'd have to wait to see how he would survive. He had been trapped in a cave with a lava flow, caused by the Moon Men melting the mountain. Taylor guessed that he would turn invisible; I guessed he would find an escape cave. Casey said he was going to die.

The Friday night picture show never got too old for us. It was almost an adventure, being somewhere where all your friends were, and everybody wanting to be there. Talking about things that weren't real, like Commando Cody or Flash Gordon, but we acted like they were. It was like a ball game, and you weren't positive how it was going to end.

Saturday we worked until noon. Late in the afternoon, we ate watermelon out on the screen porch and sang songs. Big Trek tried to accompany us with his harmonica, but he hit a lot of bad notes—except when we sang Dixie. He knew it well.

That night the grownups tried to show us how to play a new card game called Canasta. But it was hard to catch on, and Casey kept spraying the cards all over the floor when he tried to shuffle. We finally switched to Chinese Checkers.

Sunday we got to church on time, a cardinal rule, and heard the Sunday School lesson about David and Goliath. That was the story about the little shepherd boy, David, who was the least likely guy to be able to do anything about Saul's enemy, the giant Philistine.

We had all heard the story before, but this was the first time a Sunday School teacher had made such a point that we'd often see God use the most unlikely people for a big job. David just charged out there and killed the giant, Goliath, with a rock and a sling.

Casey said that personally he would have used a hand grenade.

You were supposed to take church more seriously than the picture show but church was fun too, because you got to see a bunch of the guys and talk about whatever we had done Friday and Saturday. We also got to talk about our big fishing trip that afternoon.

After church and the Sunday parking lot talk, we got home and raced inside to change clothes. We collected all of our gear and waited for Mr. Hightower to pick us up to go fishing down the river at Greenville. He had a friend with at least two boats, maybe more. The boats had outboard motors so we would be cruising up and down the mighty Mississippi. Even if we didn't catch any big catfish 'as big as a hog,' Mr. Hightower had said—it would be fun.

"Now y'all do exactly what Mr. Hightower tells you," Cousin Carol said. "And stay in the boat. That river is dangerous."

There was something in her voice when she said 'that river.' It made me think about the dead man. I guess that the river has taken a lot of bodies in all the time it's been coming down from Minnesota, or wherever it started, to the Gulf of Mexico.

But today we would have fun, especially when you had somebody like Mr. Hightower who really knew how to fish. Besides the fishing, we were close to Greenville where the dead guy was found. It was kind of spooky thinking we might hook another body like Ben Samuels and BB had done.

Our school teacher, Miss Ashley, said the Mississippi River had one of the biggest river basins in the world. It was almost as big as the Amazon's which was the biggest in the world and it was down in South America somewhere. But the Mississippi probably was the longest river in the world, depending on where it started. Nobody was sure of that. Except maybe it started in some lake in Minnesota. And no river in the world caused as many problems when it flooded. Engineers had been trying to control it since way back early in the nineteenth century, she had told us. Robert E. Lee was an Army engineer, and the army got him to try to control some part of it around St. Louis one time. And if the river could beat Robert E. Lee, there was no telling what it could do. It had some of the most dangerous whirlpools and currents that anyone had ever seen. It sure wasn't some place to go swimming.

We pulled off the highway onto a gravel road that led to a levee. Once we were across the levee, we could see the big, wide, brown river. It always looked bigger than anything else in the world no matter how many times you saw it.

Mr. Hightower greeted his friend, Mr. Smith, and introduced us. I got in the boat with Mr. Hightower and Taylor, and Mr. Smith took Casey. Mr. Hightower told Mr. Smith he could use Casey for bait if what we were using didn't work. Taylor and I laughed. Casey didn't. He probably wasn't sure if Mr. Hightower was kidding or not.

We started about a mile upriver from the bridge. The river looked a mile wide along this stretch. Like a big lake. I had never been on the river and had only crossed it in a car when we had gone to Vicksburg one time.

The time we were in New Orleans, I don't remember seeing the river up close. Although the city was built up right alongside it and even called the Crescent City, because it was in a moon-shaped crescent of the river.

Our boats remained close to the bank. Once in a while you could see a swirl that looked like water going down the bathtub drain. The whirlpools and eddies looked as harmless as the ones in the bathtub; but below the surface of the river they were fierce, we were told. Occasionally a bit of garbage would float by, a piece of paper or an empty beer bottle bobbing up and down, its neck pointed toward the sky. It was the only way you could tell the river was moving except for the eddies, because it looked like a large, wide, brown roadway. I wondered how much there was on the bottom—how much stuff you couldn't see. I kept thinking a leg or head would pop up.

We moved within what seemed like a football field distance of the bridge and turned the motors off. We left the anchors up and just floated for a few minutes. Dragon flies bobbed around us. Casey would swing his arm and yell "Git!" as if he were yelling at a yard dog.

Then Taylor got his strike, the first one of the afternoon. "I got something!" Taylor was reeling like a madman. Whatever he had hit, his strike was pulling the rod over in a big bowed arc, almost pulling the tip of the rod into the water.

"Just reel him in slowly, Taylor," Mr. Hightower said. "Here, a little less drag." He reached over and slipped the drag down on Taylor's rod. Taylor and Casey and I were cane pole fishermen. Rods and reels were new to us. "You'll get him. He's a nice one, unless it's a gar. Ya never know."

Gars were weird fish and had all sorts of wild stories told about them, none of them good. They weren't good pan fish. They looked like a barracuda. I had never caught one myself, but there were plenty of them around in lakes and bayous, and especially rivers.

I was fishing with my daddy one time when I was six or seven. He hooked an alligator gar, and just as he got it up to the side of the boat it jumped and landed in the boat. It clamped its teeth around daddy's foot, and it was sure a good thing Daddy had some good boots on. He must've smashed that gar in the head with a paddle at least ten times before he killed it. Scavenger fish is what everybody called them. But they could be dangerous, too. There had been stories of them grabbing hold of swimmers and drawing blood.

Taylor was straining, his arms taut, his left hand gripping the rod and his right hand turning the reel, trying to reel more line in than the fish took out. I kept glancing at my own line. What if he pulled a body alongside the boat, a dead man, right next to me?

Then Mr. Smith called out, "Casey's got one o'er here, a little one anyway." At the same time Taylor pulled his to the surface right next to the boat. Mr. Hightower reached over, grabbed the huge fish in the mouth and pulled him into the boat. It was no gar; it was the biggest catfish I had ever seen.

"About twelve pounds, I'd guess," Mr. Hightower said. "'Bout twenty inches long it looks like."

Casey pulled his in very fast. "About two pounds!" Mr. Smith yelled across the water at us.

Taylor was about as excited as you could be. He acted as though he caught the biggest fish ever caught. I just hoped he didn't turn the boat over. He pointed at the fish then himself. The fish was flopping around, and Taylor, flopping around more than the fish, was trying to step on it.

"Jake, can you believe the size of that thing. Must be fifty pounds."

"I think Mr. Hightower just said, 'about twelve pounds.'"

"Well, twelve or whatever. Still a big fish."

Mr. Hightower hooked the fish onto the stringer, keeping him alive tied to the boat, swimming back and forth with nowhere to go.

It was about thirty minutes before I caught my first one. Taylor had already caught two more in just a couple of minutes. Neither was as big as the first, but they were a keepable size. He acted like Simon Peter, the Great Fisherman. He kept hollering to throw my line here or there, or fish deeper, or use a roach instead of the catfish blood and mush.

I thought about hitting him in the head with a paddle. He had caught more than me, and although Casey had caught three in the other boat, they were all about the same size as one another.

Once when Mr. Hightower wasn't looking I gave Taylor the finger. I wasn't that skilled at it, and it kind of hurt my fingers. I guess as you got older your finger muscles got more developed so you got where you could do it as good as Daddy and Farley. I still wasn't sure what it meant, but since it had mortified my mother, I knew it wasn't something I should let a grown-up see me do.

Mr. Hightower and Mr. Smith had caught one each, but they weren't really fishing much. They were mostly helping us and telling us where to pitch our lines. All of us got backlash a bunch of times, not being used to reels, and Mr. Smith and Mr. Hightower had to untangle our lines. But they didn't seem to mind.

Our boats were only a few feet apart. I could see Mr. Smith spit brown every now and then, though it blended when it hit the water. When Mr. Smith wasn't watching, Casey put his hand over his mouth like he was gagging, when some brown slime ran down Mr. Smith's lower lip.

We had drifted almost under the huge bridge that crossed into Arkansas. I wondered if we were near the spot where the body was found.

"Mr. Hightower, is this where they found that dead man? I heard it was under the bridge." Taylor turned from his line.

"Well, I s'pose it is. If you believe what the newspaper says."

"You mean it might not be the spot?" Taylor asked. He had taken his eye off his line.

"No. Oh, no. That's jus' an expression of mine. I guess it's somewhere around here. But this is jus' where they found him. No tellin' where he went in. Could be miles from here, far's I know."

"Think we might find another one?" I asked.

"No. Now you boys don't worry about that. To tell you the truth, I'd forgotten about it when I thought about us comin' over here to fish. I don't want y'all getting' upset now."

"Oh, we were jus' wonderin'," Taylor said. "Don't get many murders around here. Jus' seemed kind of spooky, him washin' up in the river and all."

"Well, one is enough, I can tell you," Mr. Hightower said. "You boys just keep your minds on fishing."

By four o'clock we had caught fifteen or sixteen catfish and one gar. Mr. Hightower had caught the gar, but he didn't keep him. After fighting him for what seemed forever, he pulled him up to the side of the boat, cut the line just above the hook and let him go. He said they weren't good to eat—tasted like cotton, he had heard. The biggest catfish we had was the first one Taylor caught, although there were a couple others that were pretty close. I had caught four catfish and probably five bream, each of the bream being pretty small and I threw them back. And Casey was about oh for a hundred hitting dragon flies. I don't know for sure how many fish he caught.

Back upriver we pulled into shore, got out, and left the boats at the edge of the water. Mr. Smith and Mr. Hightower iced down the fish in big wash tubs. He said we could take the smaller ones home to eat if we wanted, but the big ones were too old and tough to eat. We just admired them for a moment then released them to swim away. We really didn't care; the fun had mostly been being out on the river and just fishing.

We pulled the boats out of the water and helped Mr. Smith load them one on top of the other in his pickup. Then we tied them down.

"Let's go into town and get something cold to drink," Mr. Hightower said.

Mr. Hightower followed Mr. Smith's pickup to a paved road that led to the highway to Greenville. Mr. Smith drove about two miles an hour. It took us about forever to get to the paved road. Taylor said it was because Mr. Smith couldn't drive fast and spit at the same time or the tobacco juice would blow back into his truck.

Mr. Hightower pulled over at a Pure Oil filling station which had a big blue sign advertising 'Be Sure with Pure.' A couple of men came out. One asked Mr. Hightower how much gas he wanted, and the other started wiping the windshield.

Mr. Hightower came around to the bed of the truck. "Okay, you boys go get yourselves a cold drink. And one of you bring me a Dr. Pepper."

He stayed to watch the man check the oil while we attacked the drink box. It was filled with ice and a bunch of cold drinks. I got an RC—a Royal Crown Cola, about the biggest size there was. We returned to the truck to help watch the dipstick get wiped. It was something they always did after looking at it. They'd wipe it off and stick it back in somewhere in the motor. The man slammed the hood, acknowledging everything under there was okay. Mr. Hightower turned his Dr. Pepper up and almost drained it in one gulp.

"Mr. Hightower, will you drive across the bridge?" Casey asked. "Just so we can see the river and go into Arkansas and look around for a few minutes? I don't remember ever goin' to Arkansas."

Taylor whacked him on the shoulder. It was rude to ask for something you hadn't been offered.

"It's okay, Taylor." Mr. Hightower smiled at Casey. "Oh, I think we got time. It won't take long. Besides, anybody who wants to see Arkansas that bad oughta get to. But I can't believe you've never been to Arkansas, Casey. A young opportunist like yourself—never been to The Land of Opportunity." That was a state motto or something; it was on all the car tags.

The sun would still be up for over an hour. We would get a good view of the river and part of Arkansas. The bridge was over two hundred feet high and you could see the big brown, snake-like Mississippi River cutting through trees and cotton fields and pastures. It was kind of like the view at Rock City, but you knew what the states were here.

It was hard to believe something as big and wide as this river started out as just a little clear stream coming out of some lake up in Minnesota. It was a mile wide where we were crossing but only about ten feet wide and two feet deep up where it started. In some places it was a hundred feet deep. It would take a freight train more than a hundred miles long to hold all the dirt that the river carried to the Gulf of Mexico every day.

It only took a couple of minutes to cross the bridge. Looking out from the back of the truck was more fun than just looking out of a car window. Once we were in Arkansas, I looked at their cotton fields. They seemed to be lined up perfectly, and you could see the whiteness spreading out just like ours. But they didn't seem like Mississippi cotton, maybe because I hadn't worked in them.

There was no one working on Sunday. Nobody was out, stooped and bent; hoeing, sweating, earning a little bit of money. It made me feel good that nobody was out there working while I was having fun. The nearest town was Lake Village and that was too far to go. Mr. Hightower turned into a short gravel driveway.

He stuck his head out of the window and yelled, "Okay, fellows, that enough for you?"

"Yes, sir. Thank you."

He spun in the gravel, turned around, and headed back across the river. We had just crossed the bridge again when he pulled over. A man walked away from the bridge. A woman was close, but as Mr. Hightower pulled up she moved away. As the man approached the truck, Mr. Hightower got out and walked toward him. "Looty. Heh, Looty. Wanna ride?"

"What's he doing out here?" said Taylor.

"Beats me," Casey said. "Remember he said he was coming to Greenville. Just the other day he said it."

"Yeah, I remember that. But I wonder why he's out here walking by the bridge."

Looty had caught up to the truck. Mr. Hightower stood at the back. He glanced at the woman who was now in the distance. "She with you, Looty?"

"She's going someplace else."

"Well, you wanna ride?"

"No, sir. I'm gonna ride the bus home tomorrow maybe."

"Well, you need a ride anywhere around here?"

"No, thank you. I'm jus' walkin'. Just vistin' some people."

"Well, if you're sure."

"Yes, sir, I'm sure. Thank you jes' the same."

Mr. Hightower climbed back into the truck and pulled away from the shoulder. We waved at Looty, and I watched the woman in the distance as she walked into the store. Then I recognized her. It was the straw-haired woman. The same one I had met on the bus. The one I hadn't said goodbye to.

CHAPTER 15

Every time I saw Looty I thought about the dead guy and the .22. Taylor and Casey and I had talked a lot about the dead guy and wondered who he was. Our thoughts got wilder each day it seemed like. We wanted to be in the middle of something big and important, I think. We had stayed up late forming our opinions of who it might be. But we couldn't come up with anyone mean enough in Cotton City to shoot someone.

There was lots of talk about Looty by the guys at the gazebo and the ones at Sunday school. And his missing rifle, and did he hide it—not lose it? Looty was a friendly, simple sort of man who didn't seem like he could harm anyone. But the talk about his using his .22 and everything since his grandmother died just seemed to make everybody talk about him over and over and over, though we'd been taught not to talk about people like that.

It seemed like he turned up every time we went somewhere. That made it hard to keep your mind off him. Since he hardly ever went far from his house, everyone was aware of him when he did. And riding the bus all over the place surely wasn't something he ordinarily did either. When the sheriff called him in to question him, it seemed almost a sure sign he was suspected of something.

But who was in his house that night when he was gone? And why couldn't he find his rifle? It all seemed kind of odd. Even the three of us knew that you could trace bullets to the gun that had fired them—if you had the gun. So a killer would get rid of a murder weapon. We had heard that lots of times on the radio program, the FBI Stories, about bullets and guns. Taylor said that he wasn't sure Looty was smart enough to know about bullets and tracing them, and that sort of thing.

I thought about Looty and how he must be lonely living by himself and everything, and having that mayonnaise jar with something in it right there on the mantle. I really hoped he hadn't done anything wrong.

I prayed a little prayer one night for him. But I didn't tell anybody. Somebody might have laughed at me. It would've been like crying for the Sullivan boys at the picture show. Looty reminded me of BB in a funny kind of way. I had known them both only a short time, but I felt a special attachment because there was something sincere about them. Now it looked like one of them was about to get in trouble.

Mr. Hightower had dropped us off. He turned down Cousin Carol's invitation to stay for supper. We stayed in the yard until he drove off so we could thank him again. We watched him drive down the gravel road, the dust rising, mixing with the orange and pink glare of the sun setting. It appeared to drop into the river, where we had spent most of the day. For a second, I thought about climbing the windmill and watching it disappear. But it was supper time and Cousin Carol was waiting on us.

When we got inside we talked about the fishing expedition, and how many were caught and who caught what. Casey mostly talked about Mr. Smith. He said he was a pretty nice old man, except he kept spitting this brown gook and usually some would dribble down his chin. Casey said it was kind of yucky, brown drool and all. Cousin Carol told him not to mention it anymore.

We talked about what we would do after supper—play kick-the-can or some other game, or maybe walk down the road to the highway to watch the cars and wave at the truck drivers to get them to blow their horns. They would do that most of the time if you jerked your arm up and down, like you were pulling on an imaginary chord.

For a while we sat on the porch and talked about baseball. Casey kept saying the Browns would beat out the Cardinals for the pennant. Taylor and I kept telling him they weren't in the same league. But he just kept being stubborn and saying that don't make no difference. Taylor tried to tell him the Cardinals were out of it anyway, that the Dodgers were going to win in the National league.

We talked about sneaking back over to Looty's house. But each one of us kept coming up with an excuse why we'd better not. I think we all were just chicken but wouldn't say so. Admitting that you were a chicken about anything wasn't something you wanted to get around.

We sat down at the table later than usual. It was leftovers and sandwiches because Cousin Trek and Cousin Carol got back from evening church late. We were tired and were going to have to work the next day. But the subject of Looty, Looty, Looty wouldn't go away.

"We saw Looty again this afternoon," Casey said.

Taylor and I said nothing, just watched the grownups for a reaction. Often grownups reacted in a way that gave you information without giving you any details. A look. It really depended. Their faces could give you a hint of whether the topic was okay.

Cousin Trek said, "Really, where 'bouts? In Greenville?" He hadn't smiled and his brow was wrinkled. This was a serious question.

"Yes, sir. On the bridge. I think he was walkin' with some lady," Casey said.

"What? What do you mean you think he was walking with some lady?" Cousin Carol asked. She passed the mayonnaise jar to Taylor. "What lady?"

"I don't know. She walked away when Mr. Hightower called out to him."

"Trek, reach in the pantry and get a new jar of mayonnaise," Cousin Carol said. The jar on the table was almost empty. Taylor was clanging the jar with his knife, trying to scrape the last of the mayonnaise from the bottom. Sounded like a fire bell.

"Did y'all recognize her?" She took the new jar and tapped against the top with the handle of her knife.

"No, ma'am," Taylor said.

I didn't tell them I recognized her. I hadn't even told Taylor and Casey yet, so I just kept quiet for the moment. I don't know why. I didn't know the straw-haired lady was with Looty, for sure. It just seemed odd that she was there along the same road where he happened to be. Maybe it was just a fluky chance she was there, maybe I would say something later about meeting her.

For a moment I had a thought of being grilled under the bright light in the sheriff's office because of information I had withheld. Someone had told them—maybe the belcher, an FBI spy—about me meeting her and I had been turned in. Taylor's double-triple fire bell clanging broke my thought.

Cousin Carol handed the jar to Cousin Trek. With a sharp twist the top came unfastened. "Here, Taylor. Now stop bangin' on that empty jar."

"Yessir."

"So, why would Looty be with some woman?" Cousin Trek said.

"I don't think he was with her," I said. "Looty said she was jus' going somewhere else. I don't think he knew her."

I felt like I had to protect Looty. I wasn't sure why. I didn't know what the straw-haired woman was doing there, and I didn't know for sure if Looty knew her. I had just met her myself the other day but I felt like I had to protect her, too. I thought about how strange she was, and I hoped Looty didn't know her. I hoped she hadn't done anything. I wasn't sure what the right thing to say was.

There was a knock at the back door. I thought Mr. Hightower might have come back for something.

"Sorry to disturb you folks at suppertime." We could hear the voice of Mr. O'Grady coming through the screen door. He was standing on the steps.

"Taylor, let Mr. O'Grady in. Don't make him jus' stand there." Cousin Trek got up and moved toward the door.

"Evenin, Billy Joe. Had your supper?" Cousin Carol asked.

Mr. O'Grady stepped past Cousin Trek and removed his hat. "Oh, no, thank you Carol. I'm fine. But thanks anyway."

"Have a seat, Billy Joe."

"Like I say, I hate to disturb you folks at suppertime, but I need to find Looty as soon as I can. He wasn't at home and

I thought maybe y'all had seen him, or maybe he'd been o'er here." In the silence, Cousin Carol and Cousin Trek looked at one another.

"Whadaya want him for?" Taylor asked.

"Be quiet, son," Cousin Trek said. "In fact, y'all go in the other room. This isn't for children." I knew we were going to get booted as soon as Taylor spoke.

Cousin Carol put her hands on our backs and shuffled us out of the kitchen. I kind of wished Farley was here right now. Anybody old enough to have a driver's license probably would have been old enough to stay and listen to grownup conversations. Old Farley could've been our spy. But he wasn't here so we had to listen through the propped open door.

Billy Joe O'Grady had been the town marshal since I could remember. He was head of Cotton City's own police force. I guess they didn't need a lot of policemen since there was hardly any crime in Cotton City. He was about fifty, I suspected, and had mostly gray hair. He wore a pistol, but I don't think he had ever shot anyone with it.

Taylor told me one time that Mr. O'Grady had shot a mad dog with a twelve-gauge shotgun. One of the town ne'er-do-wells tried to cause a stink and say it was his dog and it wasn't mad. He said the city should pay him a hundred dollars because it was the finest bird dog in the Delta, and Billy Joe had shot it just so he could be a big hero. A veterinarian examined the dead dog and concluded the dog did have rabies. He also said if that dog was a bird dog, then St. Patrick was Jewish.

"Well, Billy Joe, the boys saw him in Greenville just today," Cousin Trek said. "What's goin' on?"

"Well, I was told by the sheriff that they're gonna bring him in again. Said they were maybe gonna charge him with shootin' that fellow. Said they think they got some more evidence or some such. Told me it might be easier if I picked him up and brought him in. Sheriff said he'd come over from county and follow up with me on it."

Taylor looked at Casey and me. I wondered, what evidence? Taylor had his mouth open as if he were trying to make words out of air. Casey pulled his finger across his throat as if it was a knife cutting. They were going to arrest Looty, and it sounded like they thought he was guilty. I remembered the spot where we had fished; and Looty only a short distance away.

Looty shooting someone and throwing him in the river. It didn't seem possible. It just didn't.

"Well, Earl took the boys fishing today at the river at Greenville. That's when they saw him. Saw him walking on the road down by the bridge."

"It's just such a shame," said Cousin Carol. "That poor boy."

"He ain't exactly a boy, Carol. He's forty years old," Mr. O'Grady said.

Dishes and silverware began clinking. Cousin Carol was cleaning off the table. She was like my mother. When she heard upsetting news, she started cleaning or moving things around. My mother would even start moving big stuff around like sofas and stuff when she got upset enough. Cousin Carol was a little less drastic.

"Still, I just hate it for him. What kind of proof are they supposed to have?"

"Sheriff didn't say. Just asked me to try and find him and ask him to come in. I think they're gonna confront him with the evidence then, and arrest him."

"I'll bet they found his rifle," Casey whispered.

Taylor put his finger to his lips and "shhhed" him.

I was afraid they might open the door any second since Cousin Trek had mentioned 'the boys.' They might want us back in the room. I motioned for Casey and Taylor to move away, but Taylor just waved me off.

"What about the dead man, Billy Joe? Y'all found out who he is?" Cousin Trek asked.

Billy Joe put his hat on the table and ran his hand through his hair. "Really don't know. They say they got new evidence, but I really don't know."

"Well, let's just not say anything to the boys right now. They'll find out soon enough," Cousin Carol said.

I could see the kitchen table through the open door. Cousin

Carol had removed everything but the empty mayonnaise jar. It made me think of Looty.

We found out later that when Looty got back from Greenville, Mr. O'Grady spotted him. Looty had parked his truck downtown by the bus station. Mr. O'Grady had just kept an eye on it, someone had said. When the bus pulled in, Mr. O'Grady asked him to come over to the city jail. All Looty said was, "Yes, sir. If you want me to."

CHAPTER 16

Today was my last Saturday in Cotton City. My mother and daddy were picking me up next Friday. Taylor, Casey and I tried forgetting about Looty's problems. He had been in the Cotton City jail all week as far as we knew, but had not been sent to the county jail yet.

I guess the only thing that could have matched the local talk about Looty was something the newspapers would end up calling "the shot heard 'round the world." It was about one of the most famous baseball games ever played.

Baseball was something we played a lot of in the summer. Jackson even had its own professional team, the Jackson Senators, in the Cotton States League. We followed the major leagues and the standings and the averages all the way into football season. The crown jewel was the World Series, when everyone was glued to a radio during the first week of October and school attendance probably had a sharp drop. You were always hearing somebody whistling or humming the sponsor's song:

"To look sharp and be on the ball,
To feel sharp and be on the ball,
To be sharp and be on the ball,
Use Gillette Razor Blades today."

It was late in August and there was a lot of recent talk about the New York Giants and the Brooklyn Dodgers now that it was certain the Cardinals were out of it. And the Browns were never in it in the American League.

The Giants had been thirteen and a half games out on August 1 but had already closed the gap to eight games with over a month to go in the season. Some of the checker players at the gazebo said Leo Durocher would bring the Giants all the way back. Most of the old-timers remembered Durocher from the great St. Louis Cardinals and the Gas House Gang from 1934. They had had the great Dizzy Dean. He was from Arkansas but had married a lady from Biloxi, so they both lived in Mississippi. This was our connection to the Giants in1951.

Since we weren't working Saturday afternoon, Taylor and Casey and I were downtown talking with some guys about the Giants, and Dizzy, and Leo, and the pennant race. This led to a general discussion of baseball players and who was the greatest in the last ten years. It was always an argument that came down to Ted Williams, Stan Musial or Joe DiMaggio, who had made a hundred thousand dollars that year. One guy kept saying Bob Feller, most said pitchers and hitters were different. But he stayed with Feller.

We were lying on the grass close to the gazebo where a low-key checker game was lingering. We had our tee shirts off and some of the other boys were barefooted, those with country-tough feet. I had sissy city feet and kept my Keds on. We were just yakking and talking about most anything that came up, but mostly about baseball.

Casey was busy with one of his talents that he was sure would land him in Hollywood one day. Anyone worth his salt could put his hand under his armpit and by pumping his arm up and down make a sound that was a cross between a duck's quack and a frog croaking. But Casey could make it sound like Swanee River. He was really proud of it. One of the boys, called Nick, said he wanted to be Casey's agent. He didn't want Casey's talent wasted on something as minor-league as Hollywood; he swore he could get him onstage at the Grand Old Opry in Nashville.

But Nick said Casey needed to add some more tunes to his repertoire. Nick had suggested How Much is That Doggy in the Window and maybe White Christmas. So far, Swanee River was all Casey had been able to play. His prospects for the Grand Old Opry didn't look good to me.

"When is your brother comin' up?" someone asked me.

"Maybe this weekend, I think."

"Your parents comin, too?"

"Yeah."

Most everyone up here knew Farley and me, and a lot of them knew he had his driver's license. A guy was viewed different once he got his driver's license. He became a man-of-the-world, licensed not just to drive but to live life on the wild side—burning rubber, spinning out on gravel roads. Some even used their new freedom to dodge watchful eyes and smoke cigarettes. A driver's license was the gateway to life.

So when they asked if my parents were coming, the question they were really asking was, "Is Farley coming alone in the car?"

"Son of a dirty dog!" One of the checker players shouted a modified exclamation. It was not the traditional son-of phrase since children were present. He had slammed his fist on the table and upset the checkers. Baseball's Game of the Day on the Mutual Broadcasting System was broadcasting the Dodgers/Cardinals game. There was a socket in the light fixture of the gazebo and someone had plugged in a radio. Pee Wee Reese had just knocked in the lead run and though Reese was a good Southern gentleman, it was said around the gazebo, from Kentucky, he was playing for the enemy—the Brooklyn Dodgers.

"Now you did that jus' cause you wuz losing, you redneck low-life," his partner said.

"I did not, and anyway I wuz winnin'," the redneck low-life replied.

The two men playing were not among the checker greats of Cotton City. They were a couple of unknowns and unranked, as far as I knew. If they were of any great skill, there would be several others watching. Everybody was paying more attention to the ball game than to the checker game of these two. But to them it was an important game, I suppose. They both got up and walked to the café, perhaps to try dominoes but more likely for coffee. If they weren't great at checkers, they had better stay away from a money game. One of them had unplugged the radio and put it under his arm, so the game was over as far as we were concerned. I heard later that Brooklyn lost. Musial hit a home run in the bottom of the ninth.

Any commotion in Cotton City was easy to spot. And when a sheriff's car and a highway patrol car pulled up in front of the jail, everyone stirred. Even baseball and an exciting pennant race couldn't keep our minds off what we were thinking.

We had been so involved in the checker game, and then the police cars, that the crash of thunder scared us. We turned and looked behind us. Hugh black clouds were moving in on Cotton City.

It had not rained in two weeks, and that morning it looked as if the drought would continue. But by the middle of the afternoon the dark warning clouds had built and bubbled upward. They were caused, my daddy had once told me, by intense heat and humidity, and these were about to explode. An afternoon blackness had covered the county, and car lights were being turned on.

We ran from the gazebo toward our bikes. Big drops were falling. We needed to get home before getting drenched. Lighting flashed, followed soon by a crash of thunder, indicating the strikes were close. Riding a bike was dangerous in thunderstorms; a boy in school was killed by lightning when he was riding his bike. I wanted to get home before we got killed. It seemed everyone else feared tornadoes, but I feared lightning.

By the time we reached the highway, the clouds were blacker and the rain came down in sheets. Our mission was just to get home alive. We were soaked. I pedaled as hard as I could, with the storm closing around us, but my thoughts kept going back to the commotion at the jail. Was Looty in more trouble? Were they fixing to take him to the county jail? Or maybe to Parchman?

We reached the gravel road that led to the house. The water had turned the surface into a slick, slimy, muddy runway. The drainage ditch filled, and streams of brown water flowed down both sides of the road. Each pump of the pedals squished water through the laces of my Keds. Casey's bike didn't have fenders, so the mud spun off the rear tire and sprayed his back, turning the back of his blue overalls brown.

Cousin Carol was on the front porch when we raced into

the yard. She shook her head, her hands on her hips, frowning at our appearance. "Why didn't y'all leave before it started to rain?"

Taylor gave the traditional answer. "We forgot."

That was never a great answer, but it was the only one you had. It wasn't like we could say: "We didn't want to."

"Now y'all are completely soaked. I just don't know," she said.

Big Trek came out on the porch to view the scene. "Ahh, rain'll make 'em grow."

"Well, mud won't make them grow," Cousin Carol said. "Would you just look at this one?" This one was Casey. I think since he was born, Casey always seemed to get the dirtiest when we played, or the most food on his shirt when we ate, or the most bad things to his clothes whatever we did. Over the years Casey probably thought This One was on his birth certificate.

Without fenders on his bike, so much mud spun over him that he looked like a wet gingerbread man. Even his hair had mud in it.

She made us take our clothes off on the porch while she went inside for dry ones. Standing on the porch in our underwear was a great opportunity to moon each another. We were laughing and giggling until we heard Cousin Carol call from upstairs, "Y'all better not be doing what I think you're doing. If I catch somebody, he's going to be in big trouble."

"We're not," Taylor yelled. He put his hand over his mouth to keep from laughing.

Big Trek walked back out onto the porch. He threw a towel at each of us then sat down in the porch swing. "Did you see your daddy downtown, Taylor?"

"No, sir. We were just listening to the ballgame and sittin' around at the square."

"We saw the sheriff and the highway patrol at the sheriff's office," Casey said.

"Oh, yeah? What were they doin' there, do ya s'pose?"

"Don't know. They pulled up jus' before the storm started."

Big Trek pulled out his old briar pipe. It had a curved stem and a big bowl. It smelled wonderful. When he smoked it, it seemed as if he were contemplating all the problems over all time; smoking, moving in the swing, staring out across his beloved land. And maybe he did have solutions to all the problems, for all I knew.

He said, "Well, I hope your daddy didn't get stuck somewhere." He reached over to the open window and turned on the radio, turning the knob to get a clear station. The static from the thunderstorm was bad. "Wonder if this storm is just local or something movin' in from the west. Prob'ly just a local wash. That's what I think. But we sure need it. Cotton's gonna get stunted if it don't get some moisture."

A clap of thunder rocked the house, indicating something close-by had been hit—probably a tree just down the road.

"Good grief!" Taylor said. "That sounded like a bomb." He looked through the screen, through the wall of rain. "Well, Big Trek, whadayathink would happen if lightnin' hit the windmill? You think it would kill us on the porch?"

"Oh, I don't know." He wasn't paying attention, still fiddling with the radio. "Maybe, prob'ly not."

Cousin Carol stepped onto the porch, an armful of clothes in her arms. "Here, put these on."

"Why can't we just play in the rain in our underwear?" Casey asked.

"Because there's too much lightning. You might get killed. And if you get killed, who'd Earl Hightower have to hoe cotton?" She smiled. He smiled back. "Besides, playing in your underwear is crude. Now get these clothes on."

"I was born to be crude," Casey said.

"You're going to wish you were never born if you don't do what I say."

"The weather man jus' said there're thunderstorms all o'er northwest Mississippi and part of Arkansas," Big Trek said. "Says it must be some stuff comin' in from the west. Lots of buildup jus' for one afternoon. I still say it's local. Damn weathermen don't know what they're talkin' about most of the time. I hope Trek gets on back soon."

"I'm sure he'll be along soon," Cousin Carol said. "And I

wish you wouldn't cuss in front of these boys."

She didn't sound worried. But she probably was. If she wasn't she probably would've said a little bit more about the cussing. It had always seemed to me most mothers worried about things like danger. Next to cussing it got you their biggest lecture. My mother had said to either Farley or me at least a million times, 'you had me worried to death'. She had never said it to my daddy, at least not where I could hear, but she just got a worried look when he was late from a trip and it was raining or something.

"Well, I guess so," Big Trek said. His eyes roved the dark sky. He took his pipe out of his mouth and looked at it like he was going to talk to it. It had gone out. "And damn is in the Bible."

Cousin Carol didn't reply. She just set her teeth on her lower lip and shook her head then looked at the sky.

I remembered all the talk I had heard over the years about the Great Flood of 1927 and how it had changed people's lives in the same way it had changed the land itself—washing and scouring and moving and changing large areas and volumes of land and people. "Big Trek, do you think there is going to be a big flood like way back in 1927?"

"You mean from this little storm? Naa. This is just a little rain. In 1927 it rained for weeks and weeks. And it was raining all over the country, North and South. The rivers like the Missouri and the Yazoo all were filling up. And it wasn't just us here in Mississippi that got flooded. Arkansas got the worst. And Louisiana and Tennessee. All the way up to Illinois. And down the river below Memphis the river spread out as far as sixty miles. It was in the spring when it always rains more anyway. Why they had to dynamite some levees down in Louisiana to save New Orleans, they said. Naw, this is just a little rain, boys. Won't be any widespread floodin' today." He banged on the radio a couple more times trying to get the static out then turned it off. He relit his pipe.

The three of us watched the rain. It was so hard that if you'd run to the windmill and back as fast as you could, you'd still get soaked. The wind was passing to the southeast. Big Trek smoked his pipe and was silent after he turned off the radio. I thought maybe he was really worried about Cousin Trek and just didn't want to say it. So when he decided to tell one of his stories, I was sure it was just to get our minds off Cousin Trek.

The story was about two colored people who were killed by a panther back when Big Trek was a young boy, around 1900. The Delta was still largely undeveloped farmland, and there was still a lot of unclaimed swamp and woodlands. Alligators, bears, wild hogs, even panthers still roamed.

One night when he was fourteen, Big Trek said, he was riding home with his younger brother on an old mare. Apart from the crickets and frogs the air was still and soundless. A sudden distant, high-pitched scream jolted him and shocked his blood. I got goose bumps. Casey scooted between Taylor and me.

Big Trek said the screams came from close to the swamp, and he was so frightened he began kicking the old mare on her sides as hard as he could, trying to get away from the swamp. But her age and a lifetime of work had left her with a slow gait, no matter how hard she was kicked. Big Trek said it was the longest horseback ride he had ever made.

When they got home he told his daddy about the screams. His daddy told them to go to bed. His daddy walked outside and held up a lantern looking as far away as the light would stretch into the darkness. But he never went beyond the porch. Big Trek said that after he and his brother were sent to bed the light in the front room burned brightly that night. His mother and daddy stayed up into the early hours talking about something. But he never learned what they talked about.

The next day two colored sharecroppers had been found dead, mutilated almost beyond recognition. The man was on the porch with his throat torn away; parts of his wife had been dragged or carried to the edge of the field where it met the woods. No man could have done this, the sheriff had said.

Also, men didn't make claw marks or leave panther tracks. The thought of a wild panther about kept Big Trek and his brother close to the house for a long time.

Throughout the county there was a mild panic that year. Men kept their shotguns loaded with buckshot or slugs close to the front door. As a rule, wild animals don't attack humans unless the animals' young are threatened or they have rabies. An animal attacking someone on the front porch put everyone on alert.

Water stood in large pools around the house. We stared into the yard, absorbing Big Trek's tale.

"Now Big Trek, you shouldn't be telling these boys horrible old stories like that. They're too young." Cousin Carol had come back just as he finished the story.

"Aww, they're old enough. And anyway, it's a true story. They're gonna hear 'bout it someday anyhow. It's a growin' story." He grinned. "Like rain, ya know?"

"Just the same, I don't think it's something appropriate for them to hear. They don't have to grow up all the way right now."

Big Trek puffed and blew a smoke ring. He didn't reply.

Cousin Carol sat down next to him in the swing. She was wiping her hands with a dish rag; a troubled look covered her normal smile. "But the reason I came out here was to tell y'all that the phone is out of order. I tried to call down to the feed store to see if Trek was there, but it's dead. Must have something to do with the storm."

She walked back inside. I think she just told us to reassure us that there was a reason Cousin Trek hadn't called. Or maybe she just wanted to interrupt the story.

"Did you know the colored people, Big Trek? I mean the ones who got killed?"

"They were Ben Samuels' momma and daddy," he replied, a huge cloud of smoke rising up around his face. His stare focused across the open, soaked cotton fields.

The three of us looked at one another—Ben Samuels' parents.

After a minute I asked, "Did they ever get the panther, Big Trek?"

"No."

Taylor and Casey and I had started playing Chinese Checkers, since we couldn't go out. The rain was steady. Big Trek had remained in the swing smoking his pipe, staring down the road, which looked more like a creek now. Cousin Carol was inside and occasionally came out onto the porch to look down the road herself.

"Look!" said Casey. "I see Daddy's truck. There he comes."

We pushed our faces against the screen, trying to see through the rain. Cousin Trek's truck slid down the road. The tires seemed like wet feet in the tub, sliding to one side then the other. The windshield wipers swished back and forth trying to keep ahead of the rain. The headlights made it seem like he was driving faster than usual.

"Looks like he's home, Carol," Big Trek called into the house. But she had already come out and was waving at the truck.

Cousin Trek wore one of those yellow raincoats with a hood that made him look like a sailor on a ship's storm deck. It was the same kind we always had to wear on rainy days at school. Farley says they make you look like a loon, like a giant egg yolk with legs.

As soon as Cousin Trek got to the porch he took it off and shook it, then hung it and his hat on a hook by the screen door. He didn't seem to have his joking way that he always had. He looked at us without saying a word, beads of water ran down his face.

"Is something wrong? I was kind of worried. This is a bad storm," said Cousin Carol.

"Looty's gone. He broke out, I guess you'd say."

"What?" Big Trek asked. "Whadaya mean he broke out? I didn't know he was in. You mean he was arrested? I thought they had jus' been talkin' to him. Just holding him down there for questions."

Casey and Taylor and I sat in silence. We were scared that if we said anything we would be told to leave. Cousin Carol didn't speak either.

"He walked out the back door. He wasn't locked up or anything and at some point everyone looked around, and he was gone," Cousin Trek said.

A crash of thunder shook the house and we jerked. Big Trek opened the screen door and banged his pipe on the door sash. No one spoke. I wondered if everybody else was thinking the same thing—was Looty really a murderer?

CHAPTER 17

I awakened to Taylor nudging me, whispering. "Shhhh. Be quiet. Don't wanna wake up everybody."

It was still dark. The rain must have stopped, since I no longer heard the torrents that had worked like music, putting me to sleep. I had been sleeping so soundly that it still felt like a dream even though I was awake. "Wha..? Whadaya want?"

"Shhh. Something's goin' on. Somebody came to the house after we came to bed. It was around midnight. I heard them talkin' downstairs. Their talkin' waked me up."

"Hey, what are y'all doin'. How come y'all are up?" Casey walked in from his room. He rubbed his eyes, yawned, and sat on the bed.

"Shhh. Not so loud."

"Whdaya mean, not so loud? Y'all woke me up."

"Whisper. I think Mother is awake. The light is on downstairs. But I think she's alone. I think Daddy and Big Trek have gone somewhere."

I got up and cracked the door just enough to see a light streaming up the stairs.

"Close the door," Taylor said. "We don't want her to know we're up."

"Well, what's going on? Who came to the house?" I said.

"I couldn't see but it sounded sorta like Ben Samuels. I swear that's who it sounded like."

"What'd he be doin' here at this time of night?" I asked.

Casey was still rubbing his eyes. He flopped back on the bed.

"I don't know. But he wasn't here very long before he left. And I'm pretty sure Daddy and Big Trek went with him."

"Where did they go?"

Taylor opened the window. "I think they said they were going downtown to see Mr. O'Grady."

"What are you lookin' at out there?"

He opened the screen and pushed it out enough to stick his head out. "It's not raining. And the moon's out."

"So what?"

"So, we're goin' downtown."

We were living dangerously, for sure. Sneaking out in the early morning wasn't something you wanted to get caught doing. You'd get one of those lectures and there was always a chance you could get a switching.

It was well after midnight and the town was quiet, the streets deserted. We parked our bikes in the bushes on the edge of the square. We crept over to the windows on the side of the town marshal's office. Parked out front were two highway patrol cars, a county sheriff's car, and the Cotton City police car. Across the street we had noticed Big Trek's pickup as well as Ben Samuel's. This was a lot of cars for something like shooting chickens.

We saw figures through the open window and saw someone pass every couple of minutes, like they were pacing.

"Crud!"

"Shhh!" Taylor put his hand over Casey's mouth. "What's wrong? You want someone to hear us?"

Casey crouched like Yogi Berra and pointed underneath his legs at his butt. He had sat in a puddle. "It looks like I wet my pants. Now I'll have to hide 'em when I get home or I'm dead."

"Worry about that later," Taylor said. "We'll dang sure get killed if we get caught. Now c'mon, let's go. And keep quiet."

We sprinted for the corner of the marshal's office, staying away from the light from the window. We crouched below the ledge, trying to stifle our heavy breathing in order to hear the voices inside, clear, like a radio program.

It sounded like everyone in the room was trying to talk to Ben at the same time, and he was trying to answer them all at the same time. It was as if Ben knew some great secret and everybody in the room wanted to know it.

"Well, Ben, how in the hell do you know who she is?"

"C'mon, Billy Joe. Don't get so excited. Ben is volunteerin' to come in here." There was a sputtering and cracking of voices comin' over the two-way radio that covered the rest of what was Big Trek's voice.

"She called me, Mistuh O'Grady. She called me one night and told Julius and me. She said I had better be careful of strangers. Dat dere was one who had wanted it, and dere might be more, and they'd want Looty's."

"How would she know that?" the sheriff asked.

"She jus' said dat. She told me and Julius dat we was lucky."

Since the rain had stopped, the air was heavy and humid. As we crouched under the window, we were sweating like wild hogs. I started thinking about Cousin Carol at home. What if she went upstairs to check on us? We'd be better off getting arrested.

Everybody started talking over each other. Every now and then we heard a question about Looty—where is he? What did he do? There were so many questions about Looty, and questions about some woman who might have some information. Why were they asking Ben Samuels all these questions? I worried that right now Cousin Carol might be checking our beds.

"Maybe we oughta go home," I whispered to Taylor.

"Not now. We're about to find out something."

Casey tugged at Taylor's shirt. "I've found out enough."

"Shhh! You're just scared."

"Yeah. That, too."

"Y'all be quiet. They're gonna hear us if y'all don't shut up," Taylor said.

Then we heard another unmistakable voice. "Daddy, tell 'em what you know—what she told us. Tell 'em now. If you don't I will." It was BB. He and Ben Samuels were both in there. More sputtering and cracking obscured most of what he said.

Taylor raised his head to peek in the window, hoping for a glance at who was in the room. He dropped back down like a fallen rock. "Ben and some other men are standin' around in their raincoats. I couldn't see Looty though. I saw Daddy and Big Trek, too."

"Whodaya s'pose they're talking about? *Who is she?*" Casey asked. "What's Ben s'posed to be tellin' 'em?"

The next thing we heard was clear. Mr. O'Grady said they had better go—to get out to Looty's. That was a signal it was time for us to go, too. We didn't want to get caught out here listening at the window. We took off for the bushes in the square. From there we saw six or seven men come out of the office and move toward the squad cars. Although it had stopped raining they were wearing their yellow raincoats, all but one who wore a poncho. Silhouetted against the light from the office, BB in his old army poncho was a dark figure in the dim light. He looked like a vampire.

It was almost two when we got back to the house. No one was waiting up for us. And we had beaten Trek and Big Trek back. Casey stuffed his pants under the bed. If they hadn't dried by morning he wanted them hid good. They would have until after noontime to dry since we would be wearing our Sunday clothes tomorrow morning.

We all were still wide awake, but two things we knew were true. One was that there was a *she* involved in something; and two, the silhouette of BB in his poncho had convinced us who was at Looty's that night.

"Y'all think my pants will be dry by morning?"

"Will you stop worrying about your pants? They're gonna be dry. Momma ain't gonna check under the bed before we get back from church. Anyway, I told you not to sit down out there. I told you it was wet."

"You didn't say nothin' 'bout not sittin' down. You jus' said don't get your shoes muddy or we might get caught if we tracked it in the house. An' anyway you oughta be as worried as me. If we get caught I'm spillin' my guts. I ain't gettin' a whippin' by myself."

"Yeah, well, you'll be branded a dirty little squealer if you do. You'll be shunned in Cotton City. You'll be an outcast."

We sat up for another hour and talked in low whispers. Was BB involved in whatever Looty was involved in? Was Looty involved in anything? Was BB? As much as anything, I had begun to wonder about the 'she' who was mentioned. I probably wouldn't have thought about the straw-haired lady except I had seen her at Greenville with Looty. And she was a she.

I didn't bring the topic up to Casey and Taylor, but after we lay down I thought about her some. Was she involved somehow or just an accident that she showed up?

We decided we would go over to BB's after church tomorrow. Maybe we could ask him some questions without letting him know we were listening at the jail.

After Taylor and Casey fell asleep, I lay awake thinking about the straw-haired woman. I sat up and looked out the window. I thought about how simple she had acted. Simple of mental capacity, my daddy would say. She reminded me of Looty and his ways and habits. I remembered how she was on the bus, and the way she talked about things. She said things that were funny; but now that I thought about her, it seemed like maybe she wasn't trying to be funny. I wondered if other people on the bus were laughing at her without her knowing it, because she was different.

The skies had cleared and the full moon lighted the cotton field; a dimmer light than the sun but with a kind of a glow that seemed to rest the cotton. It was cool from the rain. As I stared across the field there was music in my head. The words of Dixie were coming from the field, like what they called background music in a picture show.

"I wish I was in the land o' cotton…

Old times there are not forgotten,"

Old times there… It wasn't a song only for some people any more than cotton was just for some people. Then my thoughts of her got mixed in with Looty and mixed in with a lot of people, like a long parade of them.

It sort of came to me—the cotton didn't get in that field by itself. People planted it. And other people tended it and took it off the stalks. And others bought it, and ginned it, and sold it, and got oil from it, and traded it, and sold and resold it for clothes and blankets and quilts and stuff.

The moonlit field made me think of Mississippi people,

because this was my home and these were people like me. No matter if you lived in the city or on a farm, or ran a store or a filling station, or played football like Johnny Vaught's Mississippi boys or were a soldier like BB who wanted to go to war for his people; or were just a lady on a bus, or a simple man who might be mixed up in the head. My thoughts seemed so strange that I thought I was dreaming. But when you dream you don't think you're dreaming, you just think things are strange.

It was like all those folks were here on the same land I was hoeing cotton on, because they were all Southern people—Mississippi people and land people. Southerners were people of the land. They didn't all have farms here like Big Trek, but they had roots here.

I thought about the blind students my grandmother had taught at the Mississippi School for the Blind. They couldn't play football, or hoe cotton or go to war either, but were part of the land because they had roots. And there was an old colored man who had no legs and scooted around the streets in Jackson on a little wooden board with metal wheels, selling peanuts and newspapers. I never knew his name, but he had roots here. All of the people were different, but their roots had made them the same. I recalled my daddy's phrase, 'Mississippi sinew.' He told me sinew was like a muscular strength that each man has or doesn't have, and groups of people have as a group. Southerners, agrarians, farmers had it. And Mississippi's was as tough and strong as anybody's, he said.

That's what I thought about Looty and the straw-haired woman—they were as different from Big Trek and Trek and Mr. Hightower, and even BB and Ben—as different as the light of the moon was from the power of the sun. And they were the same. They had roots here. Tough roots. I hoped they had done no wrong—and BB neither.

I fell asleep; and I awakened, as usual, early.

CHAPTER 18

All slicked down and pretty handsome, according to Cousin Carol, we climbed into the brown Ford. The grownups weren't as talkative as they usually were on Sunday morning. We weren't either. For one thing we were sleepy, and two, the only thing we wanted to talk about was what went on at the jail last night. We were soon to learn what went on.

We passed the New Glory Baptist Church, its gravel parking lot filled with puddles of muddy water. The colored people were carefully side-stepping the puddles in their Sunday shoes. We didn't see Ben or BB, but maybe they were already inside. I kept looking back to see if I could see them, until we were too far for me to see anything. About the time I had turned around, Cousin Carol turned and smacked Casey on top of the head.

"Stop that!" He was pickin' his nose. "Don't do that in public."

"This isn't public," he protested. "This is just regular people."

"Don't talk back."

I noticed Cousin Trek's eyes in the rearview mirror, probably lined right at Casey. Casey must have noticed too, because he didn't say anything else. He just pushed his hair back in place where he had gotten whacked then he wiped the Wildroot Cream Oil off his hand with his necktie. We pulled into the church parking lot.

Young boys weren't to know about things that were strictly for adults, like murder and crime investigations. But if you got enough boys together, there was always some information just by putting rumors and talk together, some by overhearing your parents when they didn't know you were listening.

Marshal O'Grady's son Eddie was in the Sunday School class, and he was the head knower. Whatever your daddy's job was, you knew more about that subject than everybody else your age.

"My daddy said they were gettin' close to solving the murder of that guy they found in the river."

Eddie was an okay guy, but he got a little snotty when he started telling you things about the police and all. Nobody could dispute him out loud because no one really knew what his daddy might have told him. But we were pretty sure he made a lot up.

"Oh, yeah," Casey challenged, "how come you weren't at the jail last night?"

"I coulda been if I'd wanted to."

"Yeah, sure," Casey said. Everybody in the class laughed.

"Well, maybe I could have if it weren't so late. And y'all better watch out sneaking around the jail like that. If my daddy catches y'all, he'll throw y'all in jail. I mean it. He will."

"No he wouldn't," Taylor challenged him this time. "He'd just call our parents, and we'd get a whippin', not jail."

"I'd rather be in jail," another boy said. Everybody laughed again.

Humphrey Turnipseed was also in the class. Since he had been held back in third grade, I wondered why he was still in this Sunday School class. Casey always came to the same class as Taylor because he was with his older brother. But it seemed like to me Humphrey should have been set back in Sunday School class, too. I guess they didn't want to fail a guy in Sunday School. Farley told me once that if you failed Sunday School, you probably went to hell.

Anyway, Humphrey's theory was that the dead man had committed suicide. One shot to the head. One shot to the heart. Taylor said that was the kind of thinking that would get him held back in the fifth grade.

Another boy, Benny, who was probably the smartest boy in fifth grade and always wore a bowtie to Sunday School—a clear sissy choice—said that Looty was not all there and had gone off the deep end and killed somebody. He said Looty had started by shooting chickens, and that's the way murderers did. They started with little things like chickens or yard dogs and worked their way up to people.

When he said that I thought about Casey squashing roaches for bait. I wondered if he was slowly developing into a small-town psychopath.

Benny also said he had made a study of Raymond Chandler characters on the radio programs, and that it was pretty easy to see their development from small killings to important ones. I didn't want to think about Looty being guilty. I didn't want him to be guilty because mostly, I felt sorry for him.

I didn't want to think about BB being guilty either. But what was he doing in Looty's that night if that was him in his poncho? I was hoping it was just somebody we didn't know. And I kept feeling sorry for the straw-haired lady, though I wasn't sure why.

Just then Eddie said something that got everyone's attention. "Well, I can tell you this. I heard my daddy tell my mother that they went to Looty's last night, and he wasn't there. And they couldn't find his rifle either."

I glanced at Casey and Taylor. I suspected they were thinking the same thing I was.

"Well, boys, how are y'all this morning?" The teacher walked in and we mummed-up on the crime talk. "Did y'all get plenty of rain at your houses last night?"

Various positive answers followed, and he sat down. He was a nice old man, about eighty I imagine. He wore a red tie and blue suit and had liver spots. He opened his Bible to the first couple of pages and announced, "We'll have a word of prayer and then read about Cain and Abel."

In church we sang loud and long, as usual. When we sang Blessed Assurance, I thought it would have been nice if my mother were there this weekend because that was her favorite. Farley and I were more partial to Onward Christian Soldiers since it had more action. My daddy preferred Christmas carols.

When the pastor got to going, Taylor and Casey and I squirmed and tried to look like we were paying attention to him. But our attention was on Mr. O'Grady who was two rows in front of us. I thought Casey was going to pass him a note and ask him what he found at Looty's last night. You never could tell about Casey.

I wondered where Looty was now. He hadn't gone back home, or at least the police hadn't found him there last night. That is, if Eddie O'Grady knew what he was talking about. And when I thought about Looty, I kept reminding myself of BB and what did he have to do with all this. Why would he have been in the house that night?

I didn't hear much of what the pastor said. I just stared at the back of Mr. O'Grady's head. I thought he might jump up any minute and run out on some emergency. Maybe all of a sudden he might get one of those great ideas like Phillip Marlowe did, and in a flash he would realize who the murderer was. Course it didn't happen and finally after about an hour the service was over. We all flocked to the doors.

When grownups crowd together, it's hard to get them un-crowded. Church was no different. After the service is over, most people funnel themselves out the front door so they can congratulate the pastor and shake his hand. Once outside, everyone stands around and shakes hands and some of the ladies hug and then re-hug, and the men tell either weather stories, especially those affecting the cotton crop, or baseball stories. Sometimes they talk about the upcoming football season and what the Rebels or the Bulldogs might do. And which one would win the season ending battle for the Golden Egg.

Today the crowd had dispersed into clumps of people. No one wanted to step in the puddles or mud, so they stood on the sidewalk and in the dry spots of the parking area. Occasionally someone's mother would scream at her son. "Get out of that water! You'll ruin your shoes!"

Several men, including Cousin Trek and Big Trek, were talking out of earshot with Mr. O'Grady. I was pretty sure what they were talking about today, and it wasn't about any ball games or the weather. But if you got too close they would clam up or change the subject.

Taylor and Casey and I were waiting by the car. Casey had

picked up a rain frog and was sizing him up for his leg power. In his efforts to wiggle free, the frog would kick his legs kind of like a bird trying to flap his wings. Casey said this was a decent gauge of how far he could jump.

He started sneaking up on a girl about his age named Patty. He was just about to put the frog on her shoulder when Cousin Carol screamed across the lot, "Casey Mayfield! Don't you dare! I will kill you!"

Patty almost jumped into a puddle. I think Cousin Carol's scream frightened her more than the frog had.

Just then Mr. Hightower walked over, and Casey chunked the frog in the grass. "Well, you boys workin' tomorrow or going fishin'? Ground'll be a little soft, but the sun'll dry it out pretty quick. That is if we don't get any more rain." He lit a Chesterfield cigarette and exhaled columns of smoke through his nose and mouth.

"We'll be workin', Mr. Hightower," I said. I looked at Casey and Taylor.

"Yessir," Taylor followed.

"Yessir," Casey said. There wasn't anything else he could say. He had no choice either.

We all knew that sometimes if you caught a grownup off by himself and maybe off guard, you could get the answer to a question that usually he wouldn't answer. I think that was what Taylor was after when he said, "Mr. Hightower, you got any notion where Looty is? Do you think he killed that man they found in the river?"

Mr. Hightower took another draw on his cigarette. He glanced over his shoulder in the direction of Cousin Trek and Cousin Carol, embedded in one of the grownup clumps. For a minute I thought we might get some real information. But I guess Mr. Hightower caught himself in time. Or maybe he just didn't know that much.

"Well, boys, I don't know any more than y'all know, prob'ly. Looty ran off from the jail and they haven't found him yet, I understand. It's kinda suspicious though."

"Why is it suspicious?" Casey almost interrupted. "The only

thing they know was a man was shot. Lots of people can shoot."

"Well, the man was shot with a .22, and Looty has done some shooting with a .22 and for some reason his rifle can't be found. Sounds a little suspicious to them."

"That's still not much, it doesn't seem like to me," I insisted.

"Like I said—" He flipped his cigarette into a puddle. "I really don't know that much about what the sheriff and Mr. O'Grady know. Maybe he's got more. Anyway, I got to be goin'. See y'all tomorrow." He walked toward a line of cars on the road.

I looked at Taylor and Casey. "Did he mean they were looking for Looty's rifle? I wonder why it wasn't in his house." We were to find out the next day.

After we got home Cousin Carol fixed dinner —fried chicken. There was little conversation. Nobody said so, but everybody was thinking about Looty. It was strange the way everybody seemed to feel sorry for him. He wasn't a relative or anything, but he was so harmless and alone that I think everybody felt kind of like he was a stray dog. It seemed like maybe he had killed that man.

"Daddy, do you think Looty did anything wrong?" Taylor asked.

Casey glanced at me. "Pass the chicken, please?" he asked.

There was nothing said for a moment by anybody. Cousin Carol lifted the platter of chicken and asked Casey, "What piece do you want?"

"A wing, please?"

She tried to place a wing on his plate.

"Don't let it touch my peas!" He pulled back his extended plate.

"Oh, Casey! You're such a baby. Just hush now, and take this."

Cousin Trek still had not answered Taylor, and Big Trek had said nothing either. Finally, Cousin Trek spoke.

"Well, I really don't know. What do you boys know about Looty and his doin' anything? Anything at all?"

Taylor said, "Well, sir, we heard you say yesterday when you came home that he had broken out of jail. Why would he be in jail if he hadn't done something wrong?"

"Well, nobody knows at this point. But Looty is kind of a mixed up fellow and the sheriff and Mr. O'Grady aren't sure what to think at this point. They just want to find him and make sure he's all right."

"That's enough talk about Looty for now," said Cousin Carol. "Let's talk about somethin' else."

"But—" said Taylor.

"You heard your mother. Drop it."

We finished the meal in silence, and though I had been hungry, I only ate two drumsticks. Thinking makes me eat less, I guess. Cousin Carol had asked nothing about having seconds. A courtesy that was absent today.

The dust had settled and was packed from the rain. Though water was still in the drainage ditch, it was solid enough in the middle to ride without getting muddy. We rode our bikes in single file to avoid hitting the few muddy spots, and soon pulled up in front of the B. Samuels mailbox. The gray wooden house with the chickens and tractor in the yard seemed lonelier than before, though I wasn't sure why. We wondered if BB would tell us anything.

There was a gray tarp covering the sofa and chair on the front porch. The porch overhang wasn't wide enough when the rain was blowing from the west, and Ben and BB had pulled up the tarp to keep the rain off the furniture. There was still water in the creases.

No one answered the door. We went out back, leaving our bikes stacked against the porch. BB was atop a ladder cutting a limb out of a willow tree. The storm had broken it. It was green and dangling, waiting to drop as soon as it died. Ben held the ladder, trying to stabilize it in the soft ground.

Before we could call out, Ben turned his head. "Why, hi there, young uns. Whad y'all doin' today? Y'all come vistn'?" He looked up in the tree at BB. "This un's 'bout to cut his finger off if he not more careful."

BB had his left hand wrapped around the branch and the

saw close to his thumb. "I ain't gonna cut my finger off, Daddy. Howdy fellows." He turned back to the branch and began to saw, marking the point where he would cut it. "What are y'all up to?" he said. "Got some wind with that rain yesterday."

"We're jus' ridin' around lookin' for something to do," Taylor said. He looked at me when he said it. I think he was thinking the same thing I was—that it would be easier to bring the subject up if Ben weren't there. It was easier to talk with somebody closer to your age than a really old guy. Sometimes I could say things to Farley that I couldn't to my daddy. I hoped Casey picked up the signal and didn't blurt something out like, 'Did you and Looty kill that guy?'

I worked my way behind Ben and waited for BB to look at me so I could give him some hand signals. He was sawing and had his back to me. Finally Taylor yelled something at him just to get him to turn, and I motioned with my hand that we wanted him for something. I nodded at Ben indicating I wanted BB to get his daddy to go into the house for a minute. BB kept sawing, and in a moment the limb toppled to the ground.

"Hold the ladder, Daddy. I'm comin' down."

I could see the sweat through the back of his shirt. The rain had brought a steamy and humid day. "I'll bet these boys would like some iced tea. I know I would. If you go inside and get us some, Daddy, I'll get them to help me drag this limb outta the yard. They'll earn their glass of tea." He winked at us.

Ben wiped his brow with the back of his hand. "Now Julius, dat's a gud idear. Y'all git to draggin' and I'll fetch us some tea." He turned and walked toward the house, then glanced over his shoulder at us. By the way he looked at us, I think he knew we were trying to get BB alone. He kind of nodded without comment. Ben was pretty smart for an old guy.

BB climbed down and leaned the saw against the tree. "Now what you fellows up to?"

"Did y'all know—I mean you and Ben—know the sheriff and Mr. O'Grady were lookin' for Looty's rifle?" Casey blurted.

BB said nothing.

"And they couldn't find it in his house." I couldn't hold it in.

BB looked at me. There was another pause. "Well, they said last night that they needed to find the murder weapon to check the ballistics."

"What's that?" Casey asked.

"It's some way they can tell what gun shot what bullet," Taylor said.

Just then Ben came out with the iced tea. He handed us jelly glasses filled with tea and told us to sit down under the willow tree. He returned to the house to get himself a glass.

BB took a glass and put it against his face. "Well, that's the truth, I s'pose. They ain't found the rifle." He took a large gulp of iced tea. "They just ain't found it."

"I wonder where it is?" said Taylor.

BB didn't say anything. And none of us had brought up the mention of a she. And we dang sure didn't mention a poncho. We had talked about it, and decided we'd better not even let BB know we were outside the window last night.

"Well, boys, I got to get back to clearin' limbs. Y'all better get on home. You got a big work day tomorrow. Rain's gone and the cotton's needin' attention."

Ben walked back out. He saw us getting on our bikes. "Y'all leavin'?"

All of us turned and waved. Taylor yelled, "We gotta get home, Ben. See you."

We went home without helping BB drag the limb.

CHAPTER 19

It was only four days until my family came to Cotton City to take me home.

The field had dried since Saturday's rain, but the ground was still soft. The cotton bolls were dry and the sun seemed harsher, with the wet ground throwing up steam as if punishing the Delta for taking a break. And everything looked greener after a storm. Daddy once told me it was because lightning added nitrogen to the soil. I always thought it was strange that something so deadly could also add life.

We worked like a chain gang—those convicts you sometimes saw on the side of the road, swinging sling blades and sweating in their black and white striped clothes. We were hoeing and sweating. BB set the pace. And it was a pace more than he usually set. He didn't seem like his usual cheerful self. He worked today like he was fighting. It was as if he had something he was holding in. And I had seen enough picture shows to know when a man was holding something in.

After two weeks, I had toughened to the work and the heat. I wasn't done-in as fast as that first day. Still, I was happy to see Ben's old pickup rattling down the road, a sign it was time for dinner.

We all gathered under the shade tree and sat for a minute before we started eating. Ben didn't bring anything special today like watermelon, just a couple of brown bags for him and BB.

BB took his bag from Ben and opened it. He sat on the ground next to Ben. "Ham and hard-boiled eggs? I love ham."

Ben handed BB a salt shaker from his bag. Ben didn't laugh the way he usually did. He often had a funny little story he'd punctuate with a chuckle. Sometimes the stories were funny, sometimes not. It was his chuckle that made me smile, made the stories memorable. Ben had that way about him. But today Ben was just another old man who seemed to have taken on a size of the world's troubles. I wondered if we had caused it by asking too many questions yesterday.

Perhaps the only reason BB and Ben ever confided in us was because we had shown such an interest in them. But, maybe we had asked too much.

BB placed an egg shell on the ground as carefully as if it were a piece of Cousin Carol's china. The hardboiled egg looked like a marble in his oversized hands as he sprinkled it with salt. But it didn't seem like his mind was on eggs, or eggshells, or salt, or even ham sandwiches.

He said, "I think Mr. O'Grady and the sheriff are gettin' close to findin' out who killed that man. They searched Looty's again. This time they found a pocket watch in the house. The dead man had a broken watch chain hangin' from his watch pocket when he was found in the river. That's what they said."

"But dey still didn't find no rifle." Ben looked directly at BB.

"Nope," BB said.

"How come they didn't find the watch when they looked last week?" Taylor asked.

"Maybe it wasn't there," BB said. His face looked darker than it ever had. He didn't seem positive. He appeared to be a different man.

That was curious. Why was it not there, and then there? Had Looty taken it home? Where did he get it? Did someone else put it there?

BB and Ben were talking about things they hadn't talked about yesterday, but I still felt BB was holding something back.

The roads had dried more than the fields, what with traffic and drainage ditches, so in the distance we could see a small cloud of dust following a car coming toward us. When it pulled up, the sudden stop threw the long whiplash antennae into a rhythmic flopping back and forth like a deep-sea fishing rod. It was Mr. O'Grady's police car, and Sheriff Bilbeau from the county seat was with him. No one got out for a minute or two. The dust settled. The antenna wound down. The two men got out and walked over.

We had been at the city jail for almost an hour, and Cousin Trek hadn't come down yet. He was probably out in the fields somewhere where Cousin Carol couldn't reach him.

Mr. O'Grady and the sheriff had come out to the fields to tell BB and Ben that they needed to come on into town to get this thing straightened out. We went with them, so Mr. O'Grady told us to call Cousin Trek or Cousin Carol to come down and pick us up. Taylor had tried telling Cousin Carol that we hadn't done anything wrong. But being in jail probably didn't sound very good to her. If she didn't find Cousin Trek or Big Trek pretty quick she'd be down without them. You could bet on that.

I wasn't surprised to hear BB admit that he was the caped figure we had seen that night at Looty's. He had worn his Army poncho to conceal the rifle and disguise himself, in case someone saw him at a distance.

He told Mr. O' Grady and the sheriff that because of the rumors, he had suspected Looty might have known something about the man he and Ben had found in the river. BB said he didn't think Looty was a murderer, but maybe somebody was taking advantage of him. Anyway, he knew the man had been killed with a .22 and wanted to hide Looty's rifle in case there was some connection. He had just wanted to protect Looty. A lot of people knew Looty was always popping birds and chickens with his rifle. Maybe he had shot someone—not on purpose— but just because he wasn't that smart and something might have happened, maybe an accident. BB told the sheriff that was what he was thinking when he took the rifle. It wasn't Looty's fault he was the way he was.

"I don't see why they'd put him in jail for taking a rifle. That ain't much," Casey said.

"I think it's called messin' with evidence or something." Taylor was repeating something he had heard on Big Town more than likely.

The four of us just sat in the straight-back wooden chairs in Mr. O'Grady's office. It had yellowed walls with little furnishings except for a calendar provided by Thompson's Cotton Gin and Company, a pendulum clock, and a picture of Jefferson Davis. The walls didn't have any wanted posters. There weren't many people wanted in Cotton City for high crimes, I guess. The biggest crime in Cotton City, according to Cousin Carol, was the domino game. A ceiling fan spun full blast, blowing papers on the desk and cooling us a little in the process.

Mr. O'Grady had BB in his office next to the front office where we were sitting. The door was about half way open, and we could see everybody.

Ben looked at Casey and Taylor then turned his head toward me. Ben had a gentle look that he sometimes got, and I felt sorry for him. I couldn't imagine him or BB doing anything wrong.

After a few minutes talking to BB alone, they took Ben in. We were left in the room with President Davis and Thompson's Cotton Gin, and the clock, its pendulum moving back and forth. The door remained partially open, and my chair was set so I could see everybody. I still craned my neck to look. I saw BB and Ben.

"What in the world were you thinkin,' BB?" I heard Sheriff Bilbeau say.

I looked at Casey and Taylor and whispered, "I thought he had just told him what he was thinkin'." They looked back at me and shrugged.

"I think it's one of those questions you aren't supposed to answer," Casey said. "It means you weren't thinking."

BB's face tightened and his fists seemed to clinch. He must know he had not been thinking. "I was jus' trying to help Looty. I know it prob'ly wasn't the right thing to do, but I wanted to help him."

Mr. O'Grady moved around behind BB and Ben. Both remained rigid in their seats. He took off his hat and scratched his head. He ran his hand through his hair before replacing his hat.

"Do you know you could go to prison? They don't let jail birds go to college. In case you ever planned to go."

This was getting serious. It had always been serious, but now they were talking about jail—and not just the city jail or the county jail but prison. Prison sounded a lot worse than jail. Prison was where guys like James Cagney went.

"Now, one thing we got to get straightened out is this business at the river. It's hard to believe that y'all jus' happened to be fishin' there, and jus' happened to find this body. I mean—you can see what it looks like, you taking his rifle and all."

BB's lips quivered. For a minute I thought he was going to cry. He looked scared. His mouth opened, and he took a deep breath.

"We didn't just happen to be there, Sheriff. We were invited."

For a minute the ticking of the pendulum was the only sound. Sheriff Bilbeau said nothing; he just pushed his hat back on his head and stared at BB.

Mr. O'Grady leaned forward with his foot propped on a chair and waited for the sheriff to continue.

"Invited?" Sheriff Bilbeau said. "You wanna s'plain that BB?"

BB turned toward Ben. Ben leaned forward in his chair, looked at BB and nodded.

"We were invited one night by a lady," said BB. "A lady named Sarah. She called Daddy one night and told him a story. It was a pay phone, 'cause he'd heard the operator ask for thirty-five cents."

Ben nodded in agreement.

Sheriff Bilbeau pulled up a chair right next to BB and Ben. He turned the chair around and leaned on the back with his arms folded. "Maybe you better tell us the story. Tell us what she told y'all."

The police station door swung open and Cousin Carol came in, followed by Cousin Trek and Big Trek both taking long strides to keep up with her.

"What in the world is goin' on?" Cousin Carol spoke first. "Where is Billy Joe?" Her words ran together like that radio guy Walter Winchell, hardly pausing for breath. "How long have y'all been here? Where is Ben? Where is BB? Did Earl come down? Was he out there when the sheriff got there? Are y'all all right?"

"Jus' hold on, Carol. We'll get Billy Joe out here and find out what this is all about. Now jus' calm down some," said Cousin Trek.

Mr. O'Grady came out of the interrogation room. His hands were up in front of his chest, like a pass blocking tackle fending an onslaught. "Calm down, calm down. Now ever'thing is okay with the boys, Carol. We jus' had to bring 'em in so they weren't left out there by themselves. We couldn't find Earl at the time, and we thought it was bes' jus' to bring 'em here. They ain't in no trouble."

"We're okay, Daddy," Taylor said. "But they got BB and Ben in there. They've been arrested haven't they, Mr. O'Grady?"

We waited for the answer. We weren't sure they were under arrest, or if they were just being asked questions. In a way we were afraid to know the answer. We wanted to believe BB hadn't done anything wrong.

Mr. O'Grady looked at us. He used both hands to hitch up his gun belt before turning to Cousin Trek. Big Trek didn't seem surprised, but that might be because he had seen so much in life as to not be surprised at anything.

"We're holdin' 'em until we get the report back on the ballistics, for the rifle. If it's the gun that killed that man then BB's gonna have some explainin' to do. An' Looty is gonna be wanted for murder, I'm afraid."

I squirmed in my chair.

"When did you get the rifle?" Big Trek asked.

"This mornin'." Sheriff Bilbeau came in from the other room, leaving the door open. He looked back at BB and pointed at him with his thumb. "He jus' giv' it to us. Been hidin' it all this time. I'm not sure what his intentions were. Said he was jus' helpin' Looty."

"Gave it to you?" Big Trek asked.

"Well, I think he slipped up. Might not have meant to 'give' it to us. But when we went out to Looty's Sunday early in the morning', you know, when we found the watch. Well, when we started up toward the house he said, 'Watch out there's a couple of loose boards on the front of the porch.'"

Sheriff Bilbeau paused and relit a cigar stub about two inches long he had been fooling with. "I didn't start thinkin' about it 'til after we left. I was focusin' on the watch so much. It was on the mantle next to that old jar of dirt, or whatever. Anyway I got to thinkin' about loose boards and how he'd been real careful, it seemed to me, to keep us from unloosing 'em, in case we tripped on 'em. This mornin' I got Billy Joe, and we went out and pulled 'em up. There was the rifle, carefully wrapped in an old bedspread."

I peered through the open door at BB. He jus' sat in the chair. He stared straight ahead. Not at us. Not through the open door, so I wondered if he was trying to think of something else, like scoring touchdowns or chopping cotton, or something that would take his mind away from here. He sat straight in the chair with no expression—no smile—no nothing.

"How long before y'all know if it's the gun that killed him?" Cousin Trek asked. He glanced through the door at BB and gave him a slight nod.

"They should know before the day's over. I got some people over at county lookin' at it," the sheriff said. "We'll at least have that part cleared up."

"And what about that watch?" Mr. O'Grady asked.

"What watch?" Cousin Carol asked. "This is getting to be too serious for these boys to be involved. I think we need to get them on home," she said.

We all looked at each other. A comment like that could get us pulled out of the room just when things were getting interesting.

A highway patrolman walked in. "I got a call on my radio," he said. "It wasn't the rifle. The bullet doesn't match. They'll get the official report to you in about an hour."

Our presence was momentarily forgotten with the good

news. I looked at BB. His big white smile was forming. Casey and Taylor grinned at me.

"Not the rifle?" Mr. O'Grady looked at the sheriff.

"Now what about the watch?" Big Trek said. He had said little until now. Though he talked a lot around me and Casey and Taylor, it was usually because he liked to tell us stories. But when important things were at issue he usually didn't comment unless it was pretty heavy on his mind. He always studied on things before he spoke. He stood up, banged his pipe on the trash can and walked over to the window.

" Sheriff Bilbeau and Billy Joe found a watch at Looty's Saturday night. The night Ben came over to our house. You remember, Daddy. That pocket watch," Taylor said.

Casey looked at me, a nervous grin crossing his face. We were supposed to have been asleep and not known Ben had come by. I guess no one noticed because Cousin Trek talked right through it.

"I remember, son. I'm asking them. What about it?"

"What's your point, Mr. Mayfield? We know about the watch," the sheriff said. "Looty told us she brought it before last Saturday. The last night he saw her."

Big Trek turned from his stance at the window. "Well, now you got a watch that's almost sure 'bouts from the dead man—a watch found at the home of the guy whose rifle was not the murder weapon. It seems to me what you've got is what the story-writers call an irony."

"How's that, Mr. Mayfield?" Mr. O'Grady asked.

"Well, you found evidence from a man's house that makes him look innocent—the rifle. But you also got evidence found in the same place that makes him look guilty, the watch. It's ironic. Or maybe better said, a paradox."

"Well, paradox or not, we're getting' to the bottom of this."

I could still see BB and Ben sitting in the other room. I could tell they heard the news. Ben had put his arm over BB's shoulder. Neither seemed guilty to me. Ben and BB sure looked relieved that they were no longer suspected of helping a killer.

Cousin Carol had temporarily lost interest in getting us

home and listened as intently as the rest of us. Ben and BB came into the front office. I guess they knew they weren't going to prison.

Just then, the front door opened and a deputy sheriff walked in with a man and a woman. The woman looked old and haggard. The man looked tired. It was Looty and the straw-haired lady.

Ben spoke first. "Hello, Looty. Miss Sarah."

I had never thought about her having a name. I hadn't even asked on the bus.

Her first words were to me. "Hello, Hon. How'er you doing?" She remembered me. Her lips turned up, trying to smile. But her eyes could not hide sadness.

Looty sat down. He said nothing, took out a red bandanna and wiped his brow.

Then she started talking just like she had on the bus, uncomplicated. She wasn't excited or anything; she just started telling her story in her own simple, way.

"His name was Draco Marcus, a dang carpetbagger's son from Chicago. His daddy was a carpetbagger and had come down here stealing whatever he could more'n thirty years before Draco came. Jus' trash his daddy was. And so was Draco it turns out. His daddy done told him if he wanted to make his fortune to get his-self down here in this rich Mississippi Delta land. There was plenty of ignorant hicks and dumb niggers that'd be easy to be givin' up their land. 'Jus' easy pickin's and all', he said. Didn't matter that the war had been over for almost forty years, there was plenty of folks to make easy money off of still.

"Mr. Jackson McComb had saved his land after the war and wanted it left to his slave boy who was Ben Samuel's daddy. Mr. McComb said in his will that if anything happened to Ben's daddy before Ben was twenty-one, then the land was to be kept by law with a widowed landowner hereabouts that he trusted—Elizabeth Nash. Sure enough, Mr. McComb, he died, around 1900. Ben was jus' a boy, 'bout twelve. I was a young gal then myself. Jus' fifteen.

"But ole Draco Marcus didn't know 'bout this. I don't even

know for sure he knew 'bout Ben til after that night. He just thought Ben's momma and daddy was there by theirselves."

Mr. O'Grady leaned forward. "What night…uh, Miss… uh…"

"Sarah. My name's Sarah," she almost whispered. "And I mean the night the panther supposed to done killed Ben's momma and daddy."

"Supposed to?" Sheriff Bilbeau said.

"Draco done it. He chopped them up with a machete and clawed them with a trowel to make it look like a panther got 'em. He had chopped up a panther he had trapped, and took one of its claws for to use in spreadin' tracks around. Didn't know Ben was in the room under the covers or I guess he'd killed him, too. I guess he thought if the owners was dead he could get some tax collector to sell him the land. I don't know what he thought really. He was just trash, like I already said."

"How is it you know all of this, Miss Sarah?" the sheriff asked.

She seemed to be dazed for a second. Then she looked at Looty. "Cause Draco told me. After they was killed and he found out about Ben's land going to my momma, he said he wanted to marry me and take care of me and my momma and her land. But my momma wasn't havin' any of it and told him so. He stayed around for four or five years before he realized the carpetbagging days was over. But he had me fooled, and one night he had his way with me before he left for good. And he left me my boy."

"Your boy?" someone asked.

She put her arm around Looty's shoulder.

I looked at Taylor and Casey. I wondered if they knew what was going on. I wasn't sure. I began to wonder if we were going to be told to leave. But no one told us to.

"Miss Sarah. Sarah Nash?" Mr. O'Grady said. "What happened after that?"

"I was ashamed and left my boy…" she paused to squeeze Looty's shoulder with her hand, "…with my momma. I went off to Arkansas. I married a fine gentleman who was a tent wrangler in the circus. We done alright, 'til he got killed one night went he got electrocuted by lightning."

"What did you ever hear about Draco Marcus?" Cousin Carol suddenly spoke.

"Oh, honey, not too much. Word was he was in and out of jail over the years. When he wasn't in Parchman or some other jail he was supposedly hanging out with a bunch of river rats over around Greenville."

"How come you never told anyone about him killing Ben's momma and daddy?" Sheriff Bilbeau asked. "You said a minute ago that he told you."

She lifted her head a bit to answer and the light from the ceiling reflected from the wetness in her eyes. "Didn't know before that night. All these years and didn't know. Thought it was really a panther. Not until that night. That night about three weeks ago.

"I'd taken the bus to Greenville from Clarksdale. I wuz goin' to get me some medicine from a place I know-ed about close to the river bridge. I ran into Marcus down there. He was after Looty. Somehow he'd found out that Looty wuz his son. He really got wild-eyed. Said he was too old to work, and he could sell that land and he'd git some cash. Said he'd one time chopped up two niggers, and weren't nothin' gonna stop him from getting' Looty's land now. But it'd be easier if I wuz to help him. Being as how Looty was so simple-minded like me, he said. That man didn't never love nobody but hisself."

Everyone turned toward Ben after she mentioned Marcus killing two "niggers." Now, after fifty years the truth was out. The two former slaves, Ben's momma and daddy, had been murdered. There was no panther. The claw marks and tracks had been faked. A trowel and a leg he had severed from a panther he had killed served his bloody scene, she told everybody. Ben said nothing. BB hung his head and stared at the long wooden floor boards.

"He jus' laughed and laughed." She looked down at her bag. It wasn't the same one she had had on the bus, but it was almost as big. "That's when I reached in my bag and pulled out my little pistol. I shot him twice. Then I took his pocket watch and o'er sixty dollars from his pocket. He probably'd stolen it so I figured I'd jus' steal it from him."

She had pulled out her makins' and was fumbling to put together a cigarette. Tobacco spilled onto her lap. The sheriff leaned forward and offered a Lucky Strike. "Well now, thank you, sir. You are a real gentleman."

He struck a match on the bottom of his shoe and lit her cigarette. He spoke for the first time since her arrival. "Then what'd you do, Miss Sarah?"

"I put some rocks in his pocket and drug him by his leg to the river. It wasn't that hard even for an ol' simple-minded gal like me. He had gotten a bit frail in his old age. He floated jus' a bit and got hung in some bushes. That made me think he might not float down the river for a few days. Or at least 'til the river come up. I guess I really didn't care by then."

"What kind of a gun was it, Sarah?" Mr. O'Grady broke his silence.

She took a deep draw on the cigarette, exhaled a stream of smoke and remained calm. "It was one of them little Deringer guns. Shot two bullets. Two little bullets."

"Like maybe .22 bullets?" the sheriff suggested.

"I guess," she said. "B'longed to my late husband." She took another draw on her cigarette.

"Where is the gun now?

"At the bus station in Yazoo City," I blurted out. "In a locker."

Taylor and Casey looked at me like I had lost my mind. Children were supposed to be seen and not heard. The rule was branded into our souls, especially when grownups were having a conversation. And this was definitely a grownups' conversation—murder and all.

Everybody looked at me astonished, as if I were a pot plant that had just spoken. The straw-haired lady smiled at me, smoke flowing through her nostrils.

"Now, whadaya mean, Jake?" Cousin Trek spoke first.

"Yazoo City?" said Cousin Carol.

The sheriff and Mr. O'Grady jumped in. "Do you know something, Jake?"

The straw haired lady looked straight ahead and drew on her Lucky Strike. She turned and smiled at me. "This un's a fine young fellow." Smoke poured from her nose.

CHAPTER 20

She talked for over an hour. She told them that I was right about Yazoo City, the gun being in the locker and all. I remembered asking her about the huge bag. It was the same bag that contained the cigarette lighter, the lighter that looked like a real pistol. Except that it was a pistol after all. I hadn't even thought at the time she might have put her bag in the bus station lockers. I just knew that she had gone into the bus station with it and come out without it.

She told the sheriff how she had called Ben and BB the night BB said they had "been invited," and reminded him who she was—the young daughter of Elizabeth Nash who had left town one day and never came back. She told them to drive down to the bridge where they would find a man who had wanted to take away Looty's land. She said it was the same man who once tried to get Ben's a long time ago.

"When we got below the bridge we didn't find anything at first," said BB. "She had said not to look for a man standing on the bridge or fishin' below it. We had a pretty good idea we were lookin' for somebody in it. And it didn't sound like he was swimmin' neither. At first we just saw some old beer cans and a few sardine cans where people had been eatin' while they were fishin'. Things like that. The sun was down but it wasn't dark yet, so we could still see in the water pretty good. That's when I saw him, the dead man, tangled in some old dead limbs floatin' to the bank."

The sheriff lit one of his Lucky Strikes and offered one to Sarah. She took one. BB and Ben just shook their heads and thanked him.

"Now what's this business about catchin' him on a fishin'

line? That's jus' something y'all made up?"

"Yes, sir. We didn't know what to do. Getting a strange phone call and all, then findin' a body. We didn't think we could leave him there. We'd for sure be in trouble if somebody saw us and we hadn't told anybody. We jus' took our fishin' poles and stuff so it would look like we had gone fishin'. You know, just in case. So it would look like we just happened to find him. We didn't even know if he was there, for sure."

Cousin Carol took a package of Dentyne chewing gum from her purse and handed Taylor and Casey and me a piece. She put a piece in her mouth, violating a basic rule of etiquette that ladies didn't chew gum in public.

"We hadn't done anything and we jus' worried that if we told the truth nobody'd believe us," BB said. "So Daddy and I jus' made up the story about catchin' a big catfish and all that."

Ben looked at the sheriff. "And I had jus' talked to Miss Sarah here on the phone. Hadn't seed her for forty years. I couldn't be for sure it was her. Me and Julius wuz mixed up on what to do. We worried that you mighta talked to Mr. Looty, and he thought he shoulda shot that man, even if he was his daddy. You know, on account of Mr. Looty is …you know… kinda slow. Julius here always been friends with Mr. Looty and wanted to protect him from something foolish. I'm sorry, Miss Sarah. I wuzn't tryin' to blame you"

"Well, Ben, it looks very much like she is to blame," Big Trek said.

Miss Sarah smiled as she blew smoke through her nose, as if she knew what she had done but didn't feel one bit guilty.

I think Big Trek had said it jus' to remind Ben and BB that they needn't feel afraid. I guess it really wasn't clear yet what they had done. But now I knew that the reason Ben had come to Cousin Trek's house the night of the storm was because he knew he could trust the Mayfield family.

"Well, what did you do next, Sarah?" Mr. O'Grady asked. "You were gone by the time Ben and BB got there."

"I started ridin' the bus south, away from the Delta. Thought I might go all the way to Mobile or Biloxi or someplace. I had his sixty dollars. I only got to Flora when I changed my mind. I sat there all night outside that little store where the bus stops, waiting for the bus to be comin' back the next day. I decided to go back to Clarksdale. My momma was born there. I jus' wanted to go home, I guess.

"But I wanted to go see Looty, too. My boy. He didn't know me. Didn't know who I was. But, he came to Clarksdale as soon as I called him. He hadn't seen me since he was a baby, but he knew I was his momma right away, I b'lieve. I don't know how. He jus' knew. I told him about his daddy. We went to the bridge together Sunday from Clarksdale. I showed him where his daddy died."

Looty did not break his silence, but he didn't have to. He looked at Sarah and smiled, and she returned it. It was like he was looking in a mirror and the mirror reflected his feelings with the same smile, the same plain smile.

The clock struck three o'clock reminding us we had been here over three hours. The story, the crime, all the mystery that had hung over us for the last week had all been revealed. But I had forgotten something, something the sheriff hadn't. Something Ben and BB hadn't.

The sheriff pulled up a chair and drew himself as close to Ben as he could get. "What do y'all know about this watch, Ben?" He handed Ben the watch, and we watched as he opened it.

I had never seen a man cry, not colored or white. I had been told that they did, but I had never seen it, not even in the picture show. I thought after a boy got to a certain age, he never was supposed to do it again. But when the sheriff asked Ben about the watch, Ben took on a tragic look; his eyes got wet and seemed to sparkle. BB put his arm around his daddy. Then a tear rolled down Ben's brown face. And he closed the watch.

CHAPTER 21

Our 1949 Oldsmobile was coming down the gravel road toward the house. I was halfway up the windmill, Taylor was near the top, and Casey was two steps from the bottom, all on the lookout.

I was the first to see them. "There they come. That's our car."

"Your daddy must be drivin'. Goin' too slow to be Farley," Taylor hollered down to Casey and me from his perch under the blades.

Casey was holding on with one hand, his arm outstretched, swinging back and forth with one foot on the windmill.

"Move, Casey." I was climbing down and my next step was on top of his head. "And anyway, Farley can't drive fast when he's with my mother and daddy."

Cousin Carol and Cousin Trek came out into the yard. Big Trek was rocking on the porch, and I glanced at him as we started to the end of the driveway, his pipe hooked to the corner of his mouth, hanging from a huge grin.

By the time the car stopped, we had gathered, ready for the hugging, kissing, and squealing, and handshakes, and all that comes together in a family when you haven't seen someone for more than an hour. Farley and I had given up trying to avoid it, and had accepted it like having to visit the dentist every once in a while. So you just stood in line and tried not to go limp when they squeezed you like a melon.

It had been only three weeks since I had seen my mother and daddy at the bus station. But my mother buttonholed me like I had just been rescued from North Korea. Then after kissing me like I was a pet collie, she rubbed almost all the skin off my face trying to get her lipstick off me with a tissue from her purse.

On the other hand, Daddy gave me a modest hug since I still wasn't at the handshaking age, and released me with a playful brush of my hair.

Farley just punched me in the stomach and whispered, "Good to see ya, ya little stoop." Short for stupid.

The greeting and hugs and handshakes soon subsided and we went into the house. After the bags were taken up to the rooms and everybody was arrived and greeted, Cousin Carol said, "Let's go out on the porch. It's a bit cooler out there. And I'll bring us some iced tea."

"I'll help you," my mother offered. "Ohhh! It's so good to see y'all." Greetings were like goodbyes—they seemed to linger. It was just part of life, I guess.

The rest of us went out on the porch. The grownups went to one end where Big Trek usually sat and smoked his pipe. Casey, Taylor and I went to the other. Farley wasn't sure at first where he wanted to go. He was at that awkward age where he was too old to talk with kids but too young to talk with old people. He finally came to us. I think Taylor and Casey wanted to talk about his driver's license and were glad he came to our end.

"Did Cousin David let you drive up here?" Taylor asked.

"Some of the way. I drove past Flora, then a little more. Daddy says highway drivin' is more dangerous because people go faster on the highway. He'd only let me go fifty-five."

"So, I guess that means you ain't going to New Orleans by yourself anytime soon," Casey said. We all laughed. Farley tried to pretend he wasn't insulted. But when a guy got his driver's license, he was supposed to be free.

"Well, that'll be when I get to college. That's when you can really go where you want—as long as your parents send you money," said Farley.

"Speaking of money," I said, "I made o'er eighteen dollars since I came up. Maybe Daddy'll let you use the car and take us to town tonight."

"What'll we do? Anything to do besides go to the picture show in ol' Cotton City?"

"Not since Dixie Daniels left," Taylor said. Smiles.

"Took her trained hamsters with her," Casey said. Giggles.

"What're y'all talkin' about?"

Taylor, Casey and I all tried keeping straight faces. Farley knew we were making a joke about something, but he wasn't sure just what, except it sounded like it was about him.

"Oh, never mind," I said.

Cousin Carol and Mother came out. Cousin Carol had a tray with several glasses filled with iced tea. Mother had one with a pitcher full and some sugar and iced tea spoons. We all took a glass and thanked her.

"Now y'all don't worry about that old table there. You don't need coasters. It's old and beat up and has more rings than a hundred-year-old oak."

"Yes, ma'am." We hadn't been worried about the table, but we didn't say so.

"I don't s'pose they got a pinball machine anywhere in town now, huh?" Farley asked.

"Naa, checkers at the gazebo or dominoes in the back room of the café are the only games in Cotton City," Taylor said. "And dominoes are out for us. Even if they weren't, I heard Big Trek say one time that those guys are the best in the world. 'Hard to beat a Mississippi domino player,' he said."

"But a great picture show. Flying Leathernecks, John Wayne. It's in color, too. First time it's been to Cotton City," I said.

"Okay. I can go for John Wayne."

Casey, sitting on the floor with his back to the porch screen, bellowed the length of the porch, "Hey, Daddy, can we tell 'em about the dead man and Miss Sarah and Looty and ever'body now?"

Cousin Trek and Cousin Carol had thought it better if we waited until my mother and daddy got up here before telling them about the events of the past few days. It was easier and less expensive than long distance, and I hadn't gotten into any trouble or gotten hurt so it was something that could wait.

"What dead man?" Daddy asked from his end of the porch. "And who is Miss Sarah?"

"What're y'all talkin' about?" Farley looked jealous. He had missed something big and he knew it.

Everyone at both ends of the porch began speaking at the same time. The story was told, repeated, and then someone would ask a question that already had been answered. Finally the questions and answers tapered off and everyone having absorbed as much as they could, like a Thanksgiving feast, sat back and tried to digest the episode. An occasional question here and there lingered. Sorta like mopping gravy from your plate with bread crust, I thought.

"So Draco Marcus is no more, and Sarah Nash is going to the state hospital at Whitfield for examination?" Daddy asked.

"Yeah, at least for now. I don't know if she'll end up in prison or not. Far as I'm concerned, it was justifiable homicide," Big Trek said.

"Looty and BB aren't going to jail, are they?" Mother asked.

"No. Prob'ly not. It's not clear that Looty did anything wrong himself. Maybe some misdemeanor. Looty was tryin' to help his momma, and BB was tryin' to help Looty. It's not as if they killed anybody themselves. But they did interfere a bit, 'cording to the law," Big Trek said.

All of us boys including Farley had inched our way to the end of the porch. It was easier to hear and besides, the cookies that came with the iced tea were on that end.

"Well, what about the watch?" Mother asked. "What was that about? I still don't understand. And David, please quit chewing your ice. I can't hear myself think."

"Well, anyway," Cousin Carol began, "the watch was an old one. It had belonged to Mr. McComb. It had a place for a picture in it. Apparently nobody was sure just who, maybe his wife or even his father or mother's picture, an early photo, had been in it. But when Mr. McComb left his place to Ben's parents, he also left them the watch. He had no children of his own to leave it to.

"He had taken an old photograph of them working in the field and cut the pictures out in the shape of a circle that would fit into the watch. The thing is, after Draco Marcus killed Ben's momma and daddy, he went rummaging through their house and among other things, I'm sure, stole the watch. I guess it was jus' the Lord's will that when he was rummaging he didn't discover Ben sleeping in the upper loft. Otherwise Ben may have been a panther victim."

Cousin Trek took up the explanation. "Ben didn't even know there was a watch at the time. He was just a boy in 1899. And it didn't show up until Sarah took it off Marcus' body."

Cousin Carol waved her hand at him. One of those shush hand waves. "I'm telling this, now you just wait." She looked back at my mother. "But Sarah took it to Looty's the last time she went there. And Billy Joe and the sheriff found it there the night it rained so hard."

"Why'd she take it to Looty's?" Daddy asked.

"I guess maybe she wanted Looty to keep it for BB and Ben. He was her son. I guess it was like Elizabeth keeping the land in trust for Ben's momma and daddy."

"Wonder why Marcus kept the photo inside the watch all these years?"

"Prob'ly remind him of his conquest. He was a sick you-know-what," Cousin Trek said.

"He was a dirty, damn carpetbagging Yankee," said Big Trek. Casey and Taylor and Farley and I laughed.

"Now, Big Trek," Cousin Carol said. "Please, watch your language. Even if you don't think there are ladies present, there are children here."

With his pipe in his mouth he mumbled something, maybe I'm sorry. It wasn't clear, but it was the best he was going to do.

Daddy tried to get the subject back to the watch. "Apparently, Ben saw the watch for the first time at the jail. And it was the first he had learned that his momma and daddy had been murdered."

I thought back to Ben's look when he'd been handed the watch—and his tears.

Farley was telling us everything there was to tell about cars—how to speed around curves and what to do if you fishtailed on a gravel road. Course he knew if he got caught doing something like that with our daddy's car he wouldn't be driving again until he got out of college. Daddy had let him use the car to take us all to the picture show on the condition that he was to be especially careful with us in the car. Farley kept it kind of slow going downtown; too much chance of being spotted. You were on the honor system when you drove your daddy's car, but you didn't want someone being honest for you.

The movie was pretty good, lots of action and planes shot down. John Wayne was wounded pretty bad, but he didn't die like in Sands of Iwo Jima. He just got shot and had to bail out.

Most of the time after the show was over we would hang around the square until somebody picked us up, unless we rode our bikes. But we didn't want to hang around town when we had a car to ride around in.

"Let's go out and see Looty, or BB. I bet they're home now," I said.

"C'mon Farley, we don't have to be home 'til ten," said Taylor.

"Okay, but put your head back inside the window, Casey. If you get killed, I'll get blamed."

Casey pulled himself back in. "You smoke yet, Farley?"

"Naa, I haven't decided to yet. I got some friends that do though. They can't smoke at home yet. Not even s'posed to smoke at all."

"You think Dixie Daniels smokes?"

"Prob'ly. She's in college now."

"Yeah. I bet she's a zuta geeka girlie thi or something."

"What're you talkin' about?" Taylor said. We looked at Casey and laughed. I could see in the rearview mirror Farley was laughing, but didn't take his eyes off the road.

"You know. She's in one of them fraternalty things."

"It's a sorority, you dope. If it's a girl," Farley corrected him. "And it's not a, whatever you called it. It's a fraternity. Those are kinda boys clubs like things."

"That's what I say. No girls allowed," Casey said.

"Yeah. Hamsters or no hamsters," Taylor said.

Farley didn't get our laughter.

There was a light in Looty's window. His old truck was in the yard but that didn't mean much. Farley pulled into the dusty driveway and turned off the engine and the lights. There was a moon but it wasn't bright, and our eyes hadn't adjusted to the dark. It reminded me of the night we had sneaked out.

We pulled up next to the porch, which had no light at all. I stepped up into the darkness, squinting to see the door. It was like I was stepping into a closet. I reached behind to feel for one of the guys behind me.

"Hey, Jake." Looty moved from the shadows. "Hey, Casey and Taylor. And I know you." He looked at Farley. "You're Jake's brother."

"What are you doin' out here in the dark, Looty?" Casey asked.

"Seems kinda scary," I said.

"I'm not scared. I jus' like to sit out here sometimes."

"Doncha have a porch light?" said Farley.

"Yeah. If it was on though it wouldn't be dark, I guess. And I like sittin' in the dark."

"Nice goin', Farley," I said.

"Shuddup, ya little stoop. You might have to walk home—in the dark."

Casey laughed. Farley wasn't sure if he was laughing at me or him, so he told Casey the same thing. He wouldn't really make us walk home, but I decided to change the subject. "Is BB back at his house, too?"

"I think so. They took my momma away. She killed my daddy. So they put her in the hospital."

"Yeah, we know. We're sorry and all. But we were jus' hoping they hadn't put BB in jail. He was jus' tryin' to help you."

"BB's my best friend, like a brother. He used to tell me about Andrew and Silas. That's why he helped me."

"Who're Andrew and Silas?" Farley asked.

"Two Confederates who were at Shiloh," Taylor said.

Farley's face was blank. It was fun to know something somebody a lot older than you didn't know. I knew he had never heard of Andrew and Silas Chandler.

Taylor briefly told Farley about the two boys, Silas and Andrew. Silas was black, Andrew was white. When Andrew at fifteen went off to serve in the Confederate Army, his boyhood friend Silas, age seventeen, followed him. Andrew was captured and wounded. When Andrew was released, Silas cared for his wounds, saved his life and carried him home to Palo Alto, Mississippi.

Looty was slow, and we all were quiet for a minute. All we heard were frogs croaking from the branch, crickets with their high- pitched screeching, and a yard dog barking in the distance for any number of reasons dogs barked.

The night we were sneaking around out here there were no sounds. Or maybe our fear affected our hearing. The stars were out and it was a cool night. Not real cold like the desert got after the sun went down. Deserts reflected the heat. The Delta absorbed it all day, and it released ever so slowly at night. But it still felt good. This last night for my summer in the Delta felt special. I started to say something more about Andrew and Silas and more about what Big Trek had told us about them, but Looty finally spoke again.

"BB said that my daddy was jus' a unfortunate man who thought of hisself only. He said maybe my momma would be home one day. But nobody was sure right now. He said we were lucky not to git more than jus' fussed at by the judge and sheriff."

Looty paused and stared into the night. The dog let out a long wail. Looty turned slowly in the direction of the sound. I thought he might change the subject, but didn't. "He said we could've gone to the jail where I got sent for shootin' those chickens that one time."

"Well, we're sure glad you didn't have to go, Looty," Taylor said.

"Yeah, really and truly," Casey and Farley said almost in unison. Farley just said it because he thought he should, probably. He hadn't gotten to know Looty in the last week like the rest of us had. In these three weeks I had come to know Looty as more than a simple-minded sharecropper. I felt like I had known him all my life.

"Me too. 'Bout all you git to eat is buttermilk and beans and some cornbread. Hardly ever any honey or cheese or any real good stuff or nothin'. And, I only had one Co Cola, jus' one time. One of the deputies giv' it to me."

Our eyes had gotten used to the dark now, and I could see the look on his face. It wasn't a smile or a frown, just a plain look. It reminded me of an old guy who was in the picture shows when Mother and Daddy were little. A man named Buster Keaton. I saw him in the newsreel once, but I had never actually seen him in a picture show. Anyway, that was who Looty's look reminded me of.

"And so you think BB's home too, huh?" Casey asked.

"Yeah, I guess so. Did y'all know that Andrew was in jail once? He was in a jail up North after the Yankees caught him at Shiloh."

His words returned to the black and white Confederates as if they were always present in his mind.

We told him we didn't know, because we really didn't. We had never even heard about Andrew and Silas until Big Trek had told us about them. Of course we hated to admit in front of Farley that there was anything we didn't know about the story. We had to know more about something than he did. It was our biggest power over a guy with a driver's license.

"He got what they call 'exchanged' before the war was o'er, and him and Silas went through the res' of the war together."

"You're still gonna live here, aren't you, Looty?" Casey asked. "I mean you're not gonna move away or anything, huh?"

Looty didn't answer, but I doubted he was going anywhere. He wasn't the kind of man that could really leave the home he had known all his life. Besides, what would he do? I think Casey knew it but just wanted to say something nice to Looty.

"Maybe when you come down to visit your momma you can come by and visit us," Farley said. I know he was just trying to be nice because the state hospital was just across the county line from Jackson. But it still sounded kind of dumb. 'Hey, as long as you're down visiting your lunatic mother, why not stop by and we can visit. Maybe make a day of it.'

All of us stared at Farley. Casey's teeth clenched, Taylor rolled his eyes. Farley got a little defensive. "Well, he might come by, if he's there anyhow."

We said nothing. Looty spoke. "I would like to see your house. I sure would. Maybe I'll come by if I go down there to see my momma."

It was nice the way Looty tried helpin' Farley, I thought. But I knew it would probably never happen. I doubted that Looty would ever see his mother again. She would be a lonely old lady in a hospital or prison and he would just be a simple-minded lonely man. Mother and son, apart.

Finally Taylor said, "We better get going. It's almost nine thirty."

We all said goodbye and I thought maybe we were supposed to shake Looty's hand or something like I always saw my daddy do. But we didn't know how to handle it, so we all just yelled, "See ya, Looty."

"Bye y'all," he said.

We left him on the porch. In the dark.

Our drive back to the house was quiet. Even Casey said little. I guessed everyone was thinking about Looty, same as I was. He was safe but alone in his old house, with the mayonnaise jar.

But something more was going through my mind. I thought about the big, black man who had become my friend—the reader, the worker, the football player, the war hero. And he was a Mississippian. Just like Looty. Just like me. And just like Andrew and Silas and the University Grays and Johnny Vaught. I wondered if I would ever hear from BB after this summer ended tomorrow.

CHAPTER 22

Saturday morning we got up before seven. We were going to stay for dinner then drive back to Jackson. Taylor and Casey and Cousin Trek had a 4-H club meeting at nine o'clock. For some reason known only to Farley, he went with them. Maybe he hoped there would be some farm girls there. But I stayed behind, because I knew that mostly they would be talking about things that I wouldn't be interested in, like chickens and hogs and manure. Besides, I had to pack up my gear and clothes that had gotten scattered around over the last three weeks in places not necessarily known to Cousin Carol.

After they left I pulled everything together and took off on one of the bikes, assuring my mother I would be back before dinner. I wanted to see BB before I left.

I had taken Looty's word that BB wasn't in jail and assumed he was home. Last word was he wasn't going to be in any real trouble.

I rode the two miles in about ten minutes and worked up a sweat. If it had been any other day I would have asked Ben to spray me with the hose, but not that day. That day I had to stay pretty clean. As I rode up, Ben was washing his truck with a garden hose and BB was scouring the hood with a soap-soaked sponge. It oozed with soap as he moved his hand back and forth. I guess I was surprised that he was at the house and not working in the field. I wasn't surprised that he was working at something.

"Well, looka here who's come callin'," Ben said, grinning like always.

BB dropped the sponge into a bucket then wiped his hands on his tee-shirt. He was wearing blue jeans and was barefooted.

I had worked with him on and off for three weeks and knew he was a strong man. With his tee-shirt soaked, I could see his chest muscles ripple, and from his long arms his biceps were taut as a result of hard work. I could see how he could have been a good football player. Something told me too that if he had been at Gettysburg, we would have whipped the Yankees; because I would've bet he was whipping the Communists in Korea until they shot him.

"So, you come to say goodbye?" BB said.

"Well, dat's thoughtful of you, Mr. Jake. It shore is," Ben said. "We shore gonna mis' you 'round here." He took out his handkerchief and blew his nose. Then he coughed, kind of low. "I think I gots me a sniffling cold, gittin' out in that rain the other night. Even in dis hot weather, it seems like."

"Mother says summer colds are the worst," I said.

"You know what, Jake. We need some more rain bad. And I'm gonna bet we get some soon as you leave," BB said.

I looked at BB, then at Ben. I thought maybe Ben was going to tell me what BB meant. I wondered if he was going to say I'd been a jinx or something. Finally, I asked, "Whadaya mean, BB?"

"Well, I think the Lord prob'ly held back on the rain jus' so you could work in the heat. Sometimes He's rough on a fellow just to toughen him up." He looked upward toward the sun.

I had never thought like that before, that someone could be hard on you to help you.

It seemed like BB was always saying things that seemed smart—maybe wise is what Mother would say. BB was smart and wise. Looty was simple and good. And they had a special bond between them. And they would always be special to me.

"After you leave, He'll prob'ly send us some rain. I'll just betcha," BB said once more.

This time I looked at the sun. This time I smiled.

"But next summer, if you come back, you'll be as tough as everybody else and there won't be any need for such temperin'."

"Well, I won't know until June next year if I'll be coming back. And I don't even know if Cousin Trek'll want me hoeing cotton."

Ben coughed again, putting his handkerchief up to his mouth.

"Daddy, maybe you ought to go and lie down. Take some of that cough syrup."

"Naw, I be all right. Jus' gonna shake this little cold."

BB turned back to me. "Well, he'll want you working, I'd say. If he don't, then you can help me paint this house. I need to do it before the end of next summer. Think you'd be a good house painter?"

"Oh, sure." *Painting?* "Well, I'm gonna miss y'all."

And I knew I would. It had been a summer better than anything I had ever experienced—hard work, a murder mystery, and new friends. One friend was a strange man whose mind was not much older than mine. Two others were colored men who had taught me that work was a gift. That my Confederate ancestors were fighting for their land and against those who invaded it. That Confederates were black and white, and therefore Gray. That with a lot of hard work, the Delta land grows wonderful and beautiful cotton. The best kind of cotton—Mississippi cotton. God gave the cotton and God gave the work.

I kind of wanted to say something special to them like guys did in the picture show, but I didn't know what to say. I finally told them that I hoped everything worked out for them. I didn't say "with the sheriff," but they knew what I meant. I told BB I hoped he got to go to college and I told Ben I hoped he got over his cough soon. I was afraid I'd start crying if I said I was sorry about his momma and daddy getting killed a long time ago. I waved and rode off, back to the house.

It was a big dinnertime. There were eight of us at the table. Cousin Trek and Cousin Carol had hoped that Sally would get back from summer school before today so she could visit at least one day with us, but Cousin Trek said she wouldn't be back before Tuesday.

Talk and over-talk, the clink of dishes and silverware, made it a noisy family meal. It was like Christmas or Thanksgiving with so many people trying to talk at the same time and so much food passed. Much of the talk still centered on the murder until Daddy finally changed the subject.

"Well, have you decided what you're gonna be when you get old enough, Taylor?"

Taylor had a mouth full of mashed potatoes and had to wait a second to answer, so Casey spoke right up. "I'm gonna be a crop duster."

"No, you're not," Cousin Carol said. "And you weren't asked."

"Well," said Casey, not ready to give up, "I thought it was a free country when you got grown."

"No, it's not," she said. "Crop dusting is out. Now, Taylor, Cousin David asked you a question."

Taylor was wiping his mouth with his napkin, having inhaled the potatoes. "I'm not sure. Maybe a farmer. Maybe a travelin' salesman."

"I see," Daddy said.

Big Trek looked across the table at Farley and asked him what he wanted to be.

"Might become a doctor—"

"Can I ask about it being a free country?" Casey interrupted.

"No! You may not," Cousin Carol said.

"So a doctor, eh?" Big Trek said. "Why did you decide on that?"

"So he can look at naked girls," Casey blurted. He had no sooner gotten it out than Cousin Carol picked up the butter knife from its tray and smacked him on the fingers. It not only stung, I'm sure, but smeared butter on his hand. It was all Taylor and I could do to keep from laughing, but we didn't or we'd have gotten in trouble, too.

"You are not goin' to talk like that at the table—or anywhere!"

Cousin Trek immediately took charge. "You can just go to your room 'til I come up there. Now git. Now!"

It was inevitable. Casey had been flirting with danger for three weeks. It was written in the cards for him to get a switchin' before I left.

We had only a brief look at everyone as we drove away. They all were standing in the yard, but within seconds they disappeared into the brown cloud of dust raised by our car leaving for Jackson. The top of the windmill was the last thing I saw.

As we drove back to Jackson, we passed through the little towns I had traveled three weeks before on the Trailways bus next to the straw-haired lady. Each time we slowed through one of the towns I thought of her and Looty and BB and Ben. I thought about them all the way home.

Around Christmas I got the next piece of news from Cotton City. Cousin Carol had written us a letter. Ben's cough was not caused by a simple cold or sniffle. He had advanced lung cancer, and died a week before Christmas.

Although the straw-haired lady seemed to have revealed the truth to everyone, I guess she thought it was not enough. She hanged herself in her room at Whitfield the day after Ben died.

Looty had accepted Cousin Carol's fruit cake, but turned down her offer to spend Christmas day at their house. He just wanted to be "by his-self," he had said.

I guess BB was by his-self now, too.

Epilogue

I visited several times after that until I finished high school but never again saw Looty. I don't know if he had ever gotten to see his mother before her death, but from what my parents had said, he hadn't. He lived to be an old man and died many years later, alone and at home. Taylor and Casey told me he was buried in the county somewhere.

After Ben died, BB went off to Florida and played football. He wasn't even in Cotton City the next summer to paint his house. His leg injury had kept him from being as good a player as he could have been. As it turned out, he stayed on after his playing days in Florida as an assistant football coach. His wife died in childbirth giving an only child, a son, who returned to Mississippi and was an All Conference Center at Mississippi Southern in Hattiesburg.

Casey didn't become a crop duster but he did serve as a fighter pilot in Vietnam. I guess his sixth sense was still with him since he returned home unharmed. I heard later that someone had asked him when he returned from the war if he still wanted to be a crop duster. He told them, "Crop dusting is too dangerous for me."

Farley went to Ole Miss and became a doctor. But by the time he got there, Dixie Daniels had graduated, so he had to live with his childhood memories of her. He married a girl from Hickory, Mississippi, where the welcome sign claimed it was 'The Little Town with the Big Heart'. When Farley got married, Casey told him, off to the side, that Cotton City should have a sign: 'Home of Dixie Daniels'.

Taylor went to the cow college and became an agricultural engineer. He came back to his family farm and specialized in cotton, of course. But the days of people hand-picking fields of cotton were over. The land still produced abundantly, but the harvest was highly mechanized as machine-driven cotton pickers poured through the fields in the late summer and autumn. Much was wasted, but more was harvested in a shorter period of time. Farming it somehow made farming less personal for the true agrarian. It was a numbers game and the bottom line had to run a profit or the land would be lost.

In 1952 William Faulkner had spoken to the Delta Council at Cleveland. He reminded them of freedom and spirit, of their steadfastness and honor and not just their tenure and ownership and profit of the fertile land that had been their legacy. But he wasn't sanguine: "We knew it once, had it once...Only something happened to us." Faulkner's words drew on my youth, my days in Sunday School: "God said unto them. Be fruitful... and replenish the earth..."

Another ancient memory flashed. The old signs, long since gone, about seeing seven states from Rock City: one of those things that I looked for which were never there. I hoped the land, the people, were still there. Faulkner's words reverberated. "Only something happened to us." I didn't want my old home, my roots to be something to be looked for in vain, something else that wasn't there.

A couple of years ago, BB passed seventy. He retired and returned home to the house he had been born in. It was run down, but the land had been farmed and planted on a rent basis from Mr. Hightower and Cousin Trek. I decided to pay a visit and see the man I had learned so much from almost fifty years before.

I drove up in my Blazer. The old house was dilapidated and probably beyond repair. There was a concrete slab about fifty yards away, an indication he was about to start over. I thought his hearing might be impaired, as he had his back to me and did not seem to hear my car as I pulled into the driveway.

"Say," I said as I got out. "Need some help paintin' this old house?"

He turned, slow and deliberate, like a man in his early

seventies. His eyes had not lost their keenness. I had not seen him in almost fifty years, but I suppose there is something in the structure or the topology of a man's face, even from child-hood, that marks him in another man's mind; marks him so that he is never forgotten.

"Well, I'll jus' say. It's little Mister Jake. Actually, you wasn't Mister the last time I saw you, you was Master Jake. But you was a hard workin' one." He still called me Mister. It was not out of subservience. It never had been. It was just Southern.

He didn't give me a chance to shake his hand, but grabbed me in a bear hug and squeezed me like he was wrapping up a fullback on a tackle. He was still strong. I think we both wanted to cry but we didn't. I like to think he was thinking the same thing I was thinking: too many men crying these days just for anything. We kept our tears on our hearts, but they were there. This was my black friend. Now he was old, but still as black as the first day I saw him. And still my friend.

We drove into Cotton City and went into the old café down-town. I didn't know the owners now, but whites and colored sat at the counter and tables. Once it was for whites on one side and colored on the other. The pinball machine was gone. We talked for over two hours.

His son had gone into coaching, too. He'd been a good player, mostly through hard work, since he had less natural talent than BB. But he had been a well-respected defensive coach and had been sent feelers as to him taking a head coaching job at a major university.

"You don't tell me," I said. "Well, where is it, BB? What school?"

"Well, between you and me and the fence post, Mr. Jake, it's Ole Miss."

"Really. Ole Miss? You mean—"

"I mean the first black head coach at Ole Miss," he said in a whispered voice.

I took a sip of coffee and glanced around to see if others were listening. "Is it certain he's gonna be offered the job? Will he take it?"

"Well, it's his decision. But I told him that there were a lot of white folks up at Ole Miss wanted him to have it just because he's black and because most of the players are black. Those people are about as sorry a lot as you'll find, black or white."

"You're trying to tell me something, BB. I can feel it."

BB smiled. It was that white-toothed smile contrasted against his black face. The same smile I had seen fifty years before. The only color change in BB was in his hair, now mostly white.

"Well, I told my boy, Jesse, that these people who want him as head coach are the same people who don't want white people to sing Dixie or carry their flags; the same flags that the Mississippi Grays carried. They don't care about Ole Miss and they probably won't care about you or your players. You know, Mister Jake, they tell them boys that the sound of Dixie is a sound of evil and they should shun it. They don't care that they get themselves tattooed and stick jewelry in their ears and noses, as long as they ain't Dixie boys. As far as I'm concerned, those people can go to hell. And I told Jesse that he oughta tell 'em that if you don't allow Dixie or the Bonnie Blue flags, then you don't allow me. If you start singing it like us Gray men sing it, if you teach 'em that this is their land; their land to love and work and maybe even fight for one day, then I'm your man. Because I'm not gonna lie to those young men, black or white, about their heritage. Not even for the million dollars they're offering you."

"So, you think he's gonna be the first black coach there?"

BB held his cup with both hands and took a sip. He put it down in front of him and jiggled it and looked into it like he was a seer studying the future in the small ripples of the black liquid. He looked up and smiled at me. "Nope."

I updated him on my life. I told him I had moved to Texas some thirty years earlier, had married and reared a son myself. I had served in the Navy. I had thought at the time those white uniforms looked sharp. I hadn't been sent to Viet Nam, being held in reserve to guard the Panama Canal Zone.

Texas had been a cotton and cow state forever. But there wasn't a cow college and the cotton wasn't Mississippi. I told him I had thought about moving back to Mississippi one day, but that was still in the future.

Our meeting in the old café was the last time I saw BB. He finished his new house and went back to work in the cotton fields. He would work until the day he died. I knew him well enough to know that would happen.

On my return trip along the Interstate, I realized that this was not the road of my youth that had taken me to the Delta and back to Jackson. That road winded slowly through the countryside, carrying visitors and farmers and families. It was slow enough to have memories etched, and stopping points where people and towns were local and special. And not only the destination but the journey had chronicles. The Interstate was a monster that sped people back and forth in a hurry because hurrying was essential to modernity. This monster stole land and lives and memories. It was progress. And I could see that it had begun to steal the South's identity and rob its people of their culture.

I had a long drive back to Fort Worth, plenty of time to think of childhood memories. And some of those memories are so much more vivid because of the permanence they burned into me. That August spent in Cotton City was still afire in me— the summer of mystery, murder, and working in the cotton fields. And the Giants in their remarkable race to the pennant.

They finally did win the Pennant that year, coming back from thirteen and a half games behind to win on a home run by Bobby Thomson in a playoff game. Regrettably, they were spent and had not enough left to win the grand prize. The Yankees overwhelmed them in the World Series. I guess it was like the University Grays at Pickett's charge. They took the hill but didn't have enough left to win the grand prize. And the Yankees overwhelmed them.

***

Special thanks for encouragement to:

Julie Cantrell, Oxford, Mississippi
Fred Miller, Columbia, South Carolina
James Ferguson, Oak Ridge, Tennessee